MW01127686

MURDER IN CANNES

BOOK 10 OF THE MAGGIE NEWBERRY MYSTERIES

SUSAN KIERNAN-LEWIS

SAN MARCO PRESS

Summer on the Côte d'Azur means tan bodies, wide beaches and glamorous nightclubs throbbing with the vitality of the rich and beautiful. So when Maggie Newberry arranges to meet an old boyfriend at the International Advertising Festival in Cannes, it's no surprise she begins to feel the seduction of her old life.

But amidst the glamor, beautiful clothes and brilliant creative work on display, there is also the side of the business Maggie had forgotten was always there too. The petty rivalries, the dirty deals, the betrayals, are all still front and center. When the back-stabbing turns literal and the wife of Maggie's childhood friend is accused of the murder, Maggie knows she has to help.

Along the way, she needs to fight the police, Laurent, and even her own natural instincts about who she is now and the life she left behind.

She learns the hard way that the treachery rife in her old industry has since ramped up to a whole new level—one that her quiet life as a vigneron's wife has not at all prepared her for...and one that could very well get her killed.

Books by Susan Kiernan-Lewis
The Maggie Newberry Mysteries
Murder in the South of France
Murder à la Carte
Murder in Provence
Murder in Paris
Murder in Aix
Murder in Nice
Murder in the Latin Quarter
Murder in the Abbey
Murder in the Bistro
Murder in Cannes

Murder in Grenoble
Murder in the Vineyard
Murder in Arles
Murder in Marseille
Murder in St-Rémy
Murder à la Mode
Murder in Avignon
Murder in the Lavender
Murder in Mont St-Michel
Murder in the Village
Murder in St-Tropez
Murder in Grasse
Murder in Monaco
Murder in Montmartre
Murder in the Villa
A Provençal Christmas: A Short Story
A Thanksgiving in Provence
Laurent's Kitchen

The Claire Baskerville Mysteries
Déjà Dead
Death by Cliché
Dying to be French
Ménage à Murder
Killing it in Paris
Murder Flambé
Deadly Faux Pas
Toujours Dead
Murder in the Christmas Market
Deadly Adieu
Murdering Madeleine
Murder Carte Blanche
Death à la Drumstick
Murder Mon Amour

1

Sometimes the crappiest moments in life happen in the prettiest places.

Maggie sat at the Arrivals terminal of the Nice Côte d'Azur International Airport, her demitasse espresso on the table beside her.

She'd told herself she would use this time to relax, to enjoy the feel of the sun on her face, to clear her mind and bask in a moment without a child tugging at her pant leg or an overflowing basket of laundry needing to be washed, hung or folded in her immediate future.

And maybe along the way she would be able to wash away the memory of a time spent on the Côte d'Azur that she would very much like to forget.

Unfortunately if that's what she was hoping for, she was off to a bad start.

First, it rained the whole way from St-Buvard and the minute it stopped, Maggie had to go inside the airport.

Secondly, there'd already been *two* phone calls from her husband Laurent asking where the extra car keys were and how do you get blood out of Jemmy's favorite t-shirt? Oh, and Mila's blue Aurora dress, too? Then Danielle Alexandre, Maggie's good friend and this year's co-director of the upcoming lavender festival had texted Maggie *three* times to outline the most recent problems with the lavender vendors, the display space and her concern over the weather forecast for the event.

Maggie paused to listen to the loudspeaker in the arrivals lounge. She was early. She was always early. It was one of the few habits she wasn't consciously trying to break.

Keeping an eye on her overnight bag, she stood up and walked to the arrivals board to see that Brownie's flight was already on the ground. Maggie felt a sliver of excitement at the thought of seeing him again. Brownie had been her best friend growing up and her boyfriend all the way through college. And beyond.

That role came to a screeching halt when Maggie met Laurent—a mysterious Frenchman who, at the time, had a dubious past.

Come to think of it, Laurent's past is still pretty dubious, Maggie thought.

The loudspeaker blared again to formally announce the arrival of Brownie's flight from Atlanta. Maggie went back to her seat.

She felt edgy about seeing him again. Although she'd exchanged a few texts with him over the years and kept in touch on Facebook, the fact was, there had been a rift between them when Laurent came into her life.

One minute, Brownie was her guy—as he more or less had been since she was six years old—and the next, he was history.

A wave of guilt swept through her.

And they'd never really talked about it.

Brownie was too male and too Southern to confront her or demand closure. As the female in the equation—especially a Southern one—that would have been up to Maggie to orchestrate. And somehow life got busy and she never had.

After she'd moved to France, married the sexy six foot five interloper and had two kids Brownie made the surprising jump from computer engineering into advertising—Maggie's old business—and began to serial-date a long line of sexy vapid models and no-name actresses.

Brownie had had no experience when he bought his way into his first ad agency. But then, that was advertising. It was a business that required more guts and originality than experience or diplomas. She once knew a creative director who bragged that he never hired a writer with a degree in advertising because it meant the writer had probably overthought things right out of the gate.

In spite of her advertising degree from the University of Florida Maggie had done well for the six years she worked as an advertising copywriter in Atlanta—a role in which she'd earned her agencies' highest creative honors year after year— before moving to France and giving it all up.

Brownie was right in the thick of all that now. Owner of a brash young boutique, Pixel, that was making noise throughout the Southeast and even being heard in New York and Chicago, he'd been invited to be a lead juror at Cannes this year and would even take an award home for *Top Ten Start-Ups to Watch*.

Brownie was smart. He made sure he gave his creative director her head and he didn't get in the way of the account team either. Some things Brownie just knew without being told: When the magic is right, don't want to stir the pot too much.

Maggie slid her laptop into her carry-on bag and gathered up her trash. She'd told Brownie she'd meet him at baggage claim.

He was traveling with his wife JoJo; his creative director, Bette Austin, who spent more time on the cover of Advertising Age than anyone in the business right now; and Pixel's senior copywriter, Sasha Morrison, who was up for a creative award this year.

Maggie knew she didn't have the right to feel jealous about Brownie's marriage. Especially since *she* was the one who'd dumped *him*.

But she couldn't deny that the thought of Brownie with someone else felt foreign and slightly nauseating to her. When he'd called her two weeks ago to ask if she'd be able to meet up with him at the International Advertising Festival in Cannes, Maggie had been delighted.

She'd never been to the famous festival when she'd been in the business but she knew Cannes well. And her French language skills were finally solid. She was looking forward to impressing Brownie with what a polyglot she'd become since he'd known her back in Georgia.

She hoisted her bag onto her shoulder. She'd only packed for two days and most of the weight of her bag was due to the laptop and assorted chargers. The bag was a basic canvas affair that she'd bought at a street market in Arles years ago. Danielle had surprised her one Christmas with an elaborate needlepoint that she'd added to the outside of an American flag and a French flag intertwined.

Walking through the Nice Airport among all the seriously beautiful people with their Prada bags and Chanel satchels, Maggie couldn't help feel a little shabby toting her flea market cloth bag with its garish bright colors and obviously homemade needlework.

She wished she'd brought her vintage Vuitton instead, even if it was too big for this trip. She walked to the downward escalator and tugged on her cotton jacket, suddenly wishing she'd worn something that covered her hips better.

She'd gained a few pounds since she'd last seen Brownie. Married to a man who was at the very least an amateur French chef, she was bound to. Even if Laurent didn't cook all the time, just living in France would've piled the pounds on.

How could anyone stay slim with all this amazing food, every meal of the day everywhere you looked?

Still, Maggie knew what a sweet tooth Brownie had. Surely—

with luck—his wife JoJo would be a chubby cheerful version of him?

~

JoJo Morrison looked like her last job was as one of Victoria's Secrets Angels.

Maggie spotted her and the rest of Brownie's group—from thirty yards away. They were milling about the baggage claim area and not acting at all as if they'd just slept in their clothes for past nine hours. A peal of laughter carried across the noisy concourse.

Brownie's wife was taller than Maggie but looked like she weighed at least twenty pounds less. She stood next to Brownie, her clothes draping off her in shimmers of gray silk like a runway model.

Brownie turned as Maggie approached and she felt a stab of nostalgia to see his face again. It was a little fuller than the last time she'd seen him perhaps but everything else felt like coming home again.

His blue eyes crinkled with delight at the sight of her and he flung his arms out wide to her.

"Hey, Brownie," Maggie said with a grin as he wrapped his arms around her. He held her a moment longer than she expected but Maggie thought she knew why. He'd felt it too. A moment of longing, of remembering, of being children together. Suddenly Maggie was filled with sorrow for all the years she'd missed having Brownie in her life.

"Maggie, you look gorgeous," Brownie said, breaking the spell and pulling back to regard her with pleasure.

Maggie blushed, her eyes darting to the people watching them from the side of the baggage carousel.

"I want you to meet JoJo," Brownie said, slipping an arm

around the slim goddess who stood patiently waiting for her cue. "My wife."

"I've heard so much about you," JoJo said shaking Maggie's hand firmly. "Brownie says you were the sister he never had."

Oh, is that what he said? Maggie thought, forcing down her pique.

"And this is Bette Austin, Pixel's Creative Director," Brownie said turning to a tall thin woman with black spiky hair who nodded curtly at Maggie without the benefit of a smile. Maggie knew from all the *Ad Age* feature stories she'd read that Bette was a workaholic, lived with three cats and was independently wealthy. Bette turned to focus on the carousel as if that might help her bags appear quicker.

"And Sasha Morrison, Pixel's senior copywriter," Brownie said.

Sasha grimaced a facsimile of a smile in Maggie's direction. She had thick blonde hair that fell to her shoulders. Sasha was beautiful in that just-woke-up sort of way that said she might not be totally aware of how beautiful she was. She looked very intense and Maggie wondered if that's what she herself had been like when she worked in the business and thought of little else but advertising—and winning awards.

"Sasha's up for an award this week," Brownie said. "We're very proud of her."

"That's great," Maggie said. "What client?"

"Sparks & Peter," Sasha said. "Do you know them?"

Maggie smiled apologetically. "We don't get too many American products over here," she said.

"It's British."

"Oh. Still don't know it. Sorry."

Maggie noticed JoJo slide her arm around Brownie's waist as if to claim him.

"God, it's so good to see you, Maggie," Brownie said. "But you really didn't need to pick us up. We could've taken the shuttle from the airport."

"No problem," Maggie said, smiling and wishing to God she'd let them just take the shuttle. What had she been thinking? That time hadn't passed? That his wife wouldn't be an ice queen bitch goddess? That it would be like old times?

Brownie reached over and dragged two brand-new Louis Vuitton bags off the carousel.

"Everyone good to go?" he said cheerfully.

IT TOOK LESS than forty minutes to drive to Cannes from Nice.

Maggie thought the road itself was one of the prettiest drives in France. Maybe in the world.

Going south from Nice and hugging the coast, the brilliant blue of the Mediterranean seemed to fill the sky with its relentless, unending beauty.

Maggie had been intending to take the A8 which was more inland and a faster route to Cannes, but once she started driving she knew she wanted her guests to see the curve of the white sandy beach as it undulated toward Cannes and the nerve center of the world's glamour and style.

She needn't have bothered.

Right from the start, things got wobbly. While Laurent had moved Mila's car seat out of the back there were still plenty of plastic dolls and toy army men along with a few melted crayons that Maggie had missed.

Brownie sat in front with Maggie while the three women solemnly settled into the back.

Sasha was glued to her smartphone and never once looked out at the magnificent view. The other two women—clearly furious at being relegated to the back seat—sat grim and pinch-faced as they rode through the continuous onslaught of beauty that surrounded them.

Originally, the thought of meeting Brownie and his crew and spending a day or so at the festival had seemed like such fun. As much as Maggie adored her role as mother to Mila and Jemmy, she had been looking forward to the time away.

She hadn't taken into account the thought that she might not fit in this world any more.

As Brownie chattered away on the drive, even he seemed unimpressed with the view as they drove into Antibes and then Juan-les-Pins. The village had always been a favorite of hers—ever since Roger Bentley had told her about it all those years ago. He hadn't lied either.

Well, not about that at least.

After Laurent had proposed to her, Maggie had made him take her to Juan-les-Pins and do it again properly.

With its quaint fishing boats and ancient marina, the village looked as if it hadn't been touched since the fifties.

She and Laurent had spent the weekend in a cozy *pensione* by the water, rising late, walking hand in hand along the marina and enjoying candlelit dinners of fresh seafood and homemade pasta long into the night. And while it was true they hadn't returned to Juan-les-Pins since then, she still counted it as one of the best days of her life.

As she maneuvered down the D6007 and around the *Golf de la Napoule* Maggie tried to relax. But her nerves were ramping up the closer she got to Cannes.

Cannes too had memories for Maggie.

Unfortunately, none of them good.

"I'm so glad you could meet us this trip," Brownie said as he gazed out at the bland cement apartment buildings that lined the north side of the highway. "Did you ever go to the festival when you were in the business?"

Maggie was sure she'd already told him she hadn't but she

couldn't fault him for trying to keep a conversation going. Trapped in a car with three resolutely non-speaking women had been a little short of hell on everyone.

"No, I never did," Maggie said. "I've been to Cannes, of course, but I'm looking forward to staying at the Carlton."

The Hotel Carlton—now called the InterContinental Carlton Cannes—was an historic five-star Belle Époque luxury hotel built in 1911. With its Art Nouveau architecture and breathtaking views of the Mediterranean from nearly every room, the Carlton had long been considered the ultimate in elegance and glamor on the Riviera.

Glancing in the rear view mirror as she drove into Cannes Maggie noted that Sasha still hadn't looked up from her phone.

How is it possible that anything on that phone can rival seeing Cannes for the first time? she thought in bewilderment. Was this new generation of creatives just so jaded or had they already experienced everything virtually and the reality couldn't stack up?

Maggie drove down the *Boulevard de la Croisette* with the glittering brightness of the Mediterranean on her left.

Cannes had long ago stopped being a sleepy little fishing village. Even when there wasn't a major international film or advertising festival going on there was always some major event happening that crammed the narrow roads with crowds and kept the lines long and snaking out the doors of Cartier, Hermés, Gucci, and Chanel.

As Maggie drove, the Hotel Carlton loomed ahead like the prow of a gigantic white ship. The distinctive domes on both seaward corners of the hotel were reportedly designed to resemble breasts. Whether that was true or not, one thing was certain—the Carlton was absolutely iconic of the French Riviera.

The minute Maggie pulled up in front of the hotel, Sasha and JoJo jumped out. They stood waiting for the Carlton doorman to unload the trunk while Bette unlocked her gangly legs and slowly got out of the car. Maggie saw her stare up at the majestic hotel as if unimpressed.

"I'll go with you to park the car," Brownie said but Maggie could see he had his hand on the door handle.

"No. You go on," Maggie said. "Get everyone settled in. I won't be long."

"Meet you in the lobby bar in an hour?" he said as he swung out of the car.

"Sounds good."

Maggie waited until she could see everyone and their bags were moving up the front steps into the hotel before driving off. She felt a wash of relief immediately as she did.

Had this been a good idea? The lavender fair in St-Buvard was coming up in four days and there was a lot to do before then. Plus Mila had scraped her knee last night. Laurent had laughed when Maggie offered that up as a reason why she might not come to Cannes.

She parked in a garage several blocks from the beach and hurried back to the hotel on foot, carrying her overnight bag over her shoulder. She was wearing the wrong shoes and already had a blister on one foot. She was limping by the time she made it back to the Carlton.

She took in a deliberate breath to slow herself down.

Massive alabaster columns in the Carlton lobby provided a spacious and airy feel to the hotel's entrance which was made even more elegant by the shimmering vintage chandeliers hanging every six feet throughout the lobby. The light from the chandeliers reflected onto the gleaming tetrazzini tile floors.

Two gigantic Palladian windows soared thirty feet on each side of the hotel's double entrance doors ushering in a tsunami of light that flooded the lobby with a cheerful, pristine brightness.

The lobby itself was furnished with pale silk upholstered tub chairs and populated by waiters in black ties who carried silver platters of domed-covered dishes and sparkling martini glasses.

It was when Maggie entered, gazing about in awe and delight at the famous lobby, that she caught a glimpse of herself in one of the colossal gilt-framed mirrors.

She looked bedraggled, her hair in a snarling whirlwind around her head, her tummy straining against her cotton Capri pants and her heavy shoulder bag pressing into her neck which gave her a pronounced hunched back effect.

Turning away from the mirrors, Maggie made her way with her head down through the gathering crowd of elegantly dressed people—each more sleek and tan, expensively dressed and shod and coifed than the next.

What was I thinking? she thought in dismay.

2

W ith grand royal palms lining the broad boulevard, the *Promenade de la Croisette* was dramatically visible from the patio of the Carlton Hotel. The air on the Côte d'Azur smelled sweet yet citrusy.

Maggie stood on the patio off the main bar with a white wine spritzer in one hand and found herself remembering the first time she'd ever visited the Carlton Hotel. She hadn't stayed here then. Like now, it was just drinks on the patio bar.

It was the first time she'd ever laid eyes on Roger Bentley.

Maggie felt a spasm of sadness at the thought of Roger and forced the memory away.

A quick shower in her hotel room had helped restore her optimism after the afternoon of less than pleasant surprises. That, plus a couple of phone calls from Mila and Jemmy.

Maggie smiled at the memory of their high-pitched voices, both so excited about the rabbit *Papa* had helped them catch in the garden today.

She'd felt a little unsure of herself when she came onto the patio where she was to meet Brownie. It was clear she'd brought all the wrong clothes for this trip. But then again she didn't *own* the right clothes for this trip.

As she entered the patio she spotted Brownie talking with two other advertising festival delegates. Something about the way he stood with them—hunched over and looking furtively around—bothered her.

It almost looked as if he was doing something he shouldn't be.

Now as she stood with a drink in her hand Maggie shook the image away, chalking it up to nerves on her part. It had taken only a few sips of the bright regional rosé to remind her that life was good—even planted in the middle of a group of gorgeous women dressed in outfits that cost more than Laurent's brand new mechanical crushing equipment he'd bought last winter.

"You've been to Cannes before, right, Maggie?" Brownie said as he approached. She watched the two delegates he'd been talking with slide out the door as if they couldn't leave fast enough.

"Yes, but not that much," she said. "Cannes is mostly a tourist trap. Laurent won't put up with the traffic."

"No, I meant when you came nine years ago to find Elise."

Way to put a damper on the evening, Maggie thought as the memory of her dead sister rose up before her. Did Brownie really need to bring that up? Was Maggie's murdered junkie sister really their only intersection point now?

"That's true," she said. "I was here then. Oh, there's JoJo." Maggie smiled at Brownie's wife as she glided across the tile patio toward them.

Brownie turned and kissed JoJo.

Maggie tried to remember how she and Laurent typically greeted each other. Laurent was very private and a public kiss on the patio of the Carlton Hotel would never have happened. Most likely, she'd have gotten a nod.

"I told the others we'd meet them at the restaurant," JoJo said as she took Brownie's champagne glass and sipped demurely from it.

"Excellent," Brownie said, rubbing his hands together. "Seafood, right? That's the one on...where is it?"

"*Rue Félix Faure*," Maggie said. When JoJo looked at her in surprise, Maggie shrugged. "All the good seafood restaurants are there."

"I forgot you know your way around here," JoJo said coolly, placing Brownie's champagne glass down on a nearby table and taking her husband's arm. "Shall we go?"

ONE OF NINE seafood restaurants lining the *Rue Félix-Faire, Astoux et Brun* was small with an outdoor dining area that oozed Mediterranean charm. Sasha and Bette were already seated when they arrived. Maggie assumed the Carlton Hotel concierge must have booked the table for them. *Astoux et Brun* was popular and reservations would have been necessary—at least a week in advance.

Maggie scanned the crowd of diners and wasn't surprised to hear mostly English spoken. It wasn't just that the Brits and the Yanks dominated the international advertising scene—although they definitely did—but they were the noisiest, the brashest, the most grandstanding of their breed. It was only a little past eight in the evening and already the noise had risen to raucous levels.

Surprisingly, their waiter claimed to speak no English. Maggie would have assumed that everybody in Cannes spoke English in order to support the massive Anglo tourist trade. She knew it was entirely possible the man was faking it. Listening to the obnoxious volume of the crowd rise and fall, Maggie wasn't sure she could blame him.

"Sure would be easier if there were pictures," Brownie laughed as he looked at the menu.

"You mean like Golden Corral?" Sasha asked teasingly. "Or Denny's?"

"Don't knock Denny's," Brownie said. "You'd kill for that account."

"Oh! What I could do with their Pancake Supper!" Sasha said, looking dreamily off into space. "*Stack 'em, rack 'em, pack 'em. Any way you lack 'em.*"

The table laughed good-naturedly

Sasha explained to Maggie, "See I put the joke on the end with a Southern accent."

"Clever," Maggie said biting her lip to keep from saying she'd gotten it without needing it spelled out for her. She turned and motioned for the waiter.

"Any chance you could remember you speak English after all?" she said to him in French. "Or do we really have to do this the hard way?"

The waiter shrugged, but he turned to Brownie and pointed to something on the menu and spoke in English. "Many of our American guests enjoy the *cabillaud roti*," he said.

After they all ordered their food and another two bottles of Côtes-du-Rhône, Brownie lifted his wineglass.

"I'd like to make a toast to our own dear little Sasha Morrison whose pearls of slogan jewels have fallen from her mouth—"

"Dear God, boss," Bette said sourly. "Let Sasha handle the words from now on, will you? She does write toasts you know." She glanced at Sasha. "Don't you?"

"I write anything anyone will pay me for," Sasha said with a grin.

"Okay, fine," Brownie said good-naturedly. "Here's to our amazing Sasha and the reason the board agreed to pay for the four of us to fly here to Cannes this week!"

"Four?" Bette said glaring at JoJo. "The board paid for your wife's flight?"

"Which isn't at all the point, Bette," Brownie said, trying to keep his smile in place. "To Sasha!"

They all toasted but Bette didn't drink. Maggie turned to Sasha.

"What was the winning entry that got everyone here?"

"It's a thirty second TVC," Brownie said, "but we're using the line on social media and print, too. The spot opens with a shot of a lone man standing in the—"

"She just wants to know the line, dear," JoJo said, scanning the crowd. "You can always send her the mp3 if she's really that interested."

Sasha turned to Maggie. "The line is *When it comes to financial security you can take it to the bank, because with Sparks and Peters, you're done. Well and good!*"

"Nice," Maggie said politely. Although it seemed to her that the line could be taken two ways. Especially after the recent financial skullduggery on Wall Street.

"Well, it's really just the last part that's been picked up on social media," Brownie said. "It's turned into a meme in its own right, hasn't it, Sasha? Like, '*Looking for a great deal? You're done! Well and good.*'"

"Frankly I'm at a loss to understand why it's so popular," JoJo said. "No offense, Sasha. Guess I'm not the target audience."

"Doesn't hurt my feelings," Sasha said with a shrug but her face said otherwise. The waiter arrived with the new bottles of wine effectively ending the line of conversation.

Maggie stared across the patio of diners and into the night-time streets of Cannes. In many ways it hadn't changed at all since that first time she'd come here with Roger Bentley to a restaurant very like this one.

On a nearby sidewalk vendors waved their wares of bracelets and bells, beaded necklaces and earrings. Some accompanied their sales attempts with soft crooning and guitar strumming. The music of the night mingled with the scent of olives and lemons and dusky perfumes that hovered in the air over the patio of happy diners.

Two men, clearly American by their loud voices and blue jeans, approached the table and Brownie stood up to shake hands with them. Everyone in Cannes this week was in the advertising business in one way or the other. Maggie assumed these two were representing one of the larger agencies.

Brownie's shop aside, boutiques didn't usually have the funds to make an appearance at the Cannes festival--even if they were up for an award.

"Maggie, may I introduce Rick Wilson, President of Wilson, Brut and Lewis? And this is his Creative Director, Dennis Beaker." Maggie noticed that neither man made an attempt to shake her hand.

"Are you up for an award?" she asked.

"No," Rick Wilson said without looking at her. "Just delegates enjoying the show."

"And by that, he means schmoozing and boozing," Beaker said.

Brownie turned to Maggie. "Did I mention that JoJo used to be in the business too? She worked with Rick as his Media Director."

"About a century ago," JoJo said, smiling at both Rick and Beaker.

"Can't believe you stole her away, Henderson," Rick said to Brownie. "Still haven't forgiven you for that."

"Oh, well," Brownie said with a proud grin. "I just made her a better offer."

After the two men left, Maggie was surprised to realize she'd taken an instant dislike to both of them. That wasn't unusual for her—making up her mind too quickly about people. The two men were cold, fatuous and full of themselves—not atypical at their level of advertising hierarchy.

Still. It was a habit she was trying to break.

"So you worked with them?" Maggie said to JoJo, still trying to find some level of small talk with the woman.

"She did. And so did Bette," Brownie said. "You remember how incestuous it all is, don't you, Maggie? You'd open up a vein for one shop only to move to another one six months later and do everything you could to garrote the first shop at the One Show?"

"I do," Maggie said.

"You know, guys," Brownie said. "Maggie here was a pretty big deal in her day, too."

"Brownie, don't," Maggie said, feeling the creep of heat in her cheeks.

"Oh, really?" Sasha said but she was looking around the patio for anything more interesting.

"Absolutely," Brownie said. "She was always on the short list for winning her agency either an Addy or a Clio. Weren't you, Maggie?"

"Back in the old days," Maggie said, wishing he would shut up and go back to talking about how awesome JoJo was.

"And now she writes this amazing blog about living in Provence. Don't you, Maggie?"

Kill me now, Maggie thought, trying to smile.

"That's so sweet," JoJo said as she waved to someone she knew in another part of the restaurant.

"JoJo was a killer Media director at one time," Brownie said. "Every shop wanted her. But now she plays tennis every day and shops the hell out of Lenox Square."

Maggie glanced at JoJo. Since JoJo was clearly not listening, Maggie decided a response was probably not necessary.

3

An hour after arriving, Maggie's table ordered raw oysters, *boulots,* and *oursins* to start. Then came the omnipresent and—at least in Cannes—*de rigeur* —*soupe de poisson* followed by the main dishes. For Maggie and JoJo that was a pan-seared *steak au poivre* that Maggie made a mental note to tell Laurent about. She was so focused on her meal that she forgot to see what anyone else got.

In many ways it was just a typical night in the south of France, Maggie thought as she finally put her fork down and tried to stifle a groan as she pushed back from the table.

Nonetheless, she hoped she'd still manage to do justice to the *Soufflé au Grand Marnier* that was coming.

The weather tonight was exquisite—balmy and warm with a light breeze. Even though it was nearly ten o'clock, it was still light out and Maggie could see the tips of the yachts' masts as they bobbed in the harbor nearby.

She *was* however regretting wearing the shapewear that she'd thought she'd been so clever to pack for this trip. It felt like a straight jacket now, squeezing her guts out over the top of her slacks.

Obviously she must have bought the stupid thing a size too small.

As soon as everyone finished their main dishes, Brownie's group began to talk shop. After the umpteenth reference to interactive pre-roll, brand lift, behavioral targeting, and data management platform, Maggie felt seriously out of touch. Could advertising really have changed that much in ten years? She thought she had kept her hand in pretty well—what with using newsletter subscription search phrases and key words for marketing her blog.

Clearly, she'd been deluding herself.

Not only was she grossly overweight in her size ten pants but everything she ever knew about the one thing she thought she was good at—advertising—was dated and irrelevant. Her industry—the *one* thing she'd excelled in—had moved on and left her behind.

She glanced down at her phone to see a call coming in from Laurent and was surprised to realize how much time had flown by without her realizing it. She excused herself and hurried away from the patio.

"Hey, Laurent," she said as she leaned against an old stone wall that formed the bottom of the restaurant's front façade.

"*Allo, chérie.* All is good, *oui?*" His voice was low and familiar and sparked a flood of warmth in her chest to hear it.

"It's fine. How are the kids?"

"I have managed to keep them both alive."

"Ha ha. Funny guy. I really wish you could've come."

"Not a good time of year."

"I know. Anything happening?"

"Since you left eight hours ago? *Non.*"

"Did Jean-Luc come over?" Jean-Luc was their *vigneron* neighbor and a dear friend. There was rarely a day since Maggie and Laurent had moved to St-Buvard that Jean-Luc had not come by. He and Danielle were godparents and *faux* grandparents to Maggie and Laurent's children.

"Of course."

"Am I keeping you from something, Laurent? It sounds like you're struggling to keep up your end of the conversation."

"Pas du tout."

Maggie had known when she married Laurent that he was a taciturn kind of guy and trying to prod him into being something else only ever ended in frustration. Now if she could only remember to accept that.

"I better get back," she said. "Kiss the babies for me?"

"Bien sûr."

"And keep one for yourself."

"Only one?"

Maggie laughed. "I'll be home day after tomorrow."

"Sleep well, *chérie. Je t'aime.*"

"Je t'aime aussi, Laurent."

As she disconnected, she noticed another call was coming in.

"Hey, Danielle," Maggie said. "Everything okay?"

"Oui, chérie. As long as you have ordered the tablecloths from Aix?"

"Oh, crap. I forgot. I'm sorry, Danielle. Can you do it? I don't know where my head is."

"It is not a problem. Are you having fun in Cannes?"

Maggie looked around to make sure she wasn't being overheard. "Not really."

"Oh, I am sorry, *chérie! Et pourquoi pas*?"

"Well, honestly I think I'm feeling a little the-road-not-taken here, you know?"

"Non, chérie. I am not understanding you."

"It's just that I'm seeing my former self here in the shape of a really brilliant young copywriter and...it's just very unsettling, that's all."

"You are wishing you had stayed a career woman?" Danielle's voice was abrupt with surprise.

"No, of course not. I'm just a little tired is all. And I've had three glasses of wine."

"*Ah, voila.*"

"Yeah, *voila.* You sound a little tired yourself. Everything okay? I tried to call you when I was at the airport."

"I had an appointment in Aix. I left my phone in the car."

"At least you carry it with you. Half the time Laurent leaves his at home."

"It is hard to imagine how we lived without them, is it not?"

"That's the truth. Listen, sorry again about the tablecloths, Danielle. But I'll see you tomorrow, okay?"

"You are excited for the lavender fête, *chérie?*"

"Oh, yeah, of course."

Maggie disconnected and heard the sound of Sasha's laughter ringing out over the rest. *That was the flirty laugh,* Maggie thought. The one you made when you knew every guy in the restaurant had already noticed you, was watching you, and—it went without saying—was really, really wanting you.

That's who I was ten years ago.

Even though she'd said as much to Danielle not two minute earlier, the thought stunned her.

That's who I was then.

So who would I have been if I'd stayed in the game? Would I have turned into Bette? All sharp edges and chips teetering on both shoulders? Maggie shivered. Surely not.

I was at the top of my game when I was Sasha's age, Maggie thought as she returned to the table.

Now I'm a housewife with a blog.

～

As MAGGIE REJOINED the group she saw a young man standing at their table, his hands on his hips. Even with the classic American stance, she knew before she heard him speak that he was not American. His shoes were too pointy and his shirt too blousy. Plus he wore a lime-green windbreaker.

An American male would have thought it easier to carry a sign that said *Gay* or *Alien* than wear such consciously fashionable article of clothing in public. And while Maggie had never seen an outfit like that on anyone in St-Buvard, it was practically a uniform for young French men in St Tropez and Marseilles.

The man looked at her as she approached and quickly assessed her. His expression dismissed her immediately.

I seem to have that effect on everyone here, Maggie thought as she took her seat.

"You can't be serious," Brownie was saying to the man.

"Why?" the Frenchman said, "because you didn't think of it?"

"Do we have to ask the waiter to show you the way out?" Bette asked acidly, her face twisted in a grimace of distaste as she regarded him.

"How would that be possible," he sneered, "since you speak no language but English?"

"I really think you should just move along," Brownie said, but he looked at JoJo as if looking for approval.

Pas de problème," the man said before reaching out and tipping Brownie's wineglass over and splashing the contents onto Bette's lap. She shrieked and jumped up.

"You bastard! Get out!"

But the Frenchman had already left the table and was striding across the patio toward the street.

"Can you believe he did that?" Bette said, baring her teeth. She remained standing and looked around as if expecting the waiter to come to her aid.

"Who was he?" Maggie asked.

"I am so sorry, Bette," Brownie said, handing her his napkin. She snatched it from him and threw it back in his face. "A lot of good *that* is!" Bette snarled. "A real man would have taken care of it before it got to this!"

"Don't you talk to my husband like that," JoJo said, her words like splinters of glass in the night air.

"Your *husband* in name only," Bette said with disgust as she eyed JoJo.

"How dare you!" JoJo said, her hands gripping the table so that her knuckles were white. Maggie looked from Bette to JoJo and saw what she was surprised she hadn't seen before.

The two women hated each other.

Bette wore a bright blue scarf at her throat and Maggie saw that the wine had stained it too.

"Everybody calm down," Brownie said, trying to pat his wife's hand, but JoJo moved it away to avoid his touch. "Bette's right. I should have defused the situation," he said.

"*Defused?*" Bette said, looking at Brownie in astonishment as she dabbed at her jeans with her napkin. "Did I just hear you say *defused?*"

"Would you all just shut up? Please?" Sasha said, standing up. "The whole restaurant is staring at us." She picked up her purse and turned toward the bar where there was a scrum of loud young men inside—largely American and British from what Maggie could tell.

Maggie watched Sasha weaving more than a little as she left. Not surprising. They'd killed four bottles in three hours. Maggie hoped Sasha would be okay tonight. The hotel wasn't far but it was getting late and Sasha was unfamiliar with her surroundings.

"Well, thanks for a great night," Bette said sarcastically, throwing down her wet napkin and snatching up her purse. "Where's the friggin' ladies room?"

Although Maggie had never been to this restaurant before she was pretty sure the restroom was inside near the main dining area. She gave Bette directions inside and turned in time to see the waiter appear with five perfect soufflés. He stood and watched Bette leave.

"They will fall before they return," he said, his voice full of condemnation.

"Well, the rest of us will enjoy them immensely," Maggie said. "They're beautiful."

The waiter caught her eye and nodded, slightly mollified, before setting down each of the desserts and leaving.

Brownie threw down his napkin. "This is ridiculous. Bette, wait!"

"You're wasting your time," JoJo said. "Once she gets like this..."

But Brownie was already hurrying after Bette.

"I can't believe how he babies her," JoJo said with disgust. "All his employees, in fact."

"Well, it's his business," Maggie said, watching Brownie go into the bar. He stopped as if speaking to someone.

"Yeah, that's always *his* excuse too," JoJo said.

"Well, *you* were in the business," Maggie said, clenching her jaw. "You should know how it is."

"He's changed since you knew him," JoJo said, pulling out a cigarette and lighting it up.

If you say so, Maggie thought, but held her tongue. She was surprised to see that JoJo smoked. Most Americans didn't any more. Brownie was still standing in the bar, his shoulders slumped, his back to them. Clearly Bette wasn't interested in talking with him.

"You don't think so?" JoJo said, blowing smoke over Maggie's head. She smiled in a condescending manner.

"I haven't seen Brownie in nine years," Maggie said, turning her attention to her soufflé. It had already fallen but she broke the sugar crust and spooned into the steaming center.

"He has a gambling addiction," JoJo said, pushing her own dessert away. "I'll bet you didn't know that."

Maggie felt a pang of unease. If that was true, she felt sick for poor Brownie. And if it was a lie—if it was just JoJo being jealous and wanting to upset Maggie—well, any way you looked at it, it was pretty crappy.

Brownie came back to the table and sank into his chair.

"Didn't I tell you?" JoJo said, grinding out her cigarette. "She's impossible."

"She's upset, JoJo," Brownie said with a frown as he pulled out his smartphone and squinted at the screen. "Have a little compassion, will you? She hasn't been herself since the divorce."

"Well, you have all week to smooth her feathers," JoJo said as she gathered up her cigarettes. "Although I don't know why you bother."

"I just think it helps to try to be nice," Brownie said, watching JoJo's preparations to leave. "What's the point of feeling bad if you don't have to?"

"Thank you for that Hallmark message," JoJo said disdainfully and scooted her chair back.

"Are you leaving?" Brownie's eyes were wide with dismay.

"I see my old supervisor from McCann," JoJo said, picking up her wineglass as she left the table.

Brownie and Maggie watched JoJo disappear into the interior of the restaurant. Except for the young men in the bar, the restaurant had largely cleared out. Maggie was surprised to see that they were one of only three tables still occupied on the patio.

"What the hell happened?" Maggie asked. "Who was that guy who spilled your wine on Bette?"

Brownie looked up from his phone screen and shoved his dessert plate away. "Just nobody."

"But you all knew him?"

"Not until this afternoon, we didn't," Brownie said. "He's one of the delegates. Etienne Babin I think his name is."

"When did you have time to meet him?"

"Bette and I were in the bar while the rest of you were upstairs getting ready. He and Bette had words."

"About what?"

"About nothing," Brownie said with frustration. "He's just a jerk Frenchman who hates Americans. Don't tell me you've never run into the type?"

Maggie didn't know what Brownie was driving at but decided it was entirely possible that they'd all had too much to drink. Brownie and his group would have every right to be suffering from serious jet lag. Maggie herself had driven four hours that morning and was ready to call it a night. Just as she was about to suggest it, Brownie leaned back in his chair and regarded her.

"So why didn't the big guy come? You two still doing okay? I heard biracial couples have all kinds of problems."

"Thanks, Brownie, but since Laurent and I are the same race it's a lot less tricky," Maggie said sweetly. "This is our busy time of year in the vineyard. He couldn't get away."

"Sure."

"Look, Brownie, I've been meaning to talk to you about...you know...how our breaking up all went down."

"Oh, forget it."

"No, it bothers me that we never discussed it."

"What's there to say? One minute you were my girlfriend who went to the south of France to find her sister, and the next minute you were back with some French dude you couldn't keep your hands off."

Maggie held her tongue. This was Brownie's time to get some things off his chest and she owed him that.

"What made it worse was I saw how the guy treated you," Brownie said.

"What are you talking about?"

"The way he bosses you around like it's the eighteen hundreds or something."

Maggie's mouth fell open in astonishment. "That's ridiculous."

"I had lunch with your brother Ben a few months back. He said you treat the guy like he's your lord and master."

"That...that is not true! Ben must be deranged to say something like that!"

During a difficult period in his life, Ben had come to stay with Maggie and Laurent at Domaine St-Buvard, their *mas* outside the village of St-Buvard. At the time Maggie thought everyone had gotten along fine. It was news to her that Ben thought Laurent was overbearing with her.

"I mean...it's true, with the different cultures and all," Maggie said, feeling her jaw beginning to ache, "Laurent sometimes forgets to ask instead of tell but he's never...he would never...he does *not* boss me. Quite the contrary, in fact."

"Hey, Maggie, it's none of my business if you like being dominated. Doesn't mean you're not a strong independent woman in your own right. I mean, even JoJo likes me to take control now and then. Reconfirms the sex roles, you know?"

"No, I do *not* know," Maggie sputtered. "Laurent is not like most American men. And I guess I can see how Ben might misunderstand how Laurent and I relate to each other. But I assure you, Laurent does *not* tell me what to do."

"And you're not protesting too much *at all*," Brownie said looking in the direction where JoJo disappeared as if he might catch a glimpse of her.

"I just wanted to say," Maggie said, ignoring his dig and determined to reroute the conversation, "that I felt bad about how you and I broke up. That's all."

"You mean in a burst of magical pixie dust?"

"I'm not apologizing for falling in love with Laurent—I couldn't help that. I'm apologizing for how I handled it with you."

"Yeah, well, you're forgiven. What with Elise dying in her apartment and all you pretty much had your hands full."

Maggie usually worked hard *not* to think of her sister, Elise. No good ever came of it. She brushed the thought of Elise aside now and focused on the wine in her glass. It was a lovely rosé. Laurent would know the name of it just by taste, she was sure.

"Besides, I came out just fine on the other side." Brownie looked suggestively in the direction that JoJo had gone. And that was when Maggie knew that Brownie hadn't gotten over it. Not for a minute. Not at all.

"All I can say is I'm sorry, Brownie."

"Hey, forget it."

"Could you just be honest with me for one minute?"

"Why, Maggie? What the hell would be the point of that?"

Maggie took in a quick breath as Brownie stared at her, the mask had dropped and the naked anger and hurt was finally visible.

"Is that what you think you deserve?" he said. "Honesty from me? Especially since I didn't get it from you?"

"You're right. I don't deserve it. But I'm asking you to forgive me anyway."

"Well, of course I forgive you, gal," he said with a grin, the mask firmly back in place. "After all, if you hadn't dumped me, I never would have met JoJo. Did I tell you she's an ex-gymnast?"

So much for closure, Maggie thought a few minutes later as she made her way to the ladies room. She hadn't expected Sasha to return to the table—and frankly wasn't even surprised not to see JoJo again—but for all three women to leave to find their own way back to the hotel? That was odd in anyone's book.

She left Brownie to settle up with the waiter and hurried down the small spiral staircase that led to the toilet. The bar, while still open, was now vacant. The men—and Sasha presumably—must have cleared out while Maggie was talking to Brownie.

She tapped on the unisex bathroom door. At this time of night people were often too drunk to remember to lock the door behind them when they used the facilities.

All of a sudden a loud alarm rang out from behind the toilet door. Maggie jumped back, her hand flying to her mouth.

Was it a fire?

"Hello?" Maggie called. "Is there anyone in there?" She could hear voices and the sounds of footsteps coming down the stairwell behind her.

Maggie tried to open the toilet door. It wasn't locked but she felt something blocking it.

She groped on the hall wall for the light switch and put one foot in the room. Instantly she felt her shoe—a ballet-style slipper—nearly come off her foot.

The floor was sticky.

As the hall light came on, she blinked against the sudden brightness.

The floor in the restroom was red.

Maggie's heart began to beat loudly in her ears.

It was blood.

Two men came up behind her, speaking rapidly in French, and physically pushed her out of the way. One of them was dressed as a waiter. The blare of the alarm eliminated all other sound. Over their shoulders, Maggie saw a form on the restroom floor: the body of a woman. Her eyes were glazed and her head flung back.

Maggie gasped when she recognized the bright silk scarf at the neck.

It was Bette Austin, Pixel's award-winning creative director...

... with a steak knife jammed in her throat.

4

It was surprising how quickly the police arrived.

Maggie assumed the fast response was because Cannes was a mecca for rich tourists. Law enforcement had learned long ago—whether it was a stolen wallet, a noise violation or a knife in the throat—you didn't keep the wealthy waiting.

Maggie, however, was doing precisely that at the moment. Once she'd gone screaming up the rickety spiral staircase—well, she *thought* she was screaming—Brownie told her later she was only gasping and waving her arms—everyone else seemed to take over.

It was amazing to Maggie—who was admittedly not new to finding dead bodies—that she should have been so shocked at seeing Bette's body. Maybe it was because there had been absolutely no hint or warning at all when Maggie had gone down to the restroom that there was anything sinister in the offing.

So much for any sixth sense. She had been totally taken by surprise by the horror that awaited her in the restaurant bathroom.

Had the murderer been nearby? Was he or she still in the bar area when Maggie went down? Was it possible the killer could even have been in the bathroom when Maggie was there? After all, once she found Bette's body, she never glanced into the other toilet stall. And she did remember that its door was firmly closed.

That was ridiculous. The two waiters who'd followed her down the stairs when they heard the alarm go off would have seen anyone if there had been anyone to see.

Now Maggie sat shivering in the bar of the restaurant, her favorite black ballet shoes bagged and gone. She had stepped in the blood of course. Maggie stared at her bare feet and even in the dim light of the bar saw flecks of blood on her ankles.

Bette's blood.

"You okay, Maggie?" Brownie said as he walked over to her from where he'd been talking with two French detectives.

She nodded but felt sick. She felt as if her lovely *steak au poivre* and the glistening perfect oysters on the half shell she'd consumed earlier that evening...well, just *thinking* of them made her want to find a handy trash receptacle. She forced her nausea —and her dinner—to remain down.

"I just can't believe it," she said.

Brownie sat down at the bar with Maggie and rubbed a tired hand across his face. He looked terrible.

Four detectives stood on the patio and spoke with the waiters, the cook and a few of the diners who had been in the restaurant when Maggie had come stumbling from the staircase, hyperventilating.

The archway leading to the bathroom at the bottom of the stairs was taped off but a steady stream of medical examiners and detectives continued to come up and down, most carrying plastic baggies of evidence.

Bette's body had yet to be removed.

Maggie felt cold and vulnerable. Being barefoot didn't help. She was desperate to call Laurent and hear his voice, but it was late. She was sure it had been a long evening for him too after a full day in the vineyard—pruning, raking, spraying—then making dinner for the kids and getting them to sleep. Plenty of time to tell him in the morning.

It just would be so nice to hear his voice right now.

"I think they want you to come with them," Brownie said, indicating the police.

"I know. They haven't finished interviewing me."

"They're trying to track down Sasha," Brownie said. "Someone said they saw her leave with one of the American guys in the bar."

"What about JoJo? Have you heard from her?"

Brownie stiffened. "She's not answering her phone."

Maggie watched Brownie's eyes dart around the room as if expecting to see his wife walk in any minute.

"She'll need an alibi," Maggie said.

Brownie looked at her, his mouth open. "Are you serious? Or are you just so rattled by tonight that you've lost your damn mind?"

Maggie bit her lip to keep from responding.

LAURENT SAT at the kitchen bar and sipped a glass of *marc*. He'd taken the last forty minutes to scour the kitchen as was his wont. He normally enjoyed cleaning it as it gave him time to think of his day and put things in perspective. Now as he sat and flexed the soreness out of his shoulders, he saw crumbs that he'd missed sprinkled across the kitchen's terra cotta flooring.

A wrought iron chandelier and copper range hood over the Cornue range were new additions—at Maggie's insistence—since they'd come into a little money last year. He'd fought against them. They'd seemed frivolous compared to definite needs like farm equipment or Mila's *école maternelle* expenses next year. But he had to admit they provided a level of pleasure he hadn't expected.

That was Maggie's doing of course. She often saw what he could not. And unlike himself, she saw what was missing. Not always what was there. It was a good combination, he thought. The way the two of them viewed the world so differently.

I must be tired, he thought. *I'm starting to sound like an American.*

It had taken longer than usual to get the kids down tonight. That surprised him. When Maggie put them to bed there was always so much giggling that he was sure she kept them wired and awake longer than if Laurent had just done it alone.

Perhaps it was their unease at Maggie being gone, he thought. She was rarely away from them. And the Papa was no substitute for the *Maman.*

He finished his drink. Frankly, it didn't feel good for any of them to be separated. Even for a night. It upset the natural rhythm of their lives.

He'd already fielded an annoyed phone call from Jean-Luc complaining that Danielle was upset with Maggie for not collecting some item for the fête. While Laurent thought it was all women's silliness, he would not dismiss Danielle's feelings.

As evidently—if Jean-Luc could be believed—Maggie seemed to have.

Even in her absence, the house felt full of her—her ideas, her design signatures, evidence of her presence. His eye fell on her slippers peeking out from beneath the sofa in the living room.

But it was good that she was gone. At least at the moment.

His latest project had been more involved than he'd expected. With the children out of school he'd assumed—stupidly—that Maggie would be too involved to notice what her husband was up to. She rarely came out into the vineyards other than to track down Jemmy.

But this more recent project unfortunately did not take place in the vineyard. He would have to move quickly and take advantage of her absence if he was to pull it off without her knowledge.

It was not something he enjoyed—lying to his wife. He had promised her he wouldn't do it in future and it felt wrong to be doing it now. She had made it very clear how she felt about the ends justifying the means.

But of course he would do it anyway.

He glanced at the notebook he'd been studying and rubbed his eyes in weariness. Too late for figures. Too late for plotting. Both *les enfants* would be up early and he had many things to do before Maggie returned. As he took his glass to the sink, rinsed it and set it aside, his phone vibrated on the counter.

He could see it was from Bernard Faucheux, a partner in Laurent's winery business. Domaine St-Buvard was individually licensed and operated under an alternating proprietorship that allowed Laurent to produce and bottle his own wine. After a blowup with Laurent's original partner—Adele Bontemps— Laurent had secretly bought her wine crushing operation through Bernard.

When Adele found out about that, she had been enraged.

He picked up the phone.

"*Oui*?" he said.

"I was hoping you'd still be up," Bernard said.

"What is the matter?"

"I got a call from two reporters from the magazine *Harvest*. They're interested in covering the boutique industry for our region to pitch to the international press. They intend to do it using either our boutique as the centerpiece of their story or the wine co-op in Orange."

It annoyed Laurent to hear Bernard refer to Domaine St-Buvard as if it belonged to anyone but himself.

"When?" he said.

"I've set up the meeting for the evening after tomorrow in Arles."

Maggie was due home tomorrow afternoon but Laurent had yet to sort out the details of his other, special project and now there was a conflict. He had planned to keep Maggie away from the house on the evening that Bernard was suggesting.

"I cannot make it," he said.

"Laurent, I do not need to stress to you how important this meeting is. It's not just the money. It is about our reputation in Provence and even France. Possibly even Europe."

"I'm not sure I care about that."

"Fine. But make sure the rest of your investors feel the same way. Jean-Luc for example? Will you be the one to tell him we were not the focus of a national magazine story because you couldn't be bothered?"

"*D'accord*," Laurent said with irritation. "I will come."

"On time, please. I'm sure your American wife can handle the children for one evening on her own."

"Text me the directions," Laurent said curtly before disconnecting.

Laurent knew Bernard wasn't stupid. He'd instantly deduced that Laurent's hesitation had to do with a scheduling problem involving the children. Being unmarried—and a typical Frenchman—Bernard didn't respect that. Not at all.

But as Laurent well knew—he didn't need to in order for it to become a problem.

MAGGIE HAD BEEN to the Cannes police department before.

During the drive over in the back of the police cruiser, she'd found herself praying it had somehow been remodeled or so drastically renovated—or maybe even moved to another building or section of town—so that she would not have to remember the last time she'd been there.

It was nine years ago the first time. To identify the body of her older sister Elise.

And then again six months later to bribe the head medical examiner into revealing the contents of a sealed file on that same body.

Both times had vied successfully for being the worst moments of Maggie's life.

And she'd had some pretty harrowing moments since then.

The buildings that lined the narrow cobblestoned streets in this section of Cannes were ancient and wedged tightly against one another. The eighteenth century architecture was falling down—testimony to the fact that so little had changed in this neighborhood in nine years.

Or even a hundred years.

Brownie had elected to come with her but whether to support Maggie or because he hoped there would be news about his wife, Maggie couldn't be sure. The fact that the police still hadn't found JoJo was disturbing to say the least.

Plus, with Maggie's blunt insinuations about JoJo's innocence or guilt still ringing in the air between them, the tension in the car as they drove down the narrow streets toward the police head-quarters was thick.

Maggie wasn't surprised to see the glitzy tourist section of Cannes fall away. Gone were the fifty-euro sandwiches, the jewelry boutiques and upscale clothing stores. Gone too was the harbor, the beaches, and the seemingly endless line of hotels, cafés and restaurants.

Clearly, the police department, complete with the Cannes morgue, was not a landmark the city fathers wanted to promote.

On any street in Cannes, virtually at any time of day one could detect the delectable fragrance of *couscous, coq au vin, pot-au-feu, soupe de poisson,* or *seafood paella*. But now there was only the musty, close stench of sweat and rotten vegetables in the back seat of the police car. Maggie realized she had been holding her breath.

Once at the police department, she and Brownie were escorted up a flight of stairs to a bare hallway with a series of doors. They were led to a waiting room where Brownie was instructed to wait.

The uniformed policeman then led Maggie back down the hall and opened the first door he came to. Inside was a scene out of any Law and Order TV episode Maggie had ever seen. A table, two chairs, and a long mirror, presumably two-way, was set up in the room.

Seated at one of the tables was a man who stood when she entered. He was blond, very tall, with piercing blue eyes. The police officer nodded to him and left the room, closing the door behind him.

Suddenly Maggie was so tired, she wasn't sure her legs would support her. The last time she'd glanced at her watch, it was nearly three in the morning.

God knows when she would be able to go to her bed.

"Madame Dernier?" the officer said, indicating that she should sit. "I am Detective Chief Inspector Charles Dumas."

As Maggie sat she saw her passport on the table. For a moment she thought the police had broken into her room to get it but then remembered she'd had it in her purse and had offered it up almost immediately.

I really must be tired.

"I must ask you a few questions," Dumas said, seating himself.

"I know. Because I found the body."

"Will you please tell me what happened?"

Maggie recited the events for at least the fourth time that night.

"And when did Madame Henderson leave the table after Madame Austin?"

Maggie was ready for this. After all, JoJo and Bette had exchanged ugly words. And not in soft tones. She couldn't remember who was around to hear them but there would surely be someone who would confirm it.

"About twenty minutes," Maggie said. That was plenty of time to follow Bette downstairs and do the deed if that was where the detective was leading. Except Bette hadn't pulled the alarm until nearly midnight. And that was nearly an hour after JoJo left the table.

"And Mademoiselle Morrison?"

Maggie had to think for a minute before she remembered Sasha's last name.

"Sasha left the table before Bette did."

"I see. And what time did *you* leave to go to the toilet?"

This was the tricky bit because frankly Maggie was herself the closest one to the time of death. In fact, she was right in the middle of a very narrow window of opportunity.

"I guess thirty minutes after JoJo left the table, so forty-five minutes or more after Bette went to the bathroom."

"Nobody thought it odd that Madame Austin was taking so long in the toilet?"

Maggie had asked herself this very question at least a hundred times tonight. The fact was, she'd been too engaged in her argument with Brownie to give a thought to Bette and how long she was spending in the bathroom. Truth be told, since both JoJo and Sasha had gone off to find more interesting company it wasn't at all out of the realm of possibility that Bette might have done the same thing.

"I...I guess I just thought she met someone."

Dumas wasn't writing anything down which didn't surprise Maggie. Surely he already had all the facts. Unless he was hoping Maggie would begin to tell a slightly different version—thereby implicating herself—he really was trying to understand where everyone was and at what time.

"Madame Henderson and the victim argued tonight. Is that so?"

Maggie nodded, feeling like she was betraying Brownie. She was sure the cops had asked Brownie this question and she was equally sure he'd downplayed the argument. Of course he would.

"You are being recorded, Madame. Could you speak for the recorder?"

Maggie glanced involuntarily at the big window and wondered who was in there, if anyone.

"Yes. They argued."

"Badly?"

"Well, I hadn't met either of them before today so I don't know if this was bad for them or what. Some guy had knocked a glass of wine into Bette's lap so she was pretty mad."

"And she blamed Madame Henderson for this?"

"No, if I remember right, I think JoJo said something to tick her off."

"Who was this man?"

"I have no idea but Brownie...er, Monsieur Henderson seemed to know him. You could ask him."

Dumas smiled which Maggie took as the answer that he had already asked Brownie. All of this was really just so much games-playing, Maggie thought. And at three in the morning, it was a lot less fun than it might be.

"Do you have someone to drive you back to the hotel?" Dumas asked as he handed Maggie her passport.

"I...well, I guess Brownie...I mean Monsieur Henderson and I will take a taxi."

"Monsieur Henderson is busy at the moment."

Maggie felt a wave of fear.

"Busy? Why?"

He glanced at his watch and smiled, confirming to Maggie that everyone in the whole world had officially spent way too much time watching old Poirot re-runs.

"Monsieur Henderson will be unavailable to accompany you to the hotel," he said smugly, "since his wife has been brought into the station. And he will presumably want to be with her."

"JoJo? You found her?"

"We did, Madame. Along with her fingerprints on the steak knife found shoved into Madame Austin's neck."

5

Later that morning, Maggie was sure she had just closed her eyes when her hotel room door erupted in a cacophony of pounding. She groaned as she fumbled for her cellphone to see that it was only a little after nine in the morning. That meant she'd only been asleep for four hours.

The pounding on the door continued but since Maggie had also glimpsed the fact that she had six missed calls from Brownie on her phone, she was pretty sure she knew who was making all the noise out in the hall.

She grabbed her robe from the floor and stumbled to the door. When she had gotten in that morning she'd only stopped long enough to take a quick shower and fall into bed, more tired than she ever remembered being in her life—even after childbirth.

She opened the door and Brownie stormed past her.

"They've arrested JoJo," he said. His hair was wild around his face, his eyes bleary and red-rimmed. He looked like he'd slept in his clothes, if he'd slept at all, which Maggie seriously doubted.

"I know," Maggie said. She hesitated to go to him. There was nothing about the way he stood—flexing his fists, his legs wide apart—that invited a hug. His eyes darted around the room, failing to light on any one thing.

Maggie went to the phone and ordered a pot of coffee and a basket of croissants. Then she gathered up a pair of jeans and a t-shirt and disappeared into the bathroom.

"I don't even know how to hire a damn lawyer!" Brownie shouted through the bathroom door. "And they've taken her passport. They won't let her leave the country! I contacted the American consulate and you know what they said?"

Maggie reappeared dressed and went to the window in her room. It was raining—very unusual for summer on the Côte d'Azur.

"Did they say it was a local matter and they couldn't intervene?" she asked.

"Yes! Yes! Can you believe it?"

"Did you get a chance to talk to JoJo last night?" Maggie asked.

"Just briefly and not alone," Brownie said, finally beginning to wind down a bit. He sat on the edge of Maggie's unmade bed. "I can't believe any of this is happening."

Hearing a sharp knock at the door, Maggie went to take the heavy tray from room service. She poured two coffees and handed Brownie one although caffeine was likely the last thing he needed right now.

"You have to help me, Maggie."

Maggie looked at him in surprise. "Me? How?"

"You speak French for one! I'm not even sure of half of all the stuff the cops were asking me." He looked at her sharply. "Did you tell them JoJo and Bette fought last night?"

Maggie looked uncomfortable "Well, it's the truth, Brownie. And it was confirmed by a few other people who—"

"I can't believe you told them that! *Why*? Why did you tell them?"

"Uh, because they asked and I'm not used to lying to the

police," Maggie said, feeling a guilty flush creep up her neck. But couldn't she have equivocated on that? She'd already told the police she didn't know the two women. Why hadn't she just said it didn't sound like much of an argument to her?

Because somebody killed Bette. That's why.

"It's because she's my wife, isn't it?" Brownie said hotly. "You're jealous and so you threw her under the bus."

"Okay, Brownie, I think you need to calm down. Especially if it turns out JoJo really did kill Bette—"

"How can you even say that!?"

"Well, I can say it, Brownie because she's the obvious suspect. She had opportunity, means and motive. Bada bing."

Maggie was instantly sorry about the last little flippant remark but Brownie was too upset to notice.

"I know she didn't do it," he said. "Doesn't that count for anything? I *know* she didn't do it."

Maggie reached out and put a hand on Brownie's arm.

"I know this is hard, Brownie—"

"Please, tell me you'll help me, Maggie. I know you do this kind of thing. It's all your folks talk about. They say you've solved like twenty cases since you've been in France and remember how we worked together to solve Elise's murder?"

There it was again. Now Maggie remembered *why* she'd never really reached out to Brownie. He was too big a reminder of one of the saddest times in her life. And now that he was here, it seemed he couldn't stop making her think about it.

"I have to get back to St-Buvard," Maggie said.

Brownie slumped on the bed and hung his head. "I can't believe any of this. Poor Bette."

"Did she have family?" Maggie asked softly.

He shook his head. "No. She was recently divorced and lived alone with about ten cats or something. I just can't believe this is happening."

"Has Sasha shown up?" Maggie asked.

He nodded. "She was with some guy during the critical time."

He means she has an alibi. Everybody but JoJo is in the clear.

"You could serve as an interpreter for me," Brownie said hopefully. "I'm begging you, Maggie. I can't do this alone."

"Brownie, trust me, you don't want me interfering." *Boy, wouldn't Laurent love to hear those words coming out of my mouth?*

"But I do! Unless..." He narrowed his eyes at her. "You...you don't think she did it, do you?"

"I don't know anything. I have no clue as to—"

"You think JoJo killed Bette!" His eyes were wide with shock and he stood up from the bed, knocking his mug of coffee onto the floor.

"Look, Brownie, if you want to believe she's innocent, by all means, go for it. I probably would too in your shoes. But the police aren't usually wrong when it comes to forensic evidence. They don't go on guesswork any more."

"What are you talking about? The steak knife?" Brownie was practically shouting now. "Did it ever occur to you that *of course* her fingerprints were on that knife? She ate her meal with that knife!"

"Yes, but were anybody else's prints on it?"

"I don't know what you're trying to say. What difference does that make?"

"Because, Brownie," Maggie said gently, "how would the killer be able to wipe off his or her prints but somehow manage to leave JoJo's?"

Brownie looked at her blankly, his mind clearly refusing to accept the logic of her words. He turned and moved toward the door.

"Well, if you can't help me, you can't. I guess this makes it a perfect circle, huh?" he said as he turned and glared at her by the door. "The last time I saw you, you threw my heart in the meat grinder and now when I give you the chance to make amends, you start the grinder back up again."

"That's not fair, Brownie."

"Yeah, well, welcome to my world," he said bitterly, and left the room.

Maggie sat on the chair and stared at the door, Brownie's words ringing in her ears.

Was he right?

It was true he wasn't asking her to do something easy like help clear a woman Maggie liked or believed innocent. But doing something easy like that wouldn't rate as appropriate effort to erase her previous crime against him.

He was asking her to do something really difficult.

She glanced out the window and watched the raindrops dash against the windowpanes. She was sorry she couldn't help Brownie but she needed to go home today. Home to St-Buvard and Laurent and the children. That was her world and that was where she wanted to be.

The phone rang and she saw it was Laurent. She grabbed it up and sank back into the chair, ready to be totally enveloped by her husband's love and strength.

"Hey," she said softly.

"Did you know the woman who was killed?"

Maggie wasn't sure why she should be surprised. Laurent knew everyone. His contacts—whether in the criminal underworld or the police force—were legendary. She knew Bette's murder had only been reported to the media in the vaguest possible detail.

"I found the body," she said.

Laurent cursed and Maggie wondered if the children were in earshot.

"She was Brownie's creative director," Maggie said. "And Brownie's wife JoJo is the prime suspect."

"Are you taking this call from the A8 on your way back home?"

"I...well, I've been up all night, Laurent," Maggie said, a sliver of irritation creeping into her voice. "I thought I'd have breakfast first."

"*Bon.* Have breakfast and then come home immediately. Or will you need me to come get you?"

Maggie ground her teeth and involuntarily flashed back to Brownie's smug assertions of how Laurent bullied her.

"Well, no, not being fourteen years old, I think I can manage getting home by myself. What's the big rush, anyway?"

"The big rush..." —he pronounced the word as *beeg*— "...is that you are at the center of a suspicious death...*again*...and you are not where you should be."

"Okay, I don't know what you mean by that," she said, glancing at the door where a despondent and angry Brownie had just left. "But now that you mention it, I think this might be exactly where I need to be. It turns out I have some things I need to do here first."

"Don't be *ridicule*. You will not interfere. Do you hear me, Maggie? You will leave it to the police."

Maggie sputtered. "I hear you, Laurent. Sorry if my salute is a little sloppy!"

"I am not understanding you. Just come home *maintenant*. You are needed here at home."

"What in the world for? So I can listen to your day in the vineyard? Or so I can string crepe lanterns across the village square in St-Buvard?"

"Why are you talking like this? I never should have let you go."

"Do you HEAR yourself? *Let me go?* You're not my father, Laurent, or my boss or my lord and master, much as you might like to think so."

"I have never—"

Maggie found herself standing up, a vein pulsing in her forehead.

"Sure, you have what *you* want," she said angrily. "Everything is exactly the way YOU want it."

"And this is not what *you* want? Jemmy? Mila? Life with me? What are you saying?"

"Don't put words in my mouth! This isn't about Jemmy or Mila!"

"That is *exactement* what this is about. Your life in the country raising two children instead of lying by the pool drinking *mojitos* with old boyfriends."

"Is that what you think I'm doing? Now who's being ridiculous?"

"I am done talking with you until you start making sense."

Maggie sputtered. "That is the most...I can't believe..."

But Laurent had already hung up.

～

THIRTY MINUTES LATER, Maggie found Brownie downstairs in the hotel lobby restaurant. He was staring at the screen of his phone, a cup of espresso in front of him. The floor to ceiling windows in the dining room allowed the brightness of the French Riviera to pour into the room, highlighting the Oriental Isfahan rug on the floor in a vibrant melding of blues and orange.

She went to his table. When he looked up, his eyes were full of tears. She put her hand on his.

"I'm sorry, Brownie. Of course I'll stay and help you."

"Oh, Maggie!" He lunged across the table to hug her, knocking silverware and a plate of croissants to the floor. "Thank you so much! I can't tell you what this means to me! What made you change your mind? Never mind. It doesn't matter. Thank you."

She ordered a coffee from the waiter and Brownie faced her with a brave smile.

"What's the first thing we need to do?" he asked.

"Well, we should talk to everyone who was at the restaurant last night."

Brownie frowned. "That's a lot of people. But if you think so."

"Have you had any luck finding an attorney?"

Brownie shook his head and reached over and held Maggie's hand.

"If you knew JoJo, you'd know she could never do something like this. She's the sweetest, most gentle creature, Maggie. She truly is."

Just because I don't like JoJo doesn't mean she's guilty. Some of the biggest jerks I've known have yet to kill anyone.

"And do you know *why* I know she couldn't have done this?" he persisted.

"No, why?"

"Because she suffers from a rare pathology where she has a clinical aversion to blood."

Maggie cocked her head. "Really?"

"Yes. She literally passes out at the sight of it. So you see there's no way she could have... created that much blood all over poor Bette."

Maggie nodded. "Is this in her medical files back in Atlanta?"

"Absolutely. It happened twice in the last year. Both times documented."

"That's good. I'm not sure it'll be enough to get her released. But it's a good start."

"You know what I think, Maggie?"

The waiter delivered Maggie's coffee. She felt tired but more from her fight with Laurent than lack of sleep. It was all she could do to keep Laurent's words from reverberating in her head. Had Brownie and Ben been right all along?

Was Laurent a male chauvinist and somehow Maggie had just never noticed?

"Maggie?"

She shook her head and smiled. "Sorry. You were saying?"

"I think JoJo was framed."

"Really? But who would do that?"

Brownie looked away. "Well, I don't know, do I? But look at the facts. The cops talked to the people who JoJo was with at the time of the murder and they all said she was with them. She doesn't have a drop of blood on her which is good because she'd pass out if she had, and we only have the forensics guy's word that the same steak knife found in Bette's throat is the one that JoJo was using."

"Are you saying *the cops* are trying to frame JoJo?"

"Well, I don't know who's trying to do it. Maybe the real killer switched the knife out. That makes more sense, doesn't it?"

"But why go to all this trouble to implicate JoJo? Is she important in some way?"

"No. Never mind. It's a stupid idea. Forget I said it."

As Brownie turned to dump sugar in his cold espresso, Maggie couldn't help the feeling that it was at least possible that JoJo had been framed. But that wasn't the thing that bothered her.

It was the sudden realization that if JoJo *had* been framed—somehow Brownie knew *why*.

6

Maggie gnawed a fingernail and looked down the avenue where she stood with Brownie in front of the Carlton Hotel. It had stopped raining and now the steam was rising off the pavement all around her.

She was wearing a simple cotton skirt with espadrilles and a clingy black tunic. Back in St-Buvard she would have been downright stylish as she did her market shopping, a basket on one arm, Mila's sticky hand in the other.

Here in Cannes she might as well be wearing a sign that said *Frumpy Tourist*. Gone were the days when an unwieldy map or a camera around your neck told the world you weren't from around here. Now it seems you just needed to wear shorts or last year's blue jeans to announce your cluelessness.

Brownie's suggestion that the police were trying to frame JoJo had bothered Maggie at first but she soon banished her discomfort by reminding herself that Brownie was upset. He would be leaping at any and all theories to explain why JoJo was a suspect. If Laurent were being held for a murder he didn't commit, Maggie would probably be thinking some fairly outlandish things too.

The key phrase of course being *for a murder he didn't commit*. The problem was, Maggie wasn't at all sure that applied to JoJo.

"I tried to call Sasha," Brownie said. "But she's not answering her phone. Big surprise. She's probably so hung over she's still in bed."

"We'll get to her when we come back," Maggie said. She moved out of the way of an entourage heading toward the front door of the hotel. The woman at the center was elderly and bone thin. She'd obviously had face work so there was no way to determine her real age. She clutched a tiny trembling poodle in her arms. Two tall handsome men flanked her, but whether they were sons, lovers or bodyguards, Maggie couldn't tell.

She waited for them to pass and then maneuvered Brownie out of the flow of pedestrian traffic down the stairs to a stone bench across from the Carlton's private beach.

"I need to go back to the police station," Brownie said. "To see if they'll let me see JoJo. Will you come and translate for me?"

"I thought you had an appointment to see her later today."

"I do but they might let me in sooner if I show up unannounced."

"Can you tell me again about the guy who dumped the drink in Bette's lap last night?" Maggie asked. "How was it y'all knew him?"

Brownie ran a hand through his hair. He looked brittle and worn. His eyes were bloodshot. Now that she thought about it, he hadn't looked that great when Maggie picked him up at the airport yesterday morning either.

He just looked a whole lot worse now.

"Supposedly he's some local character," Brownie said. "Everybody knows him. He's a known troublemaker."

"You said you had words with him before we even went to the restaurant."

Brownie nodded.

"He was at the bar at the Carlton," he said. "Bette and I were having a drink while we waited for you and Sasha and JoJo to come down and he made some kind of anti-American crack."

"In French?"

"What?"

"Etienne Babin is a French delegate. So did he speak French to you?"

"Well, I don't remember. I guess he spoke English or else how would we know we were being insulted, you know? I didn't think anything of it but Bette got pissed off."

"Can you remember what he said to her?"

"Something like *Why do all these Americans come and try to ruin the festival for decent people?*"

"Really?"

Brownie looked at her. "Why?"

"Well, it just seems a strange thing for him to say. I mean the Brits and the Americans usually walk off with all the big awards so I can see maybe him saying something along the lines of feeling cheated. But how do the Americans *ruin* the festival? And why just the Americans? And he said *decent people*?"

"I don't know, Maggie," Brownie said with frustration, his Adam's apple bobbing furiously. "Those may not have been his exact words. It's the gist of it, though."

"And Bette responded to him?"

"Oh, hell, yeah. She said the French were about as creative as they were brave—something like that."

"That was a crack about the war?"

"Yep."

"What was her problem? Did she hate the French?"

"Hey, chill out, Maggie. Nobody hates the French. Well, maybe Bette did, come to think of it. At least she didn't respect them."

"Any idea why?"

"No, but when Etienne left the bar, he was shooting daggers at Bette."

"And then he showed up at the restaurant and knocked a wine glass in her lap."

"Yes! So it seems to me *he's* the one the cops should be looking at."

"You told them about Etienne?"

"Of course. I mean, they wrote his name down but they still arrested JoJo."

Brownie ran a hand across his face and Maggie could see his hand was shaking. He'd been up all night. Hell, he probably wasn't even over his jet lag. Her heart ached for him. She was sure this was not at all what he had imagined in his week on the Côte d'Azur.

"I think we should split up," she said. "See if you can find the McCann-Erickson person that JoJo was supposedly talking to last night."

"*Supposedly*?" Brownie glared at her. "You know Maggie, if you're just doing this to placate me and you're really not on board—"

"No, I am. It's just how I tend to view things until I have facts, you know? Please stop getting your feelings hurt every time I utter an unguarded thought."

"You're right. Sorry. I'm on edge." He looked at his shoes. "I just feel so helpless."

"I know, I know. So let's get busy. Go find the McCann person —what's his name?"

"George Foley. He's in charge of their social media."

"Find him and ask him what he told the cops. Because they wouldn't have arrested her if Foley had given her an alibi."

"So you're saying he *wasn't* with her at the time of the murder?" Brownie looked at her with confusion in his brown eyes.

"I don't know, Brownie. That's what we're trying to find out. Talk to him. Ask him what he told the police."

Brownie nodded and looked down the street. The festival's opening ceremonies were tonight. There wouldn't be panels or viewings anywhere until tomorrow. Almost everyone at the festival was either walking on the beach, eating somewhere along the promenade or getting drunk somewhere.

"Okay. Where are you going?"

"I'm going back to the restaurant," Maggie said. "The waiters saw everything and everyone. No way they didn't know where JoJo was. Or Bette for that matter."

Brownie looked optimistic for the first time since last night. It saddened Maggie to see it. Everything she was doing was being done to reassure him. But while the theory that someone had framed JoJo was interesting, it was hardly likely.

In her experience, if a thing looked like a duck and quacked like a duck...then get ready to start scraping duck doo-doo off the bottom of your shoe.

BROWNIE WATCHED Maggie disappear down a side alley toward the direction of the little marina and last night's restaurant. He felt a surge of love for her as he watched her go. From this distance, the way she walked and swung her hair reminded him of when they were kids. He got a sudden flashback of when both their families would go up to the mountains together. Maggie was always so much fun. Always ready for a hike or a swim. She listened to him. She made him laugh.

He smiled sadly. Definitely the one who'd gotten away.

He walked back toward the hotel. From its front steps you could just see the ocean twinkling in blue diamonds over the horizon of sand and the signature bright blue cabanas. He stood off to the side with his phone in his hand and punched in the number.

"What the hell happened?" a voice answered as way of greeting.

Brownie was shocked at how viscerally overcome he felt just to hear his voice. It was all he could do not to scream into the phone.

Brownie took in a long breath and said the words he'd been practicing all morning. He fought to say them calmly. His stomach bucked as he ground out the words.

"Well, let's see. There was a terrible accident last night that you opted to take advantage of."

"That's one way to look at it. Let me ask you, Brownie, do you think I don't talk to the other delegates? That I don't hear things? Do you think I'm stupid?"

"No. I...I just...I don't know. Look, I admit, I faltered for a moment, that's all."

"So we're good now?"

"As soon as you clear my wife! Don't think I don't know you're behind this."

"I just need you to confirm that we are back on track."

Brownie took in a long breath and let it out. "It was a misunderstanding, for God's sakes," he said mechanically, his eyes on the horizon, as he fought to hold it together.

"A fairly serious one, I'd say. Just ask poor JoJo. I understand they haven't even allowed her to change clothes or shower."

Brownie bit a hole in his lip to keep from screaming.

"So do we have a recommitment to our original agreement?" the voice asked pleasantly.

Brownie's voice shook with the effort to maintain control.

"Yes, dammit. I've already said so."

"Fine. Just remember, Brownie. It can always get worse."

~

THE BATHROOM at *Astoux et Brun* was still roped off with police tape but that didn't stop the restaurant from doing a brisk lunchtime business.

Maggie went to the bar. She saw their waiter from last night— and he saw her—but he was busy. It occurred to Maggie that questioning restaurant staff probably worked better when they weren't in the middle of the lunch or dinner rush.

She turned to the bartender across the shiny mahogany bar. She was an older woman with sharp eyes and she'd been watching Maggie closely since she walked in.

"Campari and soda, please," Maggie said and took a seat at the bar.

The woman turned to make the drink and set it down in front of Maggie on a tiny pink napkin.

"Your French is very good, Madame," she said.

"That's because I live here," Maggie said, sipping the drink. It was thirst-quenching but as usual, she thought it looked prettier than it tasted.

"In Cannes?" the woman said.

"No. Near Aix," Maggie said. "Did the police talk to you about last night?"

The woman's eyebrow rose in an arch.

"Why do you want to know that?"

Maggie shrugged. "The woman who was killed was in my party."

The woman nodded and studied Maggie as if trying to decide if she would say more.

"I did not work last night," she said finally. "Who was your waiter?"

Maggie pointed him out to her.

"That's Martin," the bartender said. "I'll send him over to you."

"Thank you. I appreciate it."

Maggie tried to let the effects of her drink push away the ugly words she'd exchanged with Laurent this morning. Had she over-reacted? Now that she had some distance from the conversation, it felt like she might have. She pulled out her phone to see if she'd missed a call from him. Nothing.

Was he waiting for *her* to call *him*? After *he* hung up on *her*? Remembering that little detail made a burst of anger rocket through her.

"You are wanting to talk to me, Madame?"

Maggie looked up to see their waiter, Martin, standing in front of her, a serving tray tucked under his arm.

"It's about what happened last night," Maggie said. "I was hoping you might tell me what you told the police."

He shrugged. "I only told what was the truth."

"Always a good policy. And that was?"

"I saw Madame...JoJo, I believe her name is? I saw her go down the stairs to the toilet after the other loud-mouthed American."

So the cops had a witness that JoJo had gone down after Bette? No wonder they arrested her.

Still. There was nearly an hour's lag between when JoJo supposedly went down to the toilet and Bette pushed the emergency button.

"Right afterward?" Maggie asked.

He shrugged again. "They were both down there at the same time, Madame. *C'est façile.*"

Maggie tried to make sense of this. Had JoJo gone down to confront Bette? Was Brownie mistaken about her blood pathology?

"Is that all, Madame? I have a living to make and your coun-trymen do not tip for poor service."

He gave a smirk that Maggie wasn't able to interpret. Either he was insulting her or inviting her in on the joke. She admitted she was generally the last person to know when a French person meant anything nonliteral by what he said.

Just look at her marriage.

She watched the waiter go and then put a five-euro note on the bar and collected her bag. As she was leaving she saw someone she recognized sitting alone at one of the outdoor tables. It was that guy Brownie had introduced her to last night —Wilson.

She approached his table. He pushed his empty wine glass toward her without looking up.

"Another," he said.

"I guess you heard what happened to Bette Austin," Maggie said.

Wilson looked at her then and frowned. Maggie supposed many women might consider him attractive. He was in his early to mid thirties with thick brown hair and brown eyes. He had long eyelashes too. But the eyes that peered out from them were flat and mean.

"I'm sorry," he said. "You are?"

"We met last night. I'm Maggie Newberry Dernier. A friend of Brownie's."

"Oh, right. Yes, well, it's terrible. I think we're all in shock."

As he spoke, his eyes raked Maggie from her breasts to her shoes. She was a little startled that he'd be so obvious about it but then it had been awhile since she'd been in the business and she'd clearly forgotten how many tools there were in the industry.

"I was wondering if you spoke to Bette last night," Maggie said, keenly aware that the jerk hadn't even offered her a chair. That was probably just as well. Maggie swore she could smell his aftershave from where she stood. Like industrial lemons drowning in saccharine.

"Nope. I barely knew her," he said, leaning back in his chair as if to view Maggie better.

In spite of herself, she felt self-conscious. It was a warm day but instead of dressing for the weather as she might normally, she'd chosen to wear a long tunic today that hid her tummy and hips. She hated herself for being so vain. She made a mental note to go on a diet as soon as she was back home.

"How about JoJo? She used to work for you, right?"

"What's this all about? We've all of us already spoken to the frog detectives," he said with a sour look on his face.

"JoJo was arrested for the murder," Maggie said, hoping to shock him into being a little more helpful.

He appeared to already know. His face was impassive. He even shrugged and looked back at his bowl of fish stew. His cellphone lay next to his plate.

"I'm not at all sure what you're doing at this festival, but if you think you're going to play the housewife version of Columbo while I'm trying to enjoy my lunch, you're mistaken."

His reference to the wall-eyed and exceedingly frumpy Detective Columbo wasn't lost on Maggie but she forced away her pique. In her experience, as soon as she reacted on an emotional level to something a witness told her, she was bound to miss the crucial piece of information that made all the difference.

"I just thought you might want to make sure your friend JoJo wasn't indicted for a crime she didn't commit," Maggie said.

He laughed rudely, a loud barking sound that made several other diners turn in his direction.

"Whatever made you think that? Because Brownie and I are such chums? Or because JoJo used to work for me?" He pushed his plate away and Maggie felt a sliver of satisfaction. For whatever reason, she'd gotten to him. Now she just needed to find out why.

"Besides," he said, standing up and signaling the waiter for his bill. "I don't know what game you're playing but trying to imply that Bette's death had anything to do with the advertising festival is a very dangerous one to play."

Maggie caught her breath with a gasp of surprise. Because up to that moment, she'd assumed that Bette's death was personal.

It hadn't occurred to her that it might be connected with the advertising festival.

7

Laurent stared out the kitchen window at the back garden. From here he could see the slate walkway as it wound crookedly from the patio toward the vineyard. Three years ago he'd spent several long days lining the walk with lavender and rosemary as part of his *potager*. Bees were flying in aerial circles above the path. Little Mila sat on the slate, her chubby legs stretched out in front of her with a lapful of lavender sprigs.

He turned away from the sight and slid his phone across the counter in frustration.

He'd called their usual babysitter but Mimi was on vacation in Paris with some school friends. He'd called Danielle—the children's de facto French grandmother—but she was unavailable because of the upcoming lavender festival and had too much to do to get ready for it.

"Papa! Mila is in the garden!" shouted Jemmy as he burst into the kitchen. His face and hands were covered with some indeterminate grime, but his eyes were wide with excitement.

"Okay," Laurent said absentmindedly as he glanced back at his phone.

Who else was there to call?

The question instantly reminded him of his fight with Maggie —something he had been working hard all morning to shove from his mind. What was the matter with her? What could possibly have happened in Cannes to make her speak to him as she did?

Stop thinking of it or you'll end up driving to Cannes with two screaming children in the backseat to fight it out with her.

He felt a shiver of memory. Cannes was where he and Maggie had met. It was where they'd courted—although neither of them had known it at the time.

It was where they—

"*Papa!*"

Laurent turned toward the large cookstove where he had two copper bottom pots simmering with chicken broth. It was hot in the kitchen and he'd need to cool the soup before refrigeration.

"*Papa!*" Jemmy said more insistently.

Laurent blew a long shock of hair from his face in irritation. If it weren't for Maggie's absence, he would be overseeing the pruning of the new shoots today.

What could Maggie be thinking? he wondered. Had her friend Brownie grown a backbone since Laurent had last seen him? That hardly seemed likely. But if Brownie was in fact married to a murderess, perhaps he had more depth than Laurent had given him credit for. In any case, it was grossly ill mannered for Brownie to suggest that another man's wife stay and do the job that was his own to do.

Perhaps I should go to Cannes after all? A vision of Brownie with his bowtie, his plaid slacks and his wide earnest eyes quickly dissolved the image Laurent had been forming in his mind of punching him in the nose.

Nobody could change that much.

Brownie was weak. He was reaching out to his ex-girlfriend who—of all the many things that could be said of her—was not at all weak. *Of course* he would reach out to Maggie. And naturally, guilt-stricken because of how she had ended things with him, Maggie would be willing.

Merde.

"Papa!"

"What?" Laurent said with annoyance as he picked up his phone again and debated calling Maggie.

Jemmy stood in the doorway to the kitchen, his face already tanned by the sun, his lips purple from the berry bushes that lined the vineyard.

"I just need to know because of..." Jemmy's eyes widened as he saw a plate of *saucisson et fromage* on the counter. "Oh! Is it lunchtime yet?"

"It is not. Where is your sister?"

"She's found a new friend for Hoppy."

Laurent went to the stove and pulled down a large well-used skillet and banged it onto the burner, then adjusted the flame as he reached for the olive oil. "Ah yes?" he said, distracted. "A new friend?"

"Uh huh. I just came because I couldn't remember—do the bands on the neck mean he's friendly or not friendly?"

Laurent stopped in mid-reach for the olive oil on the shelf and turned on his heel to stare at his son before snapping off the stove and bolting out of the kitchen through the French doors and into the garden.

MAGGIE TOOK her time walking back to the Carlton from the restaurant. She knew from experience that walking was a great way to get her thoughts moving. And while she hadn't learned anything earth shattering at the restaurant, she did feel certain hints tugging at her consciousness around the edges.

She wasn't sure exactly what she had learned from the

conversation with either Martin or Wilson. One thing was certain: they were both holding back something.

As she walked and felt the sun on her hair she tried to remind herself that it was a beautiful June day in the south of France. Although it was true she *lived* in the south of France, life kept her so busy—running errands, tending to the children, managing her own business and helping Laurent with the vineyard—that just like anybody else, she often found herself ignoring the beauty around her.

From this route back to the hotel she couldn't see the marina but she was easily able to imagine the moored boats with their sails bobbing and fluttering in the breeze as the picture of languid south of France serenity.

"Oh my gosh, Maggie! Is that you?"

Maggie looked around and saw a woman walking down the sidewalk toward her. The woman was tall and dressed in in an asymmetric miniskirt with a nearly see-through camisole top. Her outfit was snug and form fitting but she had the body to pull it off. She walked with a quick, assured step—the confident stride of someone who expected others to step aside for her. Her grin matched her walk and Maggie's mouth fell open.

"I don't believe, it," Maggie said. "Courtney?"

Courtney Doan flung her arms around Maggie as people streamed by them.

"I can't believe I found you!" Courtney said. "I ran into Brownie and he said you were here. Oh, darling, you look amazing!"

Maggie felt dazed. Courtney looked like she had not changed a bit in the last decade. Still dressed to the nines and slim as a model. Even her face looked unlined and placid as if she'd just stepped out of a spa.

There'd been a time when Maggie and Courtney had been nothing short of inseparable. Both had entered the business at roughly the same time working at the same agency. They'd gone bar hopping most evenings after work, laughing, gossiping about industry contacts and clients.

They were about the same age and so totally focused on their jobs—looking great and totally enjoying being young and alive in a very hot business. They'd worked together at McKelly & Payne's agency before Maggie moved on to Selby & Parker's. A couple of years later Maggie met Laurent and left the country.

"Are you here for an award?" Maggie asked.

"My shop is, yes," Courtney said.

"Your shop? You own your own agency now?"

"I do, darling, yes," Courtney said with a musical laugh. "I guess I thought you would have heard about it. I have done for nearly six years." "

"Wow. I've really been out of touch."

"Do you have time for a drink later? To catch up? I've got a thing right now but I'm dying to talk."

"Me, too. How about this evening?"

"This evening is the opening ceremonies,. But just before? Where are you staying?"

"The Carlton."

"Perfect. Let's meet in the bar at five. We can go to the ceremonies together. Who are you here with? No, don't tell me," Courtney laughed. "Just like old times. Tell me tonight. Maggie, darling, you look wonderful. I can't wait to catch up."

Courtney gave her another hug and then hurried off down the sidewalk. Maggie watched her for a moment wondering where she was going and whom she was meeting. It wasn't like Courtney to be alone. She probably had an exciting lunch date.

Maggie turned back to the hotel, stunned and discomfited by the chance encounter.

Courtney Doan. They'd been so close at one time. Besties. Through thick and thin. Some wild adventures sure. But mostly just pals navigating the often choppy seas of the advertising game in Atlanta. Having each other's backs.

And enjoying the ride the whole way.

RICK WILSON WATCHED Maggie Newberry as she walked away from the restaurant.

Of course he remembered her. Nine years ago when she was working in the business, he had watched her regularly walk up to the awards podium at every annual Addy Awards show in Atlanta.

She wouldn't remember *him* of course. He was just a junior art director in those days.

But he knew *her*.

Everyone knew Maggie Newberry's story. How she started and how she'd ended up. She'd quit the business—turned her back on it like it was nothing—and moved to France to live on a vineyard with her French chef husband and two kiddies.

Personally, Rick thought it was pathetic and now that he'd seen her up close twice and spoken to her—something she wouldn't have deigned to allow back in the day—he was sure of it.

Truth be told he'd had a bit of a crush on her back then. He flinched at the memory and drank down the contents of his wine in one gulp.

Perhaps a little comeuppance might be added to the mix with his arrangement with Brownie? Wouldn't *that* be sweet?

"Monsieur? Another glass?"

Wilson looked at the waiter and then pulled out a hundred euro note from his wallet and slid it across the table to him.

"I think you might have been mistaken about what you saw last night, Martin. American women all look alike, don't you think? Are you sure you saw Madame Henderson? Really?"

The waiter looked at the money but didn't take it.

"Am I to tell the police this new information, Monsieur?"

"I don't think that will be necessary. Just anybody else who asks."

The waiter nodded. "Then I think you are right, Monsieur. The light was bad. I can't be sure it was her. In fact, I now realize it wasn't her at all."

The waiter took the money and left the table.

Wilson threw down the obligatory euro-coin tip and gathered up his phone and wallet with anticipation welling up in his chest. He turned his face to the sun.

This year's festival was promising to be his best yet.

8

The first thing Maggie did when she reached the hotel was go straight to Brownie's room. He didn't answer her knock. All the rooms were on the same floor so she went to Sasha's room next. Sasha didn't answer either. Maggie had gotten Sasha's phone number from Brownie so she stood out in the hall and called it but it went to voicemail.

Maggie looked down the hall where Bette's room was. A yellow tape had been crisscrossed over the door. Maggie made a mental note to call Charles Dumas in case he might be open to sharing anything he'd found in there. She doubted he would. Most police detectives were reluctant to share their information before the jury had pronounced a verdict.

And they were a long way from that.

While she considered the information she'd gotten from Rick Wilson to be sketchy at best, at least it made her think that Bette's death might have something to do with the festival and she was pretty sure that was *not* a direction the cops were going in by holding JoJo. Maggie still wasn't sure JoJo *wasn't* guilty but she owed it to Brownie to exhaust every avenue of his wife's possible innocence.

She scrolled through her missed calls on the chance that she might have gotten a call from Laurent and somehow hadn't heard her phone ring. *Fairly impossible but you never knew.*

There was nothing.

Just seeing how stubborn he was in not calling her back made her mad all over again and she stiffened her resolve to stay and work the case.

How dare he treat me like I'm a child? Does he not hear himself issuing orders?

She put in a call to Brownie and was surprised when he picked up.

"Hey, Maggie," he said in a dejected voice.

"Hey. Did you find anything?"

"Find anything?"

"You know, with George Foley? The guy JoJo was talking to at the time of Bette's death?"

What was with Brownie? He sounded stoned.

"Oh, right. He said he wasn't with her for more than a few minutes."

"Okay. Well, I'll try to talk to him too. Maybe I can get him to remember more details. How about Sasha? Have you talked to her?"

"No, but I ran into the guy she was with last night. So at least I helped confirm *her* alibi. As if she needed it. Only about ten people saw her leave with him."

"Are you okay, Brownie? Were you sleeping?"

"I needed to close my eyes for just a few minutes before going to the police station."

Maggie began walking back to her own room.

"That's good. Rest is important. Listen, Brownie, I was wondering if the Twitter handle for the festival was something special that I can't guess at?"

"Twitter handle?"

"You know, hashtagInternationaladvertising? Or hashtagIFOA?"

"Oh, sorry. Right. Uh, it's hashtagIFOA. Why?"

"I'm going to ask the festival goers if anyone saw anything."

"I don't think that's a good idea." Suddenly Brownie seemed more awake.

"Are you kidding? It's a great idea," Maggie said. "You'd be surprised what people see or hear and the French police are hopeless at using social media to investigate."

"What...what are you going to say?"

Maggie entered her room and went to the table where her laptop was sitting.

"I'm just going to ask if anyone talked to Bette Austin last night and, if they did, to please contact me."

"Okay. I guess. Sure."

"Go back to sleep, Brownie. Get some rest."

After she hung up, Maggie tapped her fingers on her laptop for a moment wondering why she felt weird about her exchange with Brownie. It probably meant nothing. Not speaking the language and all, the guy was losing it because his wife was being held for murder in a foreign country and he was helpless.

Satisfied with this interpretation of Brownie's odd behavior, she quickly posted the tweet and put a call into Detective Dumas.

He picked up on the first ring.

"*Oui*?"

"Hello, Chief Inspector Dumas," Maggie said formally. "This is Madame Maggie Dernier. I was wondering if you could tell me if you found anything in Bette Austin's hotel room yesterday when you—"

"*Non*," he said and hung up.

Maggie stared at her phone with her mouth open.

So rude!

Without stopping to think, she punched in another number. It too was answered immediately.

"Maggie?" Roger Bedard said with surprise when he picked up.

"Hey, Roger. I need your help."

She was surprised to hear him laugh. She and Roger had a complicated history and laughing on the rare moments when she reached out to him was not at all compatible with that history. She brushed away the warning signs of what that might mean. If he could help her, she needed to at least try.

"A friend of mine's wife is being held on suspicion of murder," she said. "I need to get a look at the police file on her."

There was a pause on the line.

"Does Laurent know you're doing this?"

"Of course." *That wasn't a lie. Laurent does know. He just doesn't approve.*

Another long drawn-out pause shot a wave of irritation through Maggie.

Good God! Is Brownie right? Have I lived over here so long that I don't even realize how subjugated I've become? Why don't I just tell Roger that I can do what I want without my husband's permission?

But she knew the answer to that. Because if she said that, first of all Roger would *absolutely* not help her and second of all, he'd call Laurent straight away.

Because regardless of whatever rivalry there was between Roger and Laurent, Maggie knew that men—at least in France—would always stick together.

"Which murder is this?" Roger asked.

"The one that happened last night in Cannes."

"So you're in Cannes?"

"I am. Can you help me, Roger?"

"I will get back to you." He hung up. Maggie stared at her phone. *This seems to be becoming a habit with the men in my life.*

Maggie sat on the edge of the bed. Her room at the Carlton was a suite with separate sitting areas and a small balcony facing the Mediterranean with a tiny bistro table and one chair. The view was stunning.

She felt a sliver of anger at the fact that Laurent still hadn't called her back. Was that deliberate? Was he trying to manipulate her? She had to admit Laurent didn't usually play games. But the result was the same of course. If he didn't call, he knew it would drive her crazy.

She tried to focus on something else and as she gazed out at the azure sea, she found herself wondering *why* Martin the waiter might lie.

Why did Maggie think he wasn't telling the truth?

It was true that Maggie didn't like JoJo and was only too willing to believe she was capable of the crime. But she also had quite a bit of experience with people who lied.

And there was something about the way Martin told his story that didn't ring true.

She knew it in her bones—he had lied to her.

Did that mean JoJo *wasn't* down in the toilet with Bette? Or just that Martin hadn't seen her? And if he hadn't seen her—who paid him to say he had? Because of course, why else lie?

In other words, is Brownie right? Is JoJo being framed?

Maggie got up and went to the bathroom to splash water on her face and freshen her make up. It wasn't like she was going to try to compete with anyone at the festival but she could at least try to look like she hadn't just dragged herself out of bed.

Speaking of which...

Maggie moved back into the sitting area of the suite and put in another call to Sasha. This time she answered.

"Who is this?" Sasha said, sleepily.

"Hey, Sasha," Maggie said. "It's Maggie. Brownie's friend? I just wanted to make sure you're okay."

"Huh? What?"

"Well, you know. Everything with Bette and all. Did the police talk with you a long time?"

"Who is this?"

For the love of God. Am I invisible? We ate dinner together last night!

"Maggie Newberry," Maggie said patiently. She deliberately didn't give her married name just in case—on a long shot—Sasha might recognize her better by her maiden name.

Back in the day, everyone would have known her.

"Oh, okay. Sorry. I'm wrecked. Why are you calling?"

"No reason. Are you going to the opening ceremonies tonight?"

"Probably."

"Well, maybe I'll see you there."

"Yeah, okay." Sasha disconnected. Maggie sat holding the phone and trying to make sense of it. Was the girl just hung over? Maggie had listened hard to see if she could detect anyone else in the room with Sasha but hadn't heard anything. Did it matter? Was Sasha even remotely a suspect?

Brownie said she went home with someone who alibied her. Not that she needed it. Sasha had been seen with no fewer than five men in the bar at the time that Bette was being murdered in the toilet below.

"I THINK she intends to talk to Foley, herself," Brownie said into the telephone. His hand was clammy as he gripped the receiver.

"Didn't you tell her you'd already talked to him?"

"I did but I'm not sure she was satisfied."

"Why you ever thought it made sense to involve your house-wife friend, I have no idea."

"I did it," Brownie hissed, "because I thought she might throw a curve ball into things. You know, distract the cops. But if she talks to Foley—"

"So what if she does? He'll just tell the truth as he knows it. And that can't hurt us. Don't worry so much. Everything is fixed."

Brownie sat down on the edge of the bed, the phone to his ear and chewed his lip.

"Tell that to JoJo," he said.

"That's on you."

"I accept that," Brownie said between gritted teeth. "But what I want to know now is *how* will it be fixed? I talked to Wilson this morning and he actually threatened me! I can't believe you got me involved with this, Dennis."

"And I can't believe you're not *thanking* me, Brownie. When I first came to you with the offer you couldn't snap it up fast enough. Did you inherit money in the meantime?"

"No! No. I just...I just wasn't sure it was a good idea after all."

"I don't know what made you think you could back out like you were holding a bad hand or something. Didn't make me look too good, I can tell you."

"Look, I'm sorry. I told Wilson this morning that I'd play ball and I will. Just...can you tell me *when* JoJo will be freed?"

"These things aren't automatic, Brownie. Just make sure you do your part and she'll be released. Rick's got it all worked out. Meanwhile, how about a quick visit to Monte Carlo for a run on the machines to calm your nerves? Say, the minute JoJo is released? Have you ever been?"

"Look, Dennis, what I want to do more than anything after the vote is hop on a jet and go right back to Atlanta. What with Bette and all, things are kind of spoiled for me here in a major way. You see that, right?"

Dennis sighed dramatically. "If you say so. I mean, here you are in the south of France—the most exquisite place on earth— and you can't wait to run back to Peachtree Street? The simple truth is you're a redneck, Brownie. You can put a bowtie and chinos on it but the end result is the same."

"I'm fine with that," Brownie said tightly. "How do I know Rick will do what he says?"

"God, you're a cretin! I guess you don't. You'll just have to trust us." Dennis laughed and hung up.

Brownie wiped the sweat from his hands and noticed they were shaking.

The joy that had been his just a few hours ago seemed like a long way away. Now he just needed to get the hell out of Cannes with his life still intact.

9

Well, clearly Maggie was going to have to be the bigger person.

She hated when that happened.

She paced around her room for precisely ten minutes, checking her twitter feed and her phone simultaneously. She was beginning to feel as if she'd created this drama between her and Laurent. It was true he'd been bossy with her but that didn't mean that's who he was with her intrinsically, she reasoned.

How could she be married to him for eight years and only *now* figure out he was a domineering male chauvinist?

It just didn't make sense.

She would call him back, ignore the fact that he so rudely hung up on her, and explain to him—like a mature adult—that she had a responsibility to a friend that she needed to honor. If Laurent ranted and raved, she would simply remain cool and above it.

As she dialed the phone, she had to admit she'd never seen Laurent rant or rave in the whole time she'd known him. Not his style at all. But he definitely had other ways of letting her know he was displeased.

Just like any good king.

The phone rang five times on his end before he picked up.

"Are you on your way back?" he said as he answered.

Unbelievable! That is not at all conciliatory! Am I the only one being forced to act like an adult?

"No," she said evenly. "I told you I have a few things I need to do here first."

"I have a business appointment in Arles tomorrow night," he said flatly. "There is no one to watch Mila and Jemmy."

Maggie was well aware that Laurent had a history of lying to her when he thought it was for her own good or the good of the family or mankind in general. But they had come to an agreement last year where they both acknowledged that lying was a bad thing for their marriage. Laurent had promised he wouldn't do it again.

She reminded herself that the promise itself could be a lie but up to now she'd chosen to believe it and until proven otherwise, didn't feel it was fair to doubt him.

"What kind of business meeting?"

"That is irrelevant."

Did he really just say that to me? Is the vineyard business none of my business? Maggie felt heat flushing through her body.

"Who else is coming to this meeting?"

"Nobody you know," he said, his voice full of the strain she normally never heard in him.

That's what twenty-four hours of nonstop childcare will do to you.

"I'm sorry," she said. *Be strong be strong be strong.* "But you will just have to make other arrangements for tomorrow."

"I won't forget this, Maggie."

Whoa. Laurent had *never* threatened her before. Plus he rarely called her by her name.

He must really be mad. He must be beyond mad.

All the more reason for her to stick to her guns.

She saw a phone call coming in from Danielle and realized

immediately that it would easier to stick to those guns if she were off the phone with Laurent.

"I need to go," she said. "I have another call coming in." She disconnected and let out a long breath as she connected with Danielle.

LAURENT TRIED to remember a time he had been this cross with Maggie. She had been stubborn before—many times before—but never to the point of out and out insurgency.

He frowned. Well, of course that was not true. The fact was, life with Maggie was generally even keeled and placid. It was easy to forget the times she went her own way—deliberately lying or misleading him in some cases—in the process.

But this! How possibly could the wife of an old boyfriend be the reason to cause such problems between them? Maggie never even spoke of Brownie. Laurent knew for a fact she was not in touch with him. How was it possible the man and his problems had grown to such importance in one short day?

He drummed his fingers against the counter and picked up the phone again.

Maggie won't like it, he thought. *She won't like it one bit.*

He dialed the number.

A young girl answered. "*Allo?*"

"*Allo*, Chloe. This is Monsieur Dernier. Is your father at home?"

"Papa!" the girl called and then came back to the phone. "He's coming."

Laurent congratulated himself for thinking of this. He would solve his problem and punish a naughty wife all in one.

Very tidy.

"*Oui?*" Bedard said as he picked up the phone. "Laurent?"

"Can Chloe babysit for me tomorrow evening?"

"You can bring the children here? That's no problem."

Laurent expected to detect the unasked question: *Where is Maggie that she couldn't watch the children?*

But the tension that unspoken question would have provoked didn't happen. Instead, there apparently was no curiosity at all.

It was as if Bedard already knew that Maggie was in Cannes. And why.

Had Maggie already reached out to Bedard for help? What was she up to? Laurent thought back to nine years ago in Atlanta when he first met Brownie.

Laurent's memory of the man had been that he was harmless, deeply in love with Maggie, and chronically unsure of himself. While Laurent didn't claim to have the last word in handling women, one thing he knew well enough was that there was a certain kind of woman—and his beloved *femme* was definitely one of them—who appreciated a strong man to match her.

Maggie would have tired of little Brownie before the walk had been completed down the aisle. Of that Laurent was sure.

But because of the culture in the American South and the history of their two families, they would have stuck it out until the end—happiness be damned.

Laurent didn't think for a moment that Maggie might be wondering about whether she'd picked correctly in her choice of husbands. That didn't mean, however, that she wasn't assessing her life in other ways.

He sighed. It was a very American habit and one Maggie never seemed to tire of.

He was sure it wasn't seriously problematic. How could it be? Maggie shared the two greatest joys of her life—both under the age of seven—with him. As the father of her children, he had the ultimate of all head starts on anyone vying for her affection. No, *that* wasn't seriously a concern.

But it didn't mean it didn't need to be addressed.

"A<small>RE YOU ALL RIGHT</small>, *CHÉRIE*?" Danielle asked. "You sound as if you have been running."

"No, I'm good," Maggie said. "I was just talking to Laurent. Sorry about that." She opened her laptop to look at her Twitter account.

"You know the lavender fair is four days from now, yes?"

"Of course, Danielle."

Maggie saw on her screen that there were several responses to her tweet.

Someone calling himself *@luvsFranco* tagged @betteaustin and tweeted: *the racist got her just desserts #hateabully.*

What's that all about? Maggie thought as she scrolled down to the next tweet.

@LMelange posted: *anyone surprised about Bette? #bitch #longoverdue*

Maggie couldn't believe how ugly these tweets were. So was Bette not popular? Or were these tweets not representative of how people felt about her? Brownie would know. She'd put a quick call in to him as soon as she got off the phone with Danielle.

"Maggie?"

"Yeah, sorry, Danielle," Maggie said. She saw that some people had seen her tweet request as an opportunity to post a few jokes at the expense of the French. That wasn't too surprising considering they were in France. The Brits and the Yanks were particularly brutal. Still...some of them *were* funny.

"I *said*, Maggie, that you promised you would be home this afternoon. We have much work to do."

"I did?" Maggie directed her attention back to the phone call. "I can't believe I said that. But I can't do it, Danielle. A woman's been killed here; someone I had dinner with last night."

"Are the police asking you to stay? Are you a person of interest?"

"Well, no. It's not like that."

"You have made an obligation to your village, Maggie," Danielle said sternly.

"Yeah, well, I love how all of a sudden it's *my* village," Maggie said lightly, trying to ease Danielle out of what was sounding more and more like a very indicting tone of voice. "Half the time the guild tries to lose my invitation to the monthly suppers."

"I am expecting you home *today*, Maggie. I need your help. As you promised."

"Well, I'm sorry, Danielle," Maggie said, feeling her temperature rise. "I can't do it. I told you I'd be there for the festival and I will but—"

"I do not need you to stroll the festival with a basket in your arm like a tourist!" Danielle burst out. "I need help getting it organized!"

Maggie had never heard Danielle raise her voice. Not to Jean-Luc when he'd had too much to drink, not to the little brats who rode their motor bikes through the carefully planted lines of grape vines on Danielle's property.

This was new.

"I don't know why you're getting so upset," Maggie said. "I'd think *you* of all people would understand that a murder takes priority." Last winter, Danielle had helped Maggie discover the murderer of their village's new American bistro chef.

"I do *not* understand!" Danielle said shrilly. "There is much work to be done! I cannot do it myself! All of the kiosks have not arrived and Madame Belmont is insisting on selling her olive oil soaps at the same time. The separate smells would be ghastly. *You* were to deal with this."

"Danielle, I swear I'll be there *before* the actual fête but someone's been killed. And I really think that trumps handing out lavender sachets at a country fair."

"Thank you for making clear where your priorities are."

Danielle hung up. Maggie sat staring at her phone, stunned.

Is she serious? Does she know what the word priority means? Of course murder is more important!

But an underlying knot of doubt in her chest began to throb uncomfortably.

It wasn't the lavender fair of course. It was the promise she had made to Danielle. The promise that Danielle could count on her. *That* was the priority Danielle was talking about.

As soon as the idea penetrated her thoughts, Maggie shoved it aside.

She hadn't always been a plump housewife in the countryside with only a stupid blog and a half-ass lavender fair as her claim to fame!

Maggie stood up in frustration but the burning sensation in her chest wouldn't go away. She'd never heard Danielle so mad. A wash of guilt spread over her and she paced the room to try to shake away the feeling. As she did, she heard footsteps outside in the hallway.

And then an envelope appeared from under the door.

10

Maggie picked up the envelope and listened as the footsteps hurried away. Every fiber in her being told her to open the door and confront whoever had left this note. But she hesitated. For whatever reason, whoever had left it did not want to see Maggie.

She ripped open the envelope hoping it would reveal the identity of the writer.

It didn't.

It was only one sheet of paper—taken from the back of the blank notes section that came in every festival goers' package.

The words were printed in a vibrant dark pink ink with a fountain pen: *Talk to Bert Jamison and H.O Yang. Both tell a very different story*

In case there was any doubt that the note had been written with a fountain pen, there was a tiny drop of ink at the corner of the page. Maggie turned it over but there was nothing else to see. The edges were perforated where it had been ripped out of the back of the conference brochure, making Maggie believe the sender was a part of the advertising festival.

Well, that stood to reason, didn't it?

She went to her laptop, called up the festival website, and quickly did a search for each name. Bert Jamison was an account executive with Dempsey, Baja and Carruthers, a British ad agency out of Bristol. Yang was a freelance copywriter from Hong Kong.

Did that mean these two had information about Bette's death? The note said *a very different story*. Different from what? From what the cops thought? Would Jamison or Yang be able to exonerate JoJo? Or point the finger at someone else? If that was so why haven't they come forward? Why didn't the writer of the note give this information to the police?

Maggie glanced at her phone and debated calling Dumas but decided she wasn't in the mood to be hung up on.

As she looked at her phone, a text appeared from Laurent.

<Mila said you promised a goodnight story tonight.>

Maggie sighed and lay down on the hotel bed.

Do I really wish I was living a different life? If we were to go back to Atlanta—assuming Laurent agreed to go—an assumption the size of Mount Vesuvius—would the kids be happy? Would he? Would I?

She felt another spasm of unhappiness at the thought of how angry Danielle had been. How was Maggie ever going to apologize to her? How, short of packing her bags and leaving right this minute, was she going to fix it?

Another chime came from her phone. This time it was a text from Courtney.

<Cannot wait for the new old times to begin!> There were assorted drinking emojis accompanying the text.

It was almost impossible for Maggie to believe that she and Courtney were the same age. Courtney literally looked not to have aged a moment.

I thought single girls were supposed to age faster because they were more stressed about money and having to do everything themselves.

Courtney didn't look stressed. She looked like she had massages and salt sea scrub facials on a weekly basis.

Maggie couldn't remember the last time she'd had an uninterrupted shower.

Speaking of which, she glanced at the time and decided she had just enough to shower and track down either Jamison or Yang before she needed to meet Courtney.

AN HOUR LATER, Maggie entered the Carlton bar. She knew when it came to the advertising industry in France, this bar was the preferred starting point for any serious business meetups. Forget Madison Avenue or anything it might offer in the way of martinis or a client lunch. The Carlton Bar and Lounge had a revered history. Advertising careers were made—and lost—in this bar.

A ten-foot mirror served as the backdrop to the gleaming mahogany bar itself, reflecting the hundreds of bottles and crystal decanters in front of it. The overall look was glamour with a strong 1920's vibe. Chairs were covered in soft turquoise and jade tufted leather with faux gems embedded in the tabletops.

Maggie had skipped the tummy shaper today and opted for leggings and a sleeveless tunic that hid her hips and stomach. After carrying kids and helping Laurent out in the vineyard for the last seven years, her arms were fairly toned and tanned. At least she wasn't ashamed of them.

It had been easy to track down both Jamison and Yang. She just called their rooms and asked to meet with them. Interestingly, neither even asked what it was about.

Did that mean they were expecting her to call?

She found them now sitting together at the bar. They both turned in her direction as she approached.

The bar was still fairly busy at this time of day. It was just the right time for cocktails before dinner and Maggie spotted other festival delegates—most of them easily identifiable by their badges and lanyards but also by the studiously bored looks that only the self-conscious "creative types" think they can pull off.

She hoped she'd never looked like that when she'd been in the game.

"Mr. Jamison? Mr. Yang?" she said, shaking hands with both of them. "Thank you so much for meeting me."

Bert Jamison was young and if not handsome, at least had a lively look in his eye that made one give him a second look. As a Brit in advertising, Maggie imagined he was probably amusing, if not naturally so then at least struggled to hold up the burden of representing his homeland's reputation for wit.

H.O. Yang on the other hand was good looking in a smooth, bland way. He had greeted Maggie in a genial manner without actually having to smile.

She seated herself at the bar and ordered a Cosmopolitan.

"Are you both delegates at the festival?" she asked, knowing perfectly well that they were. After all, that was how she'd gotten their phone numbers and knew they were staying at the Carlton. But she wanted to ease into her questions.

She had a habit of putting people off by barging in and asking probing questions right off the bat. Laurent always chided her for not spending more time asking people about their ailments or children before blurting out whatever it was she wanted from them.

"Harry's up for an award in the cyber competition ," Jamison said, gesturing to Yang.

Maggie turned to him. "The H in H.O. stands for Harry?"

His smile—if that's what it was—did not enlarge. "When people learn my first name is Harry, it sort of blows the whole mysterious Oriental thing, you know?"

"Well, congratulations on the nomination. When is the vote for that category?"

"Not until the very end of the festival. Plenty of time to party and not give a crap before then."

Oh, to be young and not give a crap, Maggie thought as she glanced at his hand and noted he wasn't married. Or at least he didn't wear a ring.

"What about you, Mr. Jamison?"

"My shop paid for me to attend," he said with a shrug. "It's not as dear as where Harry has to come from. I just took the Chunnel and spent a few days on holiday driving down."

She finally reached the limits of her patience. "Did you both know Bette?"

Jamison signaled to the bartender to bring another round. "I knew *of* her, of course, but I'd never met her."

"I met her," Yang said. "She was a horror show."

"How so?"

"Does it matter? She was loud and obnoxious. Typical Yank. No offense."

Yang turned back to his drink, clearly not caring if he'd given offense. Maggie tapped her fingers on the mahogany bar. She hadn't known Bette long at all and even then just during the hours after a long plane flight. But she hadn't appeared loud to Maggie. Unfriendly, yes, but horror show?

"Can you believe that JoJo Henderson is being held for her murder?" Maggie asked, finding herself losing patience with this whole slow-questioning method.

The two looked at each other again.

"Not sure why the cops would do that," Yang said noncommittally.

"*Frog* cops," Jamison said and drained his drink. But Maggie watched his eyes. There was more there.

"Were you at the restaurant last night?" she asked.

"At the bar, yeah," Jamison said.

The bar at the restaurant was directly in the path of how one would go to reach the stairs to the toilet. Maggie felt her pulse quicken.

"Did either of you see Bette go to the toilet?"

"I missed that charming sight," Yang said sarcastically and Jamison sniggered as if his friend had said something amusing.

"Does that mean you *didn't* see JoJo go down there either?" Maggie pressed.

"I only saw one person go down or come out of the loo the whole time I was at the bar," Jamison said, turning and looking into Maggie's eyes. "Typical French bog. I could smell it from the bar. Only one bloke was anywhere near it when the alarm went off."

Maggie glanced at Yang who nodded in agreement.

"You saw a man go down to the toilets *before* the alarm went off?" Maggie said. It bothered her that these two didn't mention seeing *her*. Obviously *she* had also gone down just before the alarm went off. And she hadn't seen any *bloke* down there.

"No, we saw him come *up*," Yang said. "About five minutes before the alarm went off."

That made more sense, Maggie thought with excitement. This mystery man must have gone down to the toilet, stabbed Bette and then bolted up the stairs where he was seen by Jamison and Yang. That timeline gave poor Bette enough time to stagger to the alarm and push the button just as Maggie was coming down the stairs to the toilet.

It fit. It all fit.

"Did you recognize him?" she asked, feeling a lightness in her chest. "Was he one of the delegates?"

"Maybe. Not sure."

Maggie blew out a breath of frustration. Why did she get the feeling this was getting her precisely nowhere?

"Can you describe him?"

"Not really. It was dark and I wasn't exactly checking out the guys coming and going from the loo if you know what I mean."

More shared amusement transferred between the two. Maggie was very close to reaching over and knocking both their heads together.

"Well, thanks for talking with me," she said, leaving her drink untouched. *What a waste of time. Why did the writer of the note think these two knuckleheads knew anything?* And the fact that they hadn't seen JoJo meant precisely nothing.

They hadn't seen Bette either and she had *definitely* been in the toilet.

Just ask the Cannes Medical Examiner.

"You're done with us? That's all?" Jamison looked at her with surprise.

"You didn't see anything. And the one person you did see you can't identify. So, yes. We're done."

Jamison shrugged and signaled to the barkeep again.

"Well, I could identify him if he was dressed in the same threads," he said.

"What do you mean?"

"The dude who went down to the toilets," Jamison said. "He was wearing a bright lime green rain jacket."

11

Maggie moved away from the bar and the two delegates and found a small table by the window facing the *Boulevard de la Croisette*.

Jamison and Yang had described the clothing that the French delegate Etienne Babin had been wearing that night. The same guy who'd quarreled at Maggie's table minutes before Bette went to the toilet.

Had Etienne *not* left the restaurant after all? Had he instead swung around and, seeing Bette disappear downstairs to the toilets, followed her to finish the heated argument he'd been having with her?

Why hadn't Maggie considered him before? Because she assumed he'd left?

Had the police talked to him? Who better to be the prime suspect for killing Bette than the man who'd dropped a drink in her lap an hour before?

Breathlessly, Maggie dialed the police station again. She put a call into Dumas and received his sergeant saying the detective was too busy to speak with her.

"Fine," Maggie said, fighting down her annoyance. "Please tell him that Maggie Dernier called and that I've met two people who can place Etienne Babin—a French delegate at the advertising festival—at the scene of the murder of Bette—"

"I will inform him," the sergeant said in a bored voice and then rang off.

Maggie stared at her phone, her mouth open. Was there any reason to believe the man had taken down her name? Or Babin's name? Or knew what case her call related to? She ground her teeth.

Clearly the cops have their suspect. They're not interested in doing any more work.

Maggie drummed her fingers against the table and when a waiter came over, she ordered a split of champagne and two glasses. She glanced at her watch. Courtney was late but not by much. She dialed Brownie's number but her call when to voice mail.

Had he gone back to sleep? Was he at the police station trying to see JoJo? But if that's so, why turn off his phone?

"Maggie! Darling!"

Maggie looked up to see Courtney enter the bar. She looked like a goddess. Her slinky Jay Godfrey dress clung to her curves as she moved toward the table where Maggie was sitting. Maggie couldn't help but notice that literally every single person in the bar—but particularly the men—watched Courtney as she entered the bar. Maggie half stood so they could exchange the prerequisite air kisses and realized as she was doing it that this was not something she and Courtney did when they'd known each other back in Atlanta.

She reseated herself as the waiter came and poured the champagne.

"Champers, darling?" Courtney said with delight and Maggie wondered when she'd started talking like that.

"We're celebrating," Maggie said, feeling very brown and mousey next to the sparkling magnificence that was Courtney.

Courtney's long glossy hair draped around her shoulders in thick waves of undulating curls. Since Maggie knew there probably wasn't a hairdresser on call at the Carlton, she wondered how in the world Courtney had managed the effect.

Maggie's own hair was tied in a low slung ponytail. Normally, she counted it a victory if she managed to wash it.

They lifted their glasses.

"To old friends."

"I still can't believe you're here," Courtney said.

"I live here."

"Ha ha! Good point. So darling, tell me everything."

"Well, I left advertising. You know that. And moved to France."

"And married a hunky French chef. Don't leave that part out!"

Maggie squirmed uncomfortably at the thought of how annoyed her hunky French chef was with her at the moment.

"I'm sorry you couldn't come to the wedding," Maggie said.

"I don't remember what was going on at the time but I'm sure it was something!"

"There always is. So you've got your own shop. That's amazing, Courtney. You used to fantasize about owning your own place. I can't believe you really did it."

"You and me both. It was a lot of late nights, believe me. And you remember how we used to hate the suits so bad? Well, when you're in the corner office, I learned you have to suck up to clients even worse than the AEs did."

"But still. Your own place."

"Yeah. It was worth it. A long road but in the end..." Courtney lifted her glass of champagne as if toasting herself, "...totally worth it."

Maggie began to relax. Regardless of the differences between them now, the old feeling of relating came back in a rush when she heard Courtney's laugh. Maybe things had not changed that much.

"Do you ever miss it?" Courtney asked. "The old exciting life?"

"Not really. Not until today." They both laughed.

"We probably both went down the paths we were supposed to go down," Courtney said.

"I guess so."

"Which doesn't mean I wouldn't hire you in a New York Second if you were interested in coming back."

"You're sweet."

"I'm smart. You always were the best in the business."

"A thousand years ago."

"The things that matter about selling a product..." Courtney said with a smile, "...those things don't change. I have no doubt you still have it."

As Maggie poured herself a second glass of champagne a man appeared at the table.

"Hello, gorgeous," he said to Courtney. "Aren't you on the Promo and Activation panel?" He was tall, his accent American. He was good-looking and knew it.

"I am," Courtney said with a frown.

As disconcerting as it was to Maggie that the man did not appear to realize that there was someone else besides Courtney at the table she knew she was getting a fly-on-the-wall eye-view of how this dance used to go when she had been in the game.

She recognized the interchange between Courtney and the man. It was the sort of flirty banter that she had indulged in many times over the years when she'd been younger.

Maggie couldn't help but think that the whole process was just a tad exhausting.

"Drink later?" he asked.

"Perhaps," Courtney said. "But I'm having drinks with an old friend at the moment." Both the man and Courtney glanced at Maggie.

"All right then," he said. "Later. I'll hold you to that." He turned and disappeared without another word.

"Who was that?" Maggie asked.

"I have no idea," Courtney said with a laugh. "Someone I got eye contact with during registration yesterday. Do you think he's married?"

"I do," Maggie said. The first thing she'd noticed was the white tan line on his third left ring finger.

"Oh, well. It's not like I'm husband hunting," Courtney said.

That means she'll sleep with him and not obsess about the fact that he's not available for a real relationship, Maggie thought.

It surprised Maggie to remember that she'd heard this rationale before from Courtney. Years ago, Courtney used to say she didn't consider it wrong on her part since *she* wasn't the one who'd made a vow to someone.

At the time Maggie had not thought much about it.

Now that she was married, she had *very* specific thoughts about it.

"So tell me about Laurent," Courtney said, pulling out her compact and reapplying the layer of lipstick that had been transferred to her champagne glass.

"Well, he's a chef and a *vigneron*," Maggie said. She was about to say what an amazing father he was to their two adorable children—she had the pictures on her phone to show Courtney just how adorable—when Courtney gasped and said,

"I forgot you speak French now! That is so cool! Was it hard? I love the way it sounds!"

Maggie hesitated.

"No, not hard at all," she said. "Just grab a couple of online courses and you'll be fluent in a matter of weeks."

"Really? Because I'm desperately busy as you can imagine. I barely have time for my weekly mani-pedi. Oh! Maybe I could take the courses while I'm having my nails done!"

"Yes, you could," Maggie said. It didn't matter what she said.

Courtney would no more try to learn French then paint her own toenails. It just wasn't in her. Courtney wanted to strap on headphones, go to sleep and wake up talking like Brigit Bardot. That was Courtney.

Had that been Maggie too at one time?

"So what do you think of all the excitement?" Courtney said. "Can you *believe* Brownie's wife killed Bette Austin?"

"Well, I'm not sure she did. The jury's still out."

"Although why JoJo would kill *Bette* makes no sense at all, you know?" Courtney caught someone's eye at the bar and waved to him before turning back to Maggie. "I mean, killing *Sasha* would have made a lot more sense."

"Sasha? Why? What are you talking about?"

"Oh, darling, you miss all the gossip stuck over here in the boonies! Everybody knows Brownie was sleeping with Sasha."

THE CANNES LION Opening Gala was held at the beach opposite the Carlton. Maggie and Courtney watched a stream of people surge past their table until they finally joined the crowd.

It was hard for Maggie to believe that this throng, this blaring music, and this energy was for anything less than a country being taken over by rebels or the election of a leader the world had long been waiting for—or maybe a visit by the Pope.

But the opening gala of the advertising festival was a ceremony in its own right. Instead of ending the evening with fireworks, it started with them—bursting across a still-lighted sky as if in provocative anticipation of what was to come. The pyrotechnics exploded in synch with the vibrating nonstop music coming through the enormous speakers all along the beach.

Maggie knew there were celebrities throughout the crowd— movie stars, political rising stars, past presidents and famous has-beens—all with their own security details.

Most people walked clutching wine bottles or glasses of wine or champagne. The beach was transformed into an endless drunken *soirée* punctuated by a seemingly unending line of champagne fountains, ice sculptures that defied temperatures by remaining formed and in one piece, and table after table of delectable French pastries, each more original and extraordinary than the next.

There was a choreographed performance on the main stage by the water's edge and while some people watched the topless cancan dancers and Las Vegas-style show girls going through their elaborate dance steps, most of the crowd was content to get lost in the noise, the music and the anonymity of the world's biggest beach bash.

Banners stretched across colored, bubbling fountains of Veuve Clicquot announcing *Google Is Here to Play*, or *LinkedIn Rocks the Brands*!

Maggie thought she saw one of the original Monkees on the stage.

True to the French style, there was no recognizably organized function for meeting and talking to people. It was all just a glorious mob of gorgeously dressed or seminude people waving champagne flutes and gyrating to classic rock 'n roll.

And all of it just made Maggie feel tired. Before she'd taken the first sip of the free champagne that had been shoved into her hand, she longed to get back to her hotel room and curl up with a cup of tea.

Maggie lost Courtney within five minutes of entering the crowd and wasn't surprised not to recognize a single other person she knew after that. She had hoped she might see Brownie although it made more sense that he would still be at the police station or holed up in his hotel room, too upset to come.

What was really going on with Brownie? Maggie wondered as she elbowed her way through the crowd, trying to retrace her steps back to the street.

She'd watched him talk to other delegates—most of whom either actively avoided him or acted as if they were afraid to be seen with him. Maggie had a bad feeling in her gut about that. And a theory.

And was he really sleeping with Sasha? Was it relevant if he was? How could it not be? Could Brownie really have changed so much in nine years?

She shook her head. Of course he could. Hadn't *she*?

She'd gone from a self-centered career girl with a fanatical focus on her calorie intake and winning the next Addie to someone who organized the village clothing drive, created a blog depicting the colors and sights of her life in Provence in order to bolster the village economy, and who counted *at least* three people on this earth who mattered more to her than herself.

When had *that* happened?

She pulled out her cellphone. Even if Laurent called her, she wouldn't be able to hear his voice in all this noise. Suddenly she felt a strong desire to get back to St-Buvard.

She loved giving the kids their baths. Loved reading to them before bed and watching them settle into sleep after their busy days. She loved curling up with Laurent at night, a glass of wine in her hand and talking about nothing—from whatever pest had invaded the vineyard that day to the latest scandal to rock their little village.

The two of them laughed so much. Or rather, she laughed and Laurent's mouth quirked into a near smile. But even that meant the world to her.

Even now, when she thought of Laurent, it was the image of his eyes crinkled in a smile as he gazed at her or one of the children that came to mind.

Why had she listened to Brownie? He hadn't even been honest with her about what he was doing with Sasha! If he was anything like the old Brownie, he'd be mortally ashamed of himself.

But still. What more could she do now? She'd gotten a lead about another suspect that she'd dutifully passed on to the police —which they had just as dutifully ignored.

What more was there to do?

She missed her babies. She missed her grumpy bear of a husband. Oh, she'd straighten him out about his autocratic ways when she got home, make no mistake! But first, she wanted to feel his strong arms around her and to banish the ugly words that had happened between them.

And that was when she saw him.

He was standing at one of the beachside bars with his back to her.

Wearing a lime-green windbreaker.

12

Laurent stood in his vineyard with Mila in his arms as the sun went down and frowned.

His vineyard stretched sixty hectares. It was divided by a dirt tractor track and abutted Jean-Luc Alexandre's vineyard. The heat of the morning bore down on the tidy lines of vines and the stakes that propped them up.

Along with Jean-Luc, Laurent had two gypsies he trusted to help with the painstaking debugging and intertwining the branches. Jemmy was "helping" which of course was much more work for everyone involved than if he'd been back at the house drawing or watching cartoons on TV.

Mila was kicking to be let down and Laurent gave her a stern shake in reply. He'd already chased her down two rows, tripped over a vine and split the knee on his jeans to the general merriment of his workers and his children. He had work to do and the window for doing it was narrowing by the minute.

He knew it wasn't fair to blame Maggie for that. Her absence complicated things but having her here would only present a different set of problems. It was gratifying to lay his present concerns at her feet but she was only a part of the problem.

"Papa, Mila down!" Mila said, kicking again more forcibly.

Laurent couldn't imagine speaking to his father in the way he allowed his children to address him. But he recognized the difference and the reasons. He loved his children. They were not a constant source of shame and obligation.

He set Mila down, knowing he could not say *no* to her. He held up a finger in her face.

"*Attends, ma petite,*" he said in his best warning father voice. "If I must chase you, we go back to the house."

"*Oui, Papa,*" Mila said breathlessly. Her blue eyes were large and luminous and fringed with dark lashes. Except for her blonde hair, she looked like her mother. The eyes held no secrets. They told you everything even before you asked.

"Jemmy," Laurent barked and his son ran to him, his face already purple from the berries he'd eaten that were planted at the end of every grapevine row. "Mind your sister. You are in charge."

"*Oui, Papa,*" Jemmy said, narrowing his eyes at Mila as if to gauge the level of resistance she might give him.

Laurent watched them move off into the vineyard hand in hand.

Perhaps prayer is the best parental tactic at this point, he thought with a shake of his head.

"Maggie is still not back?"

Jean-Luc stood up from where he'd been kneeling in the dirt. At sixty-eight, he looked and acted eighty. His had been a hard life and Jean-Luc was the sort of man to make it even harder if given the chance. He took out a dirty handkerchief and wiped the grime from his neck. The sun was hot. It was always hot in June.

"Perhaps tomorrow," Laurent said.

"But you have your meeting tomorrow."

Laurent glanced at his old friend "How do you know about that?"

Jean-Luc shrugged. "I met Bernard at Le Canard. It will be good for us, yes? For the business?"

Laurent grunted but didn't answer. He wasn't at all sure what Bernard was up to but his first inclination was not to think whatever it was would benefit Domaine St-Buvard. He knew if there was an ulterior motive it would be revealed in time. He hoped it wouldn't be too late when it was.

"I'm sorry that Danielle and I could not help with the children," Jean-Luc said, but he stared at his feet as he spoke.

Laurent watched him for a moment and wondered how long Jean-Luc had been wrestling with whatever problem he had. Usually Laurent saw the old fellow more frequently. He cursed himself for not seeing it sooner. Something had happened.

"What is it?" Laurent asked abruptly. "What is wrong?"

Jean-Luc looked up and his eyes were wet with unshed tears.

"Danielle is awaiting a test result," Jean-Luc said. His face was ashen. He gripped his hands in front of him.

"What kind of test result?"

"I am not supposed to say."

Laurent felt little hesitation in trammeling other people's vows. He knew it was a failing. Maggie told him frequently. But he also knew that proud people walked away from help and suffered needlessly all the time.

He should know.

"Tell me," Laurent said firmly.

Jean-Luc shook his head as if he would resist, but he spoke clearly. "She's had two tests. And a biopsy. Cancer of the...breast."

"It is confirmed?"

"It is. Now we wait to see...how bad." Jean-Luc looked at Laurent, a worried look in his eye. "Danielle wants to tell no one."

"Not even Maggie?"

"She wants to be the one to tell her. She is emphatic about this!" Jean-Luc began to get agitated, his eyes darting around as if suddenly realizing he had betrayed his wife's wishes.

"Do not worry, old friend. If Danielle doesn't wish it I will not tell Maggie."

Laurent understood. Danielle did not want Maggie to come to her because she *should* come.

Jean-Luc relaxed but his hands continued to shake.

"Should you go home and be with her?" Laurent asked.

"She sent me away."

Jean-Luc needed to work. Laurent understood this. He glanced around the vineyard until he spotted Mila and Jemmy, their laughter melodic and sweet as it drifted over the vines.

He would keep Danielle's secret and he would support Jean-Luc the best he could. Maggie would be home soon. Perhaps a little late, but in enough time to talk to Danielle and give her the comfort she needed.

He tried to believe it.

13

Maggie hurried to keep up with Etienne as he moved stealthily through the darkening streets, each step taking her steadily higher toward *Le Suquet,* the old village.

Le Suquet was a complicated maze of winding cobblestone lanes. An ancient clock tower perched over the village facing east and overlooked the bay of Cannes. In the morning the square Maggie had just crossed would be full of produce vendors and souvenir shop owners trying to lure anyone who'd strayed from the glitz and glamor of Cannes.

Every few minutes as Maggie moved through the dark narrow alleys, she would catch another glimpse of Etienne ahead of her.

Why hadn't the police picked him up? Were they just totally disregarding any information at all if it came from her?

If Etienne killed Bette, that jacket he's wearing is crawling with the DNA JoJo needs to set her free.

The shuttered windows on either side of the close alley stared malevolently down at her. The lane seemed to become narrower as Maggie walked.

Ahead, even in the gloom Etienne's bright windbreaker stood out in the fading light.

Did he not care that he was being followed? He was doing nothing to keep himself hidden.

Where is he going?

It was a warm night but Maggie felt herself shiver periodically as if her body were trying to comfort her—or prepare her for something. Her breathing sounded loud in her ears as did her footsteps on the cobblestones. It was astonishing to her that Etienne couldn't hear them as well.

Could he?

They walked steadily for several minutes away from the row of hotels and restaurants and from the cacophony of the opening ceremony on the *La Croisette*.

The sounds of laughter, diners, and merriment carried on the air gradually faded until Maggie heard only her own footfall on the cobblestones.

Hers and Etienne's.

Where is he going?

LAURENT TOOK his drink outside to the back patio. He loved the evening alpenglow as it slowly blanketed the rows of vines, turning them into silhouettes before swallowing them up entirely. He and Maggie often sat out here once the little ones were in bed. The fading sunlight would cast dappled shadows on the ochre-washed stone walls that surrounded the patio.

Recently, he'd begun imagining his Uncle Nicolas sitting here after a long day spent tending the grapes in the vineyard. Laurent smiled. To even think such a thing was testimony to Maggie's influence on him.

It was so American to wonder what an ancestor might or might not have done or felt fifty years earlier.

But he could see why she did it. There was a pleasant sense of connection to watching the undulating hills of this vineyard—the same vineyard that Nicolas had tended so carefully for decades and all on his own—and to imagine the same thoughts that he might have had.

When you knew the land as well as Laurent did, each swell and dip in the horizon meant something; an errant vine that was constant trouble, a pocket of moles that had proved resistant to eradication, the spot where Pierre Schmidtt's pigs got out and trampled what vines they didn't eat.

It was all there in a panoply of activity and...great satisfaction.

This year's harvest would be the best yet. The blossoms had already been replaced by small green grapes and it wasn't yet mid June. It had been a hard spring of attaching the long vines to the stakes and constantly turning the soil and mowing. There had been more than the usual pests and diseases to battle too. The birds had been a bigger problem than ever.

Laurent smiled at the memory of the scarecrow he and Jemmy had fashioned. It had been Maggie's idea and it had worked well enough.

The summer's work was nowhere near done. There was more soil enrichment and the arduous task of hand-removing any remaining buds as well as carefully intertwining the branches on the wires. It was hot work and exhausting. But the harvest would come in just a few short months and while Laurent had no control over the weather, he needed everything else to be perfect. Especially after what had happened to last year's harvest.

Laurent sat down on the wooden settee and readjusted the fat Moroccan pillow Maggie had bought somewhere. He took another swallow of his drink as he watched his vineyard darken in the twilight.

The satisfaction in the work and what he had created here could not be measured in euros alone.

He grunted.

I'm as bad as Maggie.

Thinking of his wife, Laurent felt an urge to call her and give her a heads up about Danielle but he knew he wouldn't. He owed it to Danielle not to break her trust. And he owed it to Maggie to believe she would come through without prompting from him. In the end of course, he would always try to save Danielle any pain that he could, but he also believed she deserved the truth.

However Maggie handled Danielle's trust—that trust was only valuable to Danielle if it were real.

If Maggie unwittingly failed Danielle, Laurent knew she would never forgive herself.

He frowned, contemplating yet again whether or not he should tell Maggie. Just then his phone vibrated indicating a new text message.

<Are you lonely tonight, chérie?>

Laurent felt a flash of annoyance. It was his ex-partner Adele. He got texts from her every now and then. Usually they were provocative, sometimes threatening. Always mysterious.

Overall, Adele hated him now and any message she sent was first and foremost designed to upset or disconcert. He ignored them all, of course. But with Adele it didn't matter. The texts were building to something. He could only wait and find out when it happened.

He glanced at the bedroom windows above the patio. He had allowed Jemmy to keep his light on a little longer and it was still on so Laurent would need to go up and enforce bedtime. He'd expected as much. Mila's bedroom light had stayed out. The child always went to sleep quickly and slept deeply. For that Laurent was grateful. It was not a surprise to him that he would need to face off with Monsieur Jemmy however.

After all, fathers and sons. How could it be otherwise?

Before he went up, he would clear up a little problem that had been at the back of his mind all day. As a pleasant buzz reverberated through his brain from the drink, he pulled out his phone and punched in the number.

Bedard answered immediately. "*Allo?* Laurent?"

"You are busy?"

"*Non.* Working a little late and just leaving. You are calling about Maggie."

Ahhh, the satisfaction Bedard must have to say those words. But Laurent couldn't fault him. Maggie would always be completely Laurent's. He could allow a new friend a small victory.

"So she contacted you?" Laurent asked.

"She wanted the file on the American woman's death. I told her I have no jurisdiction in Cannes."

"You are not able to help her?"

Bedard sighed. "I didn't absolutely say I couldn't but the file... it is out of the question. What is she doing there anyway?"

"It was her business before she moved to France."

"Ah. Journalism, I think?"

"Advertising."

"Even worse. She can hardly profess to miss it?"

"She has not mentioned it up to now."

"Cannes can get wild during the festivals. It is not the same town as the rest of the year."

"I am aware," Laurent said dryly. At the time he'd met Maggie, Laurent was making his living in Cannes—and in all the wealthy villages up and down the Côte d'Azur. And while he and Roger had not known each other then, Laurent knew that then as now Roger Bedard had spent his career catching and prosecuting people like himself.

The key word, of course being *catching.*

Laurent didn't need to wonder if Bedard knew his background. He had a modicum of respect for the man. Of course he knew.

"The person being held for the murder is the wife of Maggie's friend," Laurent said.

"So she mentioned. But she has not been arrested. Only detained for questioning."

"Oh? There is not enough evidence?"

"I haven't seen the file. I can only assume not."

"Who is running the investigation?"

"A man named Dumas. He is an ass. Very territorial."

"As you would expect in a place like Cannes."

"Exactly. I am sure he aspires to possess his own yacht if he rubs the right shoulders along the way."

"But is he an idiot?"

"I don't believe so." There was a moment of silence between them.

"Ah, well. So you won't help Maggie in this?" Laurent asked.

"Are you asking me not to?"

Laurent thought for a moment. He knew that blocking Maggie or making things difficult for her rarely ended in her giving up her quest. If anything, she just took the harder route around to get what she wanted.

"No," he said finally. "Help her within reason, I suppose."

"That is all I would ever contemplate."

But of course Laurent knew *that* was a lie.

THE DAMPNESS in the air warned Maggie that they were near water. If she strained she could even hear the sound of water lapping against the wooden docks. Big or small, somewhere near there was a marina or harbor.

Ahead of her, Etienne stopped—almost as if he wanted to make sure Maggie saw him—and then disappeared out of the alley. Maggie paused. When she did she could hear her heartbeat pounding in her chest. If she went to the end of the alley *and he knew she was following him,* he could be waiting around the corner.

Maggie tried to think.

Should she go back? Now that she looked around, she realized this section of the old village was virtually deserted. It was unusual for there not to be *someone* hanging out a window or walking by. It wasn't that late.

But the alley was vacant and the windows shuttered tight. Not a pinprick of light escaped—if indeed there was light to be leaked.

Maggie couldn't take the chance that Babin was ahead waiting for her. And for what? So she could confront him about killing someone? Even she knew that was mad.

Gripped by indecision, she felt the surrounding silence envelop her and crank up her nervousness. She had to do something! Had she come all this way to turn back?

But if she went forward and he was waiting for her...

The minute Maggie made her decision to return to the hotel was the minute she heard the sound of a single footstep behind her.

She pivoted to run when hands grasped her shoulders from behind.

She tried to scream but terror robbed her of breath as she felt the pressure of the man's hands on her. She only made an impotent gasping sound as a strong forearm came around from behind, mashing her windpipe.

She scratched desperately at his arms as she fought to breathe.

Stars blinked and throbbed in her head as her peripheral vision tightened. She was falling, her breath leaving her in agonized rasps, as the light in the alley faded to black and then extinguished.

14

The first thing Maggie was aware of when she began to rouse—beyond the booming pain in her head—was the feeling of being rocked. She knew before she opened her eyes that she was on a boat. She was lying on the wooden floor of a small dinghy. When she moved, she saw her hands were tied in front of her.

As she struggled to sit up, she could see that they were moored in the Plateau du Milieu, near the Lerin Islands on the landward side of Sainte-Marguerite and ten minutes from the lights of Cannes.

She felt a sudden stab of memory. Laurent had brought her to these islands years ago before she really knew him. Before she knew she could trust him. They'd found a secluded clearing surrounded by eucalyptus trees and fringed with umbrella pines and had a picnic lunch...

"Why were you following me?" Etienne sat on the narrow wooden boat seat and stared at her. His French was thick and sluggish, his accent a country *patois* that Maggie would have found difficult to understand if not for the fact that so many of the old country people around St-Buvard spoke the same dialect.

Except for his bad teeth and his jittery eyes Babin might not have been bad looking. He was tall but his arms looked stunted as if they were a size too small for his body. He had a scattering of hair across his chin and jaw but his face was heart-shaped. He had full lips which he licked continually.

"I...I wanted to ask you something," Maggie said, her heart beating in triple time in her chest.

His eyebrows shot up into the greasy black hair that hung into his eyes.

"Aren't you American? I thought you were with the Americans," he said in French.

"I am American, yes."

He nodded, his eyes narrowing as if reassessing her. She'd spoken slowly and laid on the accent more than usual. The result seemed to be that he was reconsidering slitting her throat or whatever horrible thing he might have been contemplating before she opened her mouth.

"You are a friend to the bitch who maligned my country."

Maggie cleared her throat.

"You mean Madame Austin. The one who was killed last night."

He turned and spat over the side of the boat. Maggie felt her gorge rise when he did.

"She deserved to die. They all do."

It occurred to Maggie that five in the morning in a boat off the coast of a remote, thickly-forested island with her hands tied was not the best time to ask him if he had killed Bette. Even if he admitted it, it would only be because he knew she wouldn't live to tell anyone.

"Why did you hate her so?" she said instead.

Etienne's lips flattened. He slammed his fist over and over onto his knee in agitation.

Suddenly Maggie saw the box on the floor at his feet that she hadn't seen before. She only caught a glimpse of it but she saw enough: wires, a clock, and two metal cylinders.

Her heart began to pound harder.

Crazy man with a bomb. I'm trapped in a boat with a crazy man with a bomb.

"She comes to my country!" he snarled. "And offends my people! Offends *me*! She had to die as they will all die."

Maggie clenched her jaw and felt the terror ricocheting through her body.

He was looking at his watch and squinting at the Cannes shoreline. She debated asking him what his plan was but decided he was too agitated to hear her and might only be able to focus on the fact that she was American.

Best not to remind him.

She watched the Sainte-Marguerite shore. The island was dark which didn't surprise Maggie. She was pretty sure she remembered reading somewhere that Sainte-Marguerite was uninhabited. A ferry came once a day from Cannes to let tourists wander around the old prison on the island but there wasn't even a place to buy a sandwich or a bottle of water.

Babin was going to dump her here alive or dead. If there was nobody on the island to hear her screaming wouldn't help. She glanced around the boat but didn't see her purse with her cell-phone. He would have tossed it as soon as he snatched her.

He stood up and she saw the sheen of the piece of metal in his hand.

"This isn't my fault," he said as he grabbed her arm and wrenched her to her feet. "Nobody else can make them pay but me."

"What...are you going to do?" Maggie blurted.

But the way he was gripping the bar made his intentions very clear.

"Don't do this, Monsieur Babin," Maggie gasped, squeezing herself as far away from him as she could on the small boat.

"Every man and women on the *Palais des Festivals et des Congrès* will die this day!" he shouted as he waved the bar over his head, his eyes glittering with madness.

Suddenly, he swung the bar in her direction.

Maggie leaned sharply away. He missed her but the sound as the bar hit the side of the wooden boat eliminated any question of how bad it could have been. She knew he would try again. Her only chance was to get off the boat.

"No, you don't!" Etienne screamed, swinging the bar at her again. This time he took a step closer but stumbled over the box with the homemade bomb. The bar grazed Maggie's shoulder and pain ricocheted down her arm and up into her brain. She had no more time.

Etienne cursed and gripped the side of the boat to get back on his feet. Maggie leaned backward against the boat rim and pushed herself over. It went against every instinct to throw herself backward into water that she had no idea of the depth.

But the need to escape trumped everything.

She felt a hard hand grab her foot.

Panic and terror cranked up into her throat as her momentum over the side was halted. With her arms useless in front of her, Maggie was half in the boat when her head hit the cold water with a sudden ferocity.

But he hung onto her foot.

She fought desperately, kicking hard with both feet. Her eyes were open underwater. How long could she hold her breath? Could he drag her back on board?

She lashed out, twisting and squirming to free herself. His fingers dug into her flesh. Each convulsive kick on her part ignited a detonation of roaring agony where he held her only tighter. Underwater, her world was silent and otherworldly as she fought for her life.

Her breath was giving out. Her lungs burned for air. One last kick. It was all she had before she suffocated and drowned.

She felt her free leg kick him in the face.

He let go. She could feel him grabbing for her again but she slipped under the water. Almost instantly she fought to break the surface and gasp for precious air.

The minute she did, the blow slammed into the side of her skull with stunning force.

A bright incendiary pain exploding in her brain that sent her back into the dark waters where all was quiet and peaceful and black.

15

The water slapped Maggie back into terrible consciousness.

Pure panic took over as she fought to keep her head above water. The agony in her face blotted out all other sensation except the will not to drown. When her feet touched the bottom she instinctively pushed away from the boat toward the shore expecting any minute a bullet or a knife in the back.

Her hearing came back and with it the sound of a motor.

It was close.

She had no idea what other weapons Etienne might have with him in the boat.

She took in a hungry gulp of air and dove beneath the water. She swam silently, touching the bottom when she could, her legs weak and ineffective for kicking or propelling her through the placid surf.

The terror of thinking his boat might be on top of her, or right next to her, forced her to stay under until her lungs threatened to explode.

When she finally surfaced, she heard his boat in a steady, throaty purr as it trawled away from her, back toward Cannes.

She nearly wept with relief. He wasn't coming after her! She took a moment to stand quaking in the water, the surface right at her chin.

Slowly, when she had the strength to do it, she walked sluggishly through the water, her legs like concrete in the thickening surf. It took her several long minutes before she fell to her knees on the beach.

Even after the submersion in the cold water, her face was hot where he had thrown the steel bar at her. She touched her cheek with her fingers and prayed it wasn't broken. Whatever blood there'd been was washed away.

She felt the cut over her cheekbone. It was puffy and beginning to swell. As she watched Etienne's boat disappear into the darkness she sent a heart-felt prayer of thanks to God that the maniac had decided not to come after her.

Within seconds, her relief was gone.

That maniac is going to try to blow up the festival.

She looked frantically up at the dark hulking prison which loomed ominously in the distance. It was the famous prison where the Man in the Iron Mask had been kept. The sight of it sent shivers down Maggie's arms. With her hands tied in front of her, Maggie stood and scanned the inlet looking for moored boats. It was still too dark to see well. If there were boats there, her cries would likely carry away to the other side of the island and be lost.

Should she go to where the ferry docked? She had no idea of what the schedule was.

All she knew was that she was very likely the only person on this island and a psychopath was on his way to blow up the *Palais des Festival* in Cannes.

~

LAURENT AWOKE with something bothering him.

It was still dark in the bedroom. He stretched out an arm to feel the space where Maggie should have been. It was cold and empty. He sat up and rubbed the sleep from his eyes. Already he could see the morning trying to penetrate the sanctity of the room from a large north facing window.

He swung his feet out of bed onto the carpet and listened. He heard nothing. That either meant that the children were still asleep...

...Or they were awake and up to something.

He went to the window and raked up the blinds. The sun was just peeking over the horizon of the vineyard which at this time of day resembled nothing so much as a darkened hulk. Soon the sun's rays would light on fire every branch, every twig and budding grape in the field.

Laurent turned from the view to pull on his jeans and a cotton sweater. It would be hot later but the early morning was cool.

It wasn't just her absence that had upset the natural scheme of things, he thought. Maggie had been gone before. It was the rift between them, the one that had developed almost as soon as she'd gone.

That was new. That was the most troublesome part of it all.

Laurent put his watch on and then paused. Soft footsteps crept down the hall toward him. A cramp of uneasiness settled in his stomach.

Mila.

Mila without Jemmy was not good.

He went to the door and opened it to find his small daughter standing in the hall in her nightgown. Her large blue eyes were wide and frightened.

There were blood flecks down the front of her nightgown.

Laurent picked his daughter up.

"Where is Jemmy, *ma petite*?" he asked as he moved down the hall with her in his arms.

"Not his fault, Papa," Mila said. She wrapped her little arms around his neck.

Laurent glanced in Jemmy's bedroom as he passed but he didn't expect to find him there. If the boy was awake he'd be up and gone. He wouldn't stay in his room. Not when there was a world to explore. One preferably without adult supervision.

Laurent hurried down the wide limestone steps of the grand staircase that emptied into the foyer.

"Where, *chérie*?"

Mila pointed toward the kitchen.

Of course. There was nothing sharp or dangerous in the living room or dining room.

Laurent's anxiety spiked as he strode to the kitchen.

Jemmy sat on the floor in the kitchen surrounded by a pile of bloodstained towels and paper napkins. The boy looked up at Laurent, his bottom lip quivering.

The blood—*merde! So much blood!*— was everywhere.

16

The emergency room in Aix-en-Provence was like any other in France, Laurent imagined as he sat in the stainless steel encased treatment room with Mila and Jemmy. It was antiseptic, efficient, singularly unattractive and absolutely not designed to relieve anxiety on any level. But the hospital cafeteria did have a small *boulangerie* that was quite good.

As Laurent watched the emergency room physician place the last of three stitches in Jemmy's temple, Mila cuddled in his arms and nibbled happily on her *pain au chocolat*, unmindful of the smells and oppressive tension in the place.

Laurent had called Maggie three times on the drive to Aix and another two from the emergency room. He also left a series of texts describing exactly what had happened along with the fact that Jemmy was fine.

There had been no response.

"You are too old to be climbing cabinets," the physician said sternly to Jemmy. Laurent cocked an eyebrow at his unhappy son. In Laurent's opinion, the doctor's admonishments were hardly necessary when one was in the process of getting stitches in one's head. But perhaps it didn't hurt to hear them. Whether it would keep Jemmy from climbing was of course another matter entirely.

"You are a single parent, Monsieur?" the doctor asked Laurent.

"None of your business," Laurent replied pleasantly.

"*Maman* is at a conference," Jemmy said, wincing as the doctor tied off the last stitch.

"Oh, she is a *working* woman, your *maman*," the doctor said, looking at Laurent as if there must be something wrong with him.

Laurent smiled at the doctor.

"That is what he calls the regional prison," Laurent said. "You cannot blame him for relying on euphemisms, eh, *docteur*?"

Laurent stood and shifted Mila to his other arm. He put his hand on Jemmy's head across from the doctor's shocked face.

"Okay, *mon vieux*?" he said.

Jemmy nodded. "It doesn't even hurt."

"Too bad," Laurent said. He handed Jemmy a *pain au chocolat*. "But you were very brave."

Jemmy flushed with pride and took the bun.

"I just wish *Maman* could have seen how brave," he said.

Laurent felt a twist of anger in his gut at his son's words.

How could Maggie not respond to any of his texts or calls? He had told her that *Jemmy was hurt*.

What could possibly be more important than that?

As Maggie made her way to the center of the island, it occurred to her that if Babin was Bette's killer then Martin must have lied about seeing JoJo in the bathroom. But why would he do that? And how could he have missed Babin? The guy was wearing a bright green neon jacket!

One thing at least was clear. After having met Etienne,

Maggie had answered the question, *Would a sane person wear something so memorable on the night he intended to kill someone?*

Etienne was definitely not sane.

The Île de Sainte-Marguerite was heavily wooded and the trees came right up to the edge of the beach. As Maggie walked through the woods and crested the first hill she was able to turn and see the lights of Cannes in the distance.

Where was Etienne now? Was he in Cannes? Was he even now setting the bomb in place?

The sun wasn't up yet and she shook from the cold. It was hard to believe that within the hour she'd be roasting. It felt like a cold autumn morning on Whiteside Mountain in the North Carolina mountains where she and her family used to go every fall with Brownie's family when they were children.

Brownie. Just the thought of him made her sad.

He was trying so hard to show Maggie he was happy, that everything had worked out for him. *But all you had to do was spend five minutes with him to see how false that was.*

He'd married badly. *That's the part that must really bother him,* she thought. *When someone dumps you, you need to be able to show them you went on and everything worked out okay.*

Things were definitely not okay with Brownie and JoJo.

Was JoJo right about a gambling problem? If so, Maggie had never seen it coming. The Brownie *she* knew didn't have an addictive personality. He practically didn't drink. He was the only one she knew in college who didn't even try weed.

Would he talk to her about it? Would it defeat the purpose for him if she asked him about it?

She shivered violently and started to jog, hoping to warm herself up. But her wet clothes soon rubbed uncomfortably in all the wrong places. Her sandals squished in the marsh as she made her way inland. Her toes felt like they were frozen.

The minute she crested the knoll that divided the beach from the interior of the island, Maggie saw what appeared to be a village of about ten or twelve buildings. And there were lights on in some of the buildings.

There must be fishermen here! Maggie stumbled toward the village and gave a jubilant prayer of thanks for the fact of an unexpected village of simple folk and fishermen.

Now if one of them just has a cellphone.

17

Within an hour of knocking on the door of the first fisherman's shack she came to, Maggie's bonds were cut, a hot drink put in her hands, and she was on the phone to the police in Cannes.

Dumas still wasn't taking her calls so she left a message with his sergeant before putting in a call to Brownie. It went to voice mail.

Frustrated that nobody seemed to be willing to hear her warnings, she called the Carlton and announced that a bomb was going to be placed on their beach and then hung up before they could ask any questions.

The fisherman whose phone she was using frowned at her.

"Don't worry," she said. "You won't get in trouble."

He looked at his phone and it was clear he didn't believe her.

She debated putting a call into Roger Bedard. But Roger had been minimally helpful last time she called him—*as in, not at all*—and she decided it made more sense to just call the Cannes fire and emergency services with her bomb threat. Unfortunately, before she could make any more calls, the fisherman reached over and plucked the phone from her hands. He snapped a photo of her and raised his eyebrows as if in warning.

It was just as well. Maggie couldn't think of a single thing she could do other than what she had already tried to do. She was on the record for calling and warning the police. If Dumas let the disaster happen anyway, it was on him.

But that didn't make her feel any easier about it all.

As she waited for the ferry to take her back to Cannes, Maggie sat on the bench in front of the small boatyard where the ferry would dock. She picked up a glossy brochure from one of the trash receptacles and saw that the fort was now a youth hostel as well as a museum featuring recovered artifacts from ancient Roman shipwrecks.

She glanced behind her at the prison and shivered.

Île de Sainte-Marguerite was still a seriously creepy place. For centuries it had been a place of torture and despair smack dab in the heart of one of the most beautiful places in the world.

She had plenty of time to think of Laurent while she waited. He was the last person she would call. Hearing she'd gotten herself abducted in a dark alley was practically his worst nightmare and not one she wanted to prove to him could actually happen. Besides, except for the loss of her wallet and cellphone, there was no real harm done. She gingerly touched the bruise on her cheek. Well, almost.

At least she'd left her car keys in her hotel room. She could drive home without a license but not without car keys.

Maggie stretched out the kink she'd gotten in her back from sleeping on the floor of a dirty, rickety skiff all night.

And finally she thought of her meeting with Courtney. Maggie had been hesitant to compare herself to Bette the other night. She knew she hadn't started out like Bette—bitter and jaded—so it stood to reason she wouldn't have ended up like her. But it was different comparing herself to Courtney. She and Courtney had always had more similarities than differences.

It wasn't just their shared love of the work—they were both optimistic and fun loving. It was possible that Maggie was a tad less confident than Courtney, but if she wanted to look at anyone to imagine how things might have been, she only had to look as far as the beautiful, composed and thoroughly successful Courtney.

Is this envy I feel? Is it mourning for a life that might have been? Does that even make sense when I love my husband and children so much?

Maggie stared out over the Mediterranean and tried to see the speck on the horizon that would morph into the arriving ferryboat. The rising sun was illuminating the water, causing diamonds to jump and flicker on the surface. Now other boats were visible—yachts and fishing boats, one-day cruisers and sunsailers.

"Madame?"

She turned to see the fisherman who'd loaned her his phone. He was now holding it out to her.

"The police," he said sternly, clearly not happy to be on the Cannes Police department's speed dial.

Maggie took the phone. "This is Maggie Dernier," she said into the receiver.

"Madame Dernier," Dumas said. "You may now stop calling the various popular landmarks at hotels around Cannes in order to terrify the patrons and tourists."

"Well, that's certainly not what I was—"

"Monsieur Babin has been apprehended."

"Really? You got him?"

Maggie felt warmth radiating throughout her body at his words. She looked at the fisherman and gave him a thumbs up. The man shook his head and scowled.

"That was fast!" she said to Dumas. "When did you—"

"He was picked up this morning as his boat docked in the

marina. Our intention was to bring him in for questioning. The contents of his boat quickly led to his arrest."

Thank God, Maggie thought.

"And his involvement with Madame Austin's murder? Have you asked him about that? He practically confessed to me that he did it."

But Dumas had already disconnected. Maggie forced herself to dismiss any lingering annoyance that the man had once more hung up on her. She handed the phone back to the fisherman.

It didn't matter. The bad guy was caught. The murderer was in jail. JoJo would be free. And all was right with the world.

LAURENT STOOD in the doorway of Bedard's townhouse on Cours Gambetta. The children had been instantly absorbed with squeals of delight into the interior of the home by Bedard's daughter Chloe. Laurent stood now on the front steps with Bedard, both of them smoking and staring up the residential street.

Laurent had been relieved to drop the children off early since he was already in town due to the ER visit and because he had business in Aix today.

Secret business.

Plus, having the children nowhere near the scene of the crime tonight was an unexpected godsend.

Bedard's neighborhood was in the older section of Aix. The townhouse was built with a beautiful rose-colored brick all the way up to the orange tiled roof which was covered by a dramatic draping of purple bougainvillea. Laurent had encouraged Maggie to grow the flower at Domaine St-Buvard but she preferred only those plants she was familiar with, the ones that grew in her native Georgia.

In some ways, Laurent knew that Maggie was a transplant who would never really be at home in France.

"They will be fine," Bedard said.

Laurent grunted. "Better than with their father obviously."

"Jemmy was climbing in the kitchen before you were awake?"

"I dared to assume a full night's sleep might be managed."

"Ah, that was your error," Bedard said.

Laurent laughed. He knew Bedard, widowed years ago, was raising his only daughter alone and had done since she was three. If anyone knew the strain and responsibility of caring for such a fragile thing as the typical child intent on self-destruction, it was Bedard.

"My mother-in-law often spends the night with Chloe," Bedard said. "And I have a deposition in Orange tomorrow. I can drop them off in St-Buvard before lunch."

"That would be very good. Thank you, Roger."

"Not at all."

Laurent was keenly aware that the man hadn't mentioned Maggie yet. Not by word or facial expression. Not by what he'd said or left unsaid. Of course neither had he offered up information as to whether or not he'd spoken to her recently either. And of course, Laurent was not about to ask.

It was bad enough that Jemmy had given himself a three-inch gash in his forehead. But the fact that Maggie had not come rushing home when she heard...?

Laurent wasn't sure what Bedard would make of that.

He wasn't sure what *he* made of that.

"This meeting in Arles must be very important," Bedard said, throwing his cigarette butt into the pale pink petunias that lined the brick walk to his front door.

"I'm not sure that it is at all," Laurent said. He'd received a confirmation text from Bernard reminding him of the address tonight. They were meeting at a roadside restaurant outside Arles. There was something about the arrangement that felt contrived to Laurent. He couldn't put his finger on it but he didn't completely trust Bernard. He was serving as a go-between and that felt odd too.

Why would the wine reporters not just contact Laurent directly?

But he would find out in due time. In about nine hours to be exact.

Meanwhile, he would finish the last minute touches of the details of his own covert operation and now he would have the freedom to do it without having to worry about Maggie or the children. He glanced at Bedard and smiled thinly.

"I appreciate this, Roger. I owe you."

"Not at all. *Pas du tout.*"

As Laurent turned to walk back down the street toward his car it occurred to him that in the two short days that Maggie had been in Cannes she'd succeeded in upsetting most of the people who counted on her, starting with himself when she'd told him in no uncertain terms that his interests were not as important as her time with her friends from Atlanta.

First me, then Danielle, and now Jemmy.

Who has Maggie become after such a short time with these people?

18

Two hours after climbing onto the ferry from Sainte-Marguerite, Maggie staggered through the front door of the Carlton. Several delegates gave her strange looks and she was sure she smelled as bad as she looked. Thankfully, the full day of panels and viewings had begun today so the hotel wasn't busy.

She went to the registration desk to get a new room key and ordered a double American breakfast to be sent up to her room. She hurried upstairs and immediately checked her email on her laptop for any word from Laurent—highly unlikely since the man could barely be persuaded to keep his cellphone on him and certainly didn't use email if he could help it. Sure enough, there was nothing.

Once in her room, she stepped out of her clothes and into a very hot, very long shower.

The left side of her face had swollen badly and when she looked in the bathroom mirror she saw it was dramatically discolored. She didn't think anything was broken, and thank goodness no teeth seemed to be loose, but she swallowed two ibuprofen to soften the persistent ache.

When she emerged from the bathroom from her shower, she was delighted to see the table by her bed was covered with three trays of silver-domed food. Still wrapped in a towel, she lifted the lid off one dish and sat down to devour the scrambled eggs, bacon and buttered English muffins.

If she got on the road within the hour, she'd get home in time to mollify Danielle today. It was still two days before the lavender festival and while the last thing Maggie felt like doing was jumping into that project—which meant dealing with the irascible old biddies of St-Buvard—she knew for the sake of her friendship with Danielle that she needed to.

A sharp rap on the door made her frown until she thought...Brownie!

She dropped her towel on the floor and slipped into the hotel's bulky terrycloth robe and cinched the belt tight before hurrying to the door.

Brownie and JoJo stood there beaming at her.

"You did it, Maggie," Brownie said, his arm around his wife's waist, his eyes glowing with joy. "Thanks to you, JoJo is free."

Both JoJo and Brownie came into the room.

"I'm so glad!" Maggie said. "I was hoping it would be fast."

"What happened to you?" Brownie said. He frowned and lifted a hand to Maggie's face but didn't touch her.

"Ran into a door," Maggie said.

"How in the world did you manage to get me free?" JoJo said. She looked tired. She'd clearly spent the night in her makeup but there was a brightness to her eye. Maggie was pleased to see how she clutched Brownie's hand.

Maybe something good had come out of this after all?

"I didn't really do anything," Maggie said, settling on the side of the bed and pouring herself a large coffee and waving for the other two to help themselves. "I got a lead and I followed it. That's all."

"And it led you to Etienne Babin?" Brownie asked. Maggie

noticed he'd taken the time to shave. He'd nicked himself in the process and his face looked bone white against the tiny ruby cut.

"Yes. Two people saw him go down to the toilet when Bette was there. So I talked to them and just passed on what they saw."

"He *confessed*," JoJo said, shaking her head as if in wonder at it all. Maggie knew just how she felt. One moment you're terrified and sleeping in a holding cell, and the next minute you're drinking coffee from a silver service anticipating a luxurious shower in a five-star hotel.

"I was pretty sure he would," Maggie said. "He practically confessed to me this morning. I'm afraid he's really mentally...you know...off his rocker."

"I just can't believe it's all over," JoJo said. She looked at Brownie and her eyes were soft and full of love.

"You came straight here from the police department?" Maggie asked.

JoJo laughed and put her hand to her hair.

"I know I look a disaster. I didn't even stop to shower. I just wanted to...thank you."

"No thanks necessary," Maggie said. "Can't have the wrong person go to prison for a crime she didn't commit."

JoJo hesitated and then reached out to take Maggie's hand.

"I think I was a real pill to you when we first met. Can you forgive me?"

"Don't be silly. Nothing to forgive."

"It's just that..." JoJo looked at Brownie and then shook her head but Maggie thought she knew what JoJo was trying to say. JoJo had been jealous of Maggie as the childhood sweetheart, an image JoJo hadn't felt she could compete with. She'd been ready to defend her turf.

"Honestly, JoJo, forget it," Maggie said, squeezing her hand. "We're good. Okay?"

JoJo let out a sigh and then turned to Brownie.

"I'm going to see if the hairdresser can take a walk-in. Meet you back in the room later?"

Brownie nodded and kissed JoJo before she left the room. JoJo turned to Maggie one more apologetic, grateful smile.

"I owe you, Maggie," Brownie said once JoJo was gone. "Seriously."

"God, stop it, will you? Forget it," Maggie said. "Or if you want to think we're finally even after how I broke us up then I'm good with that."

"I knew I could count on you, Maggie." He glanced at her bed where her suitcase was open. "You're leaving?"

"I'm needed at home."

"Maggie the mom, huh? I'd love to see *that* show sometime. I'll bet you're amazing."

"Well, I don't know about that."

"It was great to see you again, Maggie."

"You too, Brownie. So we're good, right?"

"Absolutely and totally," he said and walked over to kiss her on the cheek. When he did, Maggie saw that the razor cut had started oozing blood.

As Brownie turned to leave Maggie couldn't help but wonder how it was that JoJo and her blood pathology had had no trouble kissing him a few minutes earlier?

19

Maggie folded her slacks and t-shirts and tucked them neatly in her bag.

So that was that.

Babin had killed Bette in a hate killing and was safely in police custody. JoJo was free, Brownie had forgiven Maggie for dumping him nine years ago and Maggie was taking her matronly plump figure back to the hinterlands to wipe noses and write blog posts about the vineyards of Provence.

All was right with the world.

So why do things still feel out of sorts?

Why did she feel like something was still off with Brownie? And why had he misdirected her about JoJo's blood pathology? And why had Martin the waiter lied to her about seeing JoJo?

Maggie stopped packing. They were just little things but they niggled. They were like grains of sand—not much in themselves —but when trapped in the waistband of your swimsuit on a summer day they were enough to drive you crazy.

She went to the room phone and called down to the front desk.

"Oui, Madame?"

"Could you please put in a call to *Astoux et Brun* for me?"

"We are happy to make the reservation for you, Madame. What time?"

"No, I want to talk to them myself, please."

"Of course, Madame. We will call back with that connection."

Maggie hung up and then turned to stand in front of the mirror trying to determine if she needed to lose five pounds or ten. If she were still in the advertising game it would have to be more like twenty. She felt a wave of irritation.

This is Laurent's fault. If it weren't for his obsession with cooking, I'd still be a size six!

Her room phone rang. Assuming it was the front desk with her connection to the restaurant, Maggie didn't bother looking at the LED display on her phone set.

"Yes?" she said into the phone.

"Where have you been? Why are you not answering your cell-phone?" Laurent said sharply.

Hearing his abrupt combative tone, Maggie was tempted to say she'd lost her phone after being attacked with a crowbar in a stolen boat before being left for dead on a deserted island. She quickly realized the satisfaction of saying it would be fleeting, but the lasting results on Laurent would be, well, lasting.

"I've been busy with a few last minute things here," she said, urging herself to take the high road and not agitate the situation any more than it already was.

"Danielle is very concerned that you will not be back in time to help her with the festival."

"That's because Danielle needs to take a serious chill pill. I *told* her I'd be back in time. Although frankly the last thing I need is another excuse to eat nonstop at twenty different food kiosks. As it is, I could no more wear the sorts of outfits I've seen here in Cannes than pilot a space shuttle to the moon."

"Then it is fortunate that your life in St-Buvard does not require you to wear those kinds of clothes," Laurent said dispassionately, "But if it matters to you then do something about it."

"Are you saying I should lose weight?"

"*Non, chérie*," Laurent said patiently. "It matters not at all to me. But if it matters to *you*—"

"So you don't care what I look like?"

Laurent gave one of his famous Gallic snorts of annoyance but before he could respond—if indeed that had been his intention—Maggie heard the low-grade trill on her end that indicated another call was coming in. It was just as well. She and Laurent clearly both needed to take a time-out.

"I'm getting another call," she said. "I'll talk to you later." She hung up and engaged the next line. "Yes?"

"Your call to *Astoux et Brun*, Madame," the disembodied voice from the front desk said.

"*Allo*? This is *Astoux et Brun*."

"Yes, thank you," Maggie said, trying to shake off her irritation with Laurent long enough to ask the questions she had in mind. "May I please speak to the waiter Martin? I am an American who dined at your restaurant two nights ago and I would like to tell him how happy I was with the service."

"*Oui, Madame. Un moment.*"

Maggie chewed a nail and sat on the edge of the bed. Her eyes fell on the remnants of her American breakfast. There was even a pot of creamy cheese grits on the tray. Her stomach growled in spite of all she'd eaten. *God, was she never going to be able to diet?* Or was she too out of the habit of denying herself?

"*Allo?*"

"Hello, Martin. This is Madame Dernier. If you remember I came in to talk to you about what you saw the night of the murder. Do you remember me?"

"*Oui, Madame.*" Maggie noticed his voice became instantly guarded.

"At that time you told me you saw JoJo Henderson go down to the toilet while Bette Austin was there."

"You must be mistaken, Madame. I never told you that."

Maggie caught her breath. Of all the things she had expected him to say, denial had not been one of them.

"You...you're saying you did *not* tell me that?"

"*Non.* You are mistaken. I never saw anyone that night anywhere near the toilet. Is that all, Madame?"

He disconnected before Maggie could answer. She sat on the side of the bed with the hotel phone in her hand staring out the window at the bright blue sky over the Mediterranean.

What just happened?

Martin definitely told me he saw JoJo. Now he's saying he didn't.

Someone has gotten to him. Someone has either paid him to lie or threatened him to recant his statement.

Which is the truth? Did he see JoJo or didn't he?

But why would anyone want to implicate JoJo...and then pull back?

Did any of this make sense?

She turned and glanced at her packed suitcase.

Does it matter? We're done here.

She walked to the window and looked out. The sun was fully up now and blazing down on the *La Croisette.* Even with all the advertising panels going on today there were still plenty of delegates strolling the promenade or parked in café tables along the beach just enjoying the day.

Who would coerce Martin into changing his story? Could Brownie have done that?

Maggie quickly discounted the idea.

Brownie didn't know enough French to order a Coke, let alone bribe someone.

But if not Brownie then who?

And more importantly, why?

LAURENT PLACED his cellphone on the café table and frowned.

Incroyable! She doesn't even act as if she knows about Jemmy! Was her phone not working properly? Has she not received my calls? How is that possible?

"Monsieur?"

Laurent glanced up to see the old man standing by his café table. He half stood in greeting and waved toward the empty seat at the table.

"I am happy to finally meet you, Monsieur Dubois," Laurent said. "Will you have lunch?"

Dubois shook his head. "A coffee only," he said as he slid a heavy envelope across the table to Laurent.

Laurent ordered the coffees before picking up the envelope. Inside were a series of five color photographs. He flipped through them, his heartbeat drumming in his chest. *Perfect.*

"You are pleased, Monsieur?" the old man said.

"Very much so," Laurent said as he tucked the photographs back in their sleeve. "And the shipment?"

Dubois waited while the waiter brought the cup of coffee and left before speaking.

"It will be as arranged," Dubois said. "My people will take care of it."

"Tonight?"

The old man looked at Laurent and smiled for the first time. "As arranged," he said quietly.

It occurred to Laurent that this was the first thing that had gone right all week—if indeed the delivery came off with no unforeseen problems.

A big if.

"You will find a little something extra in here for your trouble," Laurent said as he pulled an envelope from his jacket and placed it on the table. "And I may need your services in the future."

Dubois sipped his coffee and shrugged but his eyes were on

the envelope of money. "I am easy enough to find," he said. "For those who know where to look."

Laurent stood and pulled several bills out of his wallet. He set them by his cup then tucked the packet of photos under his arm and glanced around the café. It was an old habit and one that didn't seem worth breaking. Especially since it had served him so well so many times before. He recognized no one.

"*Au revoir, Monsieur,*" Laurent said and then turned on his heel and walked out of the café.

One visit to the hardware store on his way out of Aix and he should have all he needed. His men would of course have to handle everything else tonight but while he had not worked with them before, they came highly recommended.

The only problem was Jean-Luc. Laurent's men had been instructed how to handle him. But Laurent offered up a silent prayer that it would not be necessary.

It wasn't until two hours later as Laurent was watching Aix disappear in his rearview mirror as he headed back to St-Buvard that he found himself thinking of Maggie again. And when he did he realized that he'd not stopped thinking of her all day long. The incessant worry of what she might be doing was always there humming, grating in the back of his mind as he went through the motions of his day.

Had something happened to her in Cannes? Is it possible she was being seduced back into that life? Forget that she didn't seem to know about Jemmy which meant she wasn't reading her texts, but she didn't even *ask* about either child.

In spite of himself and for the first time since he'd known Maggie, Laurent found himself confused, worried...and genuinely a little unsure of her.

20

Her harsh words with Laurent and the bothersome questions about Martin and JoJo filled Maggie's head as she changed into clean slacks and a sleeveless top and finished packing. Fortunately she had tucked away in her overnight bag some emergency cash and a credit card which she slipped into her pocket now. Then she went downstairs to the registration desk. The same goddess who probably hired out as an extra in indie films as *gorgeous nymphet number four* smiled at her.

"You are leaving us, Madame Dernier?"

"Sadly, yes," Maggie said. The truth was she wasn't sad at all. She couldn't wait to get on the road and back to St-Buvard.

"You have a message," the young woman said.

"I do?" Maggie frowned and held her hand out for the note card. *Who would send me a message? Why not just telephone my room?* But when she saw the note, she understood why not.

MAGGIE, please feel free to stay as long as you like in Cannes. I have asked

Madame Lampé to aid me with finishing the decorations for the fête.

Sincerely, Danielle Alexandre

OH, for pity's sake, Maggie thought with annoyance. Why were both Laurent and Danielle acting like this? Maggie felt a wave of frustration which she quickly worked to tamp down.

It didn't matter. She would go home and get it all sorted out. She'd have a come-to-Jesus meeting with Laurent and she'd pull out the peppermint schnapps and go to Danielle's and not leave until they had everything ironed out.

"Your room is paid for the rest of the week by Pixel Advertising," the woman at the registration desk said cheerfully.

"I know. I'm still leaving."

"I can process you immediately but in the meanwhile there is a reception in the bar. Free champagne."

Maggie turned to see the spillover of people standing in the opening to the bar. As far as she was concerned she'd already said goodbye to everyone except Courtney. She caught a glimpse of her in the bar.

"Okay," Maggie said. "Can I leave my bag with you?"

"Of course, Madame."

Maggie headed toward the bar. She was surprised it was so full of people. Today was the first day of the juried panels and it was only a little after midday. But there was a line of people two deep in front of the bar.

She heard Courtney's laugh and found her in the midst of a crowd of six very handsome men. Maggie scrutinized their clothing. She knew if they were account types—which only made sense at Courtney's level—they certainly wouldn't be dressed in suits on the Côte d'Azur. As it was they all looked uncomfortable and incongruous in their pressed jeans and starched polo shirts. *So, not creative types*, Maggie thought with a smile.

She hesitated to approach Courtney while she was holding court. The men were listening to her. They were appreciating her with their eyes too. Courtney was after all still a knockout. But it was more than that.

They were hanging on her words.

Courtney was respected in the business. Her opinion meant something. She was *somebody*.

A man jostled Maggie spilling his drink on her sleeve and moved off without apologizing. No doubt he hadn't even noticed her. To him, she probably looked like one of the maids who made up the beds.

No, Maggie had seen the housekeeping staff at the Carlton. They *also* looked like extras for sexy indie films.

Dejected, her chest aching, Maggie turned away without approaching Courtney. But instead of going to the front desk to retrieve her bag, she felt a sudden urge to step outside and clear her head.

When she moved away from the bar to head toward the front doors, she saw a special media display of the Top One Hundred International Blogs had been erected in the foyer outside the bar. The banners touted "*International Creative Forum de Cannes* Best of Blogs." Without realizing she was doing it, Maggie stepped into the area and saw that three walls were lined with examples of what was being called the "power house winners of blogging."

She was drawn to the first display. It was touting a blog run by a large conglomerate—which meant they'd spared no expense on either the gorgeous photographs, obviously taken from all around the world or the famous writers who served as guest bloggers.

As Maggie walked down the line of displays, each blog sample was more gorgeous and arresting than the last. Each was labeled with their subscriber numbers—most well into the millions—and, when attached to a product or service, also their ROI.

What Maggie had done with her own blog was done basically on instinct. It was true she'd studied several blogs that she liked —mostly travel blogs—but for the most part she'd gone with her gut, written from the heart, taken photos of the villagers and the countryside and her own vineyard, and let the world love it or leave it as they would.

As she finished her tour of the winning Best of Blog entries, her heart swelled with pride. It was clear she was doing something right.

Her blog was every bit as fresh and provocative as the ones here.

Maybe even better. Her heart beat quickly as her mind raced to think. Should she enter next year? Did she want to see *A Provençal Farm Life* up here with these other specimens of the best blogs in the world?

Still drawn to the brilliant blue of the sky reflected on the Mediterranean, Maggie walked down the front marble steps of the hotel to the panoramic view of the seaside.

As she regarded the famous promenade that separated the Carlton from the beach, her mind was whirling. To her immediate right was an electronics store and on impulse she walked into it. She pulled out her credit card and bought a cheap disposable phone.

She needed to finish this. And one thing she knew if she knew anything was that things were *not* finished.

Maggie punched in Roger Bedard's number on the new phone from memory.

"*Allo?*" he answered.

"You never called me back," she said.

"Where are you? Are you still in Cannes?"

"I know you're busy, Roger, so this time I have a very simple request of you. If you're sitting by your computer you can probably answer it in about ten seconds."

"Have you talked to Laurent?"

Instantly, Maggie's blood ran cold.

"Why? What's happened?"

"Everyone is fine. Jemmy needed only three stitches—"

"What?" Maggie roared. She stepped off the curb into traffic and a man behind her quickly jerked her back onto the sidewalk. A car horn wailed in annoyance at the same time.

"Where are you?" Roger asked. "It sounds like you're directing traffic."

"What happened to Jemmy?" Maggie shouted. She hopped from one foot to the next in agitation and then turned back toward the hotel. She needed to get home. *Now.*

"I believe he was climbing the kitchen cabinets? I am afraid I do not have all the details."

"How do you know *any* details at all?"

Where was Laurent? Why hadn't he called her?

"You do know Mila and Jemmy are with me and Chloe, right?"

"Are you kidding? What? No! Where's Laurent?"

"He had a meeting, I believe."

Maggie dragged a hand over her face. She remembered now. His meeting in Arles. But Jemmy was hurt? How could Laurent leave him?

"I will give you my home number," Roger said. "Your children are there with Chloe and my mother-in-law. Talk to them and then call me back."

Maggie took the number and within seconds was speaking to both Jemmy and Mila. She'd talked to Jemmy yesterday afternoon. But a lot can happen very fast with an active seven-year-old boy. He gave her the exciting details of his tumble but the visit to the emergency room was clearly the biggest adventure of all.

Once Maggie was reassured that he was fine, she called Roger back.

"All is well, yes?"

"Yes. Thank you so much, Roger."

"*Pas de problème.* Now, what do you want to know?"

"I'm sure you're going to tell me the case is all wrapped up but since nobody on this side of things will talk to me—"

"You are talking about Madame Austin's murder?"

"Yes. I gave some information to the police that led to them arresting a man who was seen at the scene of the crime and I just wanted to make sure everything's tied up with a bow."

"Etienne Babin."

"Yes! That's him. What have you heard?"

"He was found with enough explosives to destroy the *Palais des Festivals et des Congrès* which, it seems, was his intent."

"But about Bette Austin...?"

"Babin has not been charged with her murder."

"But...how can that be? He confessed!"

"*Au contraire.* He swears emphatically that it was not he."

21

Maggie sat with the phone in her lap and stared at the sea, the busy *Promenade de la Croisette* was before her, the sounds of traffic a rhythmic hum in her ear. She had found a comfortable bench on the hotel side of the boulevard. The sun felt good on her face but several people walking by grimaced at her swollen and discolored cheek.

It didn't make sense.

Etienne did *not* confess?

JoJo said he had. Was she misinformed?

Now that Maggie thought about it, how would JoJo have heard that? Surely police detectives wouldn't let something like that slip—and JoJo didn't know enough French to understand it even if they had.

So had JoJo lied?

Had Etienne even *been* at the murder site?

A sudden thought hit her: What if Yang and Jamison lied to her about Etienne being there? Was it possible Maggie was set up in order to frame Etienne?

In order to free JoJo?

Whoa. That is a twisted line of logic.

Roger told her the police had no concrete leads on the case but they were working the forensics and were hopeful that a picture would emerge soon.

She glanced at her watch.

Is there a time limit on this? As in, the killer needs to distract the cops just long enough for her—or him—to hop on a transatlantic flight out of the country?

And was that any of Maggie's concern?

She stood and straightened her shoulders. It was over she told herself firmly. Her involvement—the extent of what she could do —was *over*.

She felt a sudden flush of shame as she turned back to the hotel. While it was true that Jemmy was fine *now* he could definitely have used his Mommy yesterday during what was a very stressful hour for him at the ER. Just thinking of it made Maggie want to cry. The thought of her brave boy, holding his Papa's hand and trying to be strong...

But if she were really honest she'd have to admit that her presence would have made it harder for Jemmy. She waved away the voice of reason in favor of the much more satisfying feeling of sadness and guilt.

And anger.

Why hadn't Laurent told her!? Why hadn't he called her? But she glanced down at the burner phone in her hand and knew why.

Her anger dissipated as she began to climb the broad stone steps to the hotel entrance.

The fact that her son had experienced an incident that Maggie not only wasn't a part of but had no knowledge of was not something she could accept.

At least not comfortably.

And it wasn't just what had happened to Jemmy. Maggie knew she had seriously upset one of the sweetest women on the planet when she'd put Danielle off and there was nothing—not even a dead body or an attempt to right a slight to an old boyfriend—that was more important than that.

No, the bottom line was that when it came to the things that really mattered, Maggie realized she didn't care if Bette's murder was never solved. It had nothing to do with her. JoJo was free. Maggie's debt to Brownie was discharged. Now she just wanted to be home with her family and friends.

And advertising and everyone in Cannes could go straight to hell.

ONCE THROUGH THE front doors of the hotel, Maggie was startled to see Bert Jamison, the British delegate standing alone with a champagne flute in his hand. There was a crowd huddled at the front desk which meant there would be a wait before she could grab her bag and be on her way.

She decided she could waste five minutes.

She walked up to the young man. He frowned as she approached.

"Remember me?" she said in clipped tones.

"Of course. Although I'm afraid I have nothing new to say."

"Oh, really? Not even after I tell you I'll be reporting you to the police for giving a false statement in an active homicide investigation?"

He burst out laughing, spilling his champagne on the floor and Maggie's sandal.

"I say! That is bloody amusing! Who would care? Please answer me that."

Until she'd cocked her arm, Maggie had no idea that she was going to punch Jamison in the nose, knocking his glass from his hand and causing an unfortunate geyser of blood to spurt out in all directions.

"Jesus, you maniac!" Jamison yelped, clapping both hands to his nose as blood dribbled down his shirt.

Maggie grabbed him by the arm and dragged him out of the lobby where too many people who'd come for the free champagne were now enjoying the free show.

Jamison came willingly, moaning, clutching his nose until she reached the door to the ladies' room. She stuck her head in, saw it was clear, and pulled him in behind her.

The Carlton restrooms only had cloth napkins so Maggie grabbed up a stack and wet them under the faucet before turning back to Jamison.

"Tip your head back," she instructed. She pushed the dampened cloth into his hand. "Hold this against your nose until the bleeding stops."

"I promise you that you will regret—"

"Oh, shut up," Maggie said with irritation. "It's not even broken."

"Well, it doesn't feel very nice, I can tell you." Jamison dabbed at his nose and watched her suspiciously over the cloth.

"I need you to answer my questions," Maggie said, "or I'll go to your agency and tell them you roofied my drink. Your next festival will be on the Liverpool docks for Best of Industrial Advertising."

Jamison scowled at her.

"Why did you and Yang lie to me about seeing Babin?"

"Rick Wilson paid us five hundred pounds each to do it."

Maggie's mouth dropped open.

"Rick Wilson of Wilson, Brut and Lewis? In Atlanta?"

"The very one."

"Why would he do that?"

"You'll need to ask him."

Maggie made an impatient gesture with her hand and Jamison flinched.

"I honestly don't know," he said hurriedly. "Harry and I were in the restaurant bar the night of the murder and the next morning Rick approached us with the offer."

"Did you tell the police it was Babin you saw?"

"No, that was the part of the deal. We wouldn't have to lie to the police."

"But then...who were you supposed to lie to?"

Jamison's eyebrows arched as if in answer.

"*Me?*"

"Rick just said 'anybody who asked.'"

Why had Rick Wilson wanted to feed Maggie wrong information?

"So to be clear," Maggie said, "you were paid five hundred pounds to tell me you saw Etienne Babin go down to the toilet? With the assumption that I would go to the police with it?"

"That is correct."

"Why?"

"I have no idea."

"But you in fact never saw Babin go down to the toilet?"

"I did not."

"Did you see JoJo go down there?"

"Nope. Not her either."

Maggie tried to process what this information might mean.

Martin the waiter had placed JoJo at the scene of the murder at the time of the murder. Then Martin recanted his story of seeing JoJo. At the same time, Jamison and Yang—who were paid by Wilson to lie—put Etienne Babin in the murder window.

Had Martin also been paid by Wilson?

While it was possible that none of this was against the law—since nobody had lied to the police—the result was definitely obstruction. Because the purpose of the lies was that false information be passed on to Maggie and she *had* gone to the police.

"But as it happens, I did see JoJo that night," Jamison said, going to the sink to rinse out the cloth and dab at his shirtfront.

"She was talking to the McCann media guy, right?"

"No, she was *servicing* the Saatchi's art director guy in the alley by the restaurant. And by servicing I mean—"

"I know what you mean," Maggie said, holding up her hand to stop him from proceeding. "What time was this?"

"Midnight. Just before the alarm went off."

If Jamison was telling the truth, JoJo had an alibi all along. Maybe not one she wanted to trot out for Brownie and the world to see, but she was never really in any danger of being held for Bette's murder.

Had Brownie known? *Surely not.*

"One last question," Maggie said. "What is Wilson's connection to Brownie Henderson?"

"I have no idea."

"They don't have something cooked up? Something about the festival? Maybe the votes?"

Maggie had heard of buying votes at the festival. It seemed every year someone was caught trying to influence the delegates to manipulate the outcome of a category win. If that's what Brownie was doing—and she hated herself for even thinking it—he wouldn't be the first.

"I don't know what you're talking about."

Maggie narrowed her eyes as Jamison gingerly touched his nose. She couldn't tell if he was lying. She didn't have the time or energy to find out.

"Maybe you should toddle off somewhere now," she said. "I'm feeling an overpowering urge to smack you again."

"Right-o!" he said, hurrying past her and out the restroom door.

MAGGIE FOLLOWED BEHIND HIM. She tried to keep straight in her mind the things she'd learned.

So Etienne *wasn't* at *Astoux et Brun* during the critical time?

JoJo *was* sleeping around. Which, if Courtney was right, made that marriage two for two in the infidelity department. Was that relevant?

Did Brownie know JoJo was with someone that night? That was an easier question for Maggie to answer. Regardless of what Brownie was or wasn't doing with Sasha, Maggie knew his hysteria over JoJo the morning she'd been arrested was real. She would bet her life he would never believe that JoJo could betray him.

Poor Brownie. So naive in so many ways.

At that moment, Maggie caught the titter of a distinctive laugh that hung in the air over the babble of all other conversation. She turned and saw JoJo and Brownie standing in the middle of the lobby talking to the agency creative director who'd come by the table with Rick Wilson the night Bette was killed. Dennis something. They were all three chatting away like close chums.

For some reason just seeing them together, laughing and talking animatedly, with Bette's brutal death so recent, turned Maggie's stomach.

Whatever. It wasn't her business any longer and for that she was infinitely and forever glad.

As she approached the group on her way to the desk to get her bag and leave, all three turned toward her. JoJo and Brownie beckoned her over. Maggie saw a festival packet in Brownie's hands. On it was a girlish handwriting with notes to the side.

Written in bright pink.

"Whose packet is that?" Maggie asked as she joined them.

"Huh? Oh, it's Sasha's," Brownie said. "She left it in the lobby. They were holding it for her at the front desk. I said I'd give it to her when I saw her today."

Was the handwriting on the packet the same as on the note shoved under her door? It was hard to tell. The note was written in all caps and this was in cursive. But one thing was sure—the pen was the same. Down to the same fountain pen inkblot and bright pink color. Definitely distinctive.

That note was the thing that had originally led Maggie to Jamison and Yang and ultimately to lay the murder at Etienne Babin's feet.

How was Sasha involved in this? If she sent the note she must have known about Jamison and Yang.

Now that Maggie knew that the information Jamison and Yang had given her about Etienne was false, she also knew why Sasha hadn't just handed the information straight to the police.

But if the note came from Sasha, did that mean she was in on whatever vote-scam was going on with Rick Wilson?

Maggie glanced toward the Carlton bar and saw Rick Wilson himself standing at the bar. He smirked and raised a glass to her. His response was a far cry from their meeting at *Astoux et Brun* yesterday where he pretended not to know her.

What was his deal? Was he mocking her? Had Maggie just served as a pawn in some stupid game of his?

She knew confronting Wilson was a waste of time. He wouldn't tell her the truth. She looked at Brownie who had gone back to his conversation with Dennis and JoJo.

And Brownie probably didn't know enough truth to tell.

No, Maggie couldn't help but think that somehow *Sasha* was the missing piece in all this. And one thing was for sure—for the critical time period surrounding the murder—Sasha had definitely been missing. Maggie could now pinpoint where every single person of interest was the night Bette was killed.

Everybody but Sasha.

In fact, now that she thought of it, all she really had for Sasha's alibi was a lot of gossipy assumptions passed on by sniggering misogynistic admen that the copywriter had gone home with a guy from the bar.

Finally making up her mind, Maggie strode to the elevator. This time she would not take no for an answer. This time, she would find out once and for all what was going on and who was masterminding it. And why.

As she rode up in the elevator Maggie rehearsed her confrontation with Sasha.

I know it was you who shoved the note under my door, Sasha, so don't bother trying to deny it.

I also know you're sleeping with Brownie.

Maggie frowned. Maybe she'd leave that last bit out. She wasn't sure how relevant it was and it would probably get things on the wrong foot.

She got off the elevator on the third floor and hurried down the hall.

Did Rick Wilson make you give me that note? No, that wasn't right. Sasha could just say *no.* Maggie needed to back Sasha into a corner and force her to blurt out the truth.

What is Brownie doing with Wilson? Are they buying votes? Are you a part of that?

Better. Much better, Maggie thought as she stood before Sasha's door. If *that* doesn't get Sasha backpedaling and trying to defend herself, nothing would. And in Maggie's experience, backing someone into a corner usually forced bits of the truth to squeeze out.

She plucked off the *Do Not Disturb* hanging tag on the handle and pounded on Sasha's door.

"Open up, Sasha," Maggie yelled. She waited with her hands on her hips.

No answer. She pressed her ear against the door. The Carlton was known for its vintage decor and classic architecture. Usually this was a good reason for guests to give it a bad review on Trip-Advisor about worn carpets and chipped molding and the fact that you could hear people talking through the walls—especially if you pressed your ear right up to them.

Maggie listened intently. Nothing.

She stood back in exasperation. Enough of this. Maggie

pulled out the credit card from her pocket. Another thing the Carlton's Old World charm had going for it was the ability to jimmy any of its room doors since they'd yet to graduate to a key card system.

Maggie slid the side of the credit card into the space between the lock and the doorjamb and wiggled it until she heard a distinctive click. She grasped the door handle and jerked open the door.

"Wakey, wakey," Maggie sang as she stepped into the room.

Silence greeted her. Maggie glanced at the bed. Something made her stay where she was.

A sixth sense.

She could see from the doorway that the bed had not been made. One pillow was on the floor.

It was that pillow that turned on all of Maggie's internal warning alarms. There was no reason why it should. But it did.

She took a tentative step toward the bed and that's when she saw it. The tip of a naked arm protruding from the blankets. The fingertips on the hand were blood red.

Dripping blood red.

"Sasha?" Maggie said softly, her heart thumping loudly in her throat. But she knew the girl wouldn't answer.

And she would never answer again.

22

B rownie hung up the phone. He turned to JoJo who was lounging on the bed flipping through a magazine.

"Sasha is dead," he said, shaking his head.

He felt a rush of coldness and blinked his eyes rapidly as if that might erase the words he'd just spoken.

He re-ran the sound of them in his head. They sounded as if they were from a movie. As if none of this was happening in real life. He was trapped in a sick script and couldn't escape.

JoJo sat up, the magazine falling to the carpeted floor.

"No! Oh, my God. that's terrible! How?"

Brownie sat on the corner of the bed. He put his hand to his forehead and felt the sweat beading up there. He had tried to call Sasha. For two days he'd tried! He'd pounded on her door. He'd sent her a ton of texts. Like everyone else, he'd heard that she'd gone home that terrible night with the American art director from Young and Rubicam.

He'd texted her the very next morning that he understood. He'd told her he forgave her.

Now for the first time in a very long time, he just wanted to sit down and cry.

"Brownie? How did it happen? When?"

"I don't know," he said in a daze. "But Maggie has been brought in for questioning."

"Maggie? What was she doing near Sasha? Do you think... could she...?"

Brownie turned on her.

"Don't be ridiculous!" he snarled. "Maggie has been my friend for nearly thirty years! My *best* friend since we were kids!"

"Okay, darling, calm down. I didn't mean anything..."

"She helped me get *you* off the hook for Bette's murder! And let me tell you, JoJo, she wasn't at all sure you *didn't* kill Bette."

"Well...that's just a terrible thing to tell me."

"I'm trying to say that she did it anyway. Because of her devotion to me."

"Well, maybe the two of *you* should have gotten married."

"Are you seriously going to get in a huff over the fact that someone cares enough about me to help me out when I needed them? Who are you, JoJo? Seriously. Who *are* you?"

"I'm sorry, Brownie. But honestly, don't you think you're going a little off the deep end? There wasn't anything between you and Sasha, was there?"

"I can't believe you'd even ask me that."

"Really? You can't believe it because you thought I wouldn't hear the rumors from our big McMansion in Dunwoody? Between my private tennis lessons and my mindless shopping trips to Lenox, you thought I wouldn't hear?"

Brownie put his face in his hands and burst into tears.

JoJo jumped up and ran to him.

"Brownie, I'm sorry. Please don't cry. I'm sorry."

Brownie nodded but was too overcome to speak. It felt too good to cry and get rid of the pain and the sorrow and the horror of it all.

Poor Sasha! Poor Maggie! Poor Bette! His shoulders shook with his sobs as he allowed himself to be carried away with the catharsis. JoJo sat next to him, her arm around his shoulders and her face against his neck.

Finally, he gave one last long trembling sigh and reached for the sheet on the bed to dry his face. JoJo squeezed his knee but didn't speak.

"I'm sorry," he said. "I don't know what came over me."

"Probably long overdue," JoJo said. "You and I have made a mess of things, Brownie."

He nodded. "Yeah."

"Do...do you think we can fix it?"

Brownie looked at her. JoJo's face was close to his and her eyes —so beautiful, so clear and trusting. He remembered the first time he'd seen them.

"Do you really want to?" he asked, his voice lilted upward with hope.

"I do. More than anything."

He thought about it for a moment and then sighed again.

"There's probably more things to forgive each other for," he said.

"I know."

He reached for her hand. "I'm willing if you are."

She smiled and nodded. "Good."

He went to the bathroom to splash water on his face. When he came back, he had a towel over one shoulder.

"I'm not sure I feel good about going to the awards banquet tonight," he said.

His shop was scheduled to receive an industry award. He, himself, as the principal owner would be presented with the *Top Ten Start-Ups to Watch* award.

"Oh, Brownie, you have to go."

"How can I? With Bette and Sasha murdered in the last two days? How could I stand up there and act like any of it meant anything?"

"You could if you dedicated the awards to them."

Brownie thought about that for a moment and then turned to look out the window. It was still only late afternoon. The sun in the south of France in June would stay up for hours yet.

"Maybe," he said.

JoJo went to him and wrapped her arms around his waist.

"What about Maggie?" she asked. "Is there anything we can do?"

"I don't know."

"Call her husband?"

"She will have gotten her phone call," he said.

"Should we go down to police headquarters? You know, to support her?"

Brownie knew what the offer must have cost JoJo. To go back there just hours after walking away would be more than anyone could ask of anyone. He loved JoJo for it and gave her shoulders a squeeze.

Maybe JoJo was right. Maybe they *could* fix things. He felt a rush of love toward her.

JoJo lifted up on tiptoe and kissed him on the mouth. And when he responded to the kiss she led him quietly to the bed.

FOUR HOURS after entering Sasha's hotel room Maggie was still in the police interview room. It was a different room from the one where she'd spoken to Detective Inspector Dumas the day before. This one was freezing.

She wondered if it was a ploy to make the interviewees more uncomfortable. That would make sense. She should be glad she wasn't being water boarded. After all, she was less than three miles away from one of the most notorious prisons in the history of the world. Certainly in the world of literature.

"Madame Dernier?" Dumas sat opposite her and chain-smoked.

Maggie was pretty sure the police building was a smoke-free zone but probably—like the overactive AC—it was one more tactic in Dumas's bag of tricks to make her uncomfortable. *As if finding Sasha dead wasn't uncomfortable enough.* Thank God she had had the sense to step back out into the hall without touching anything. When she did, she'd glanced up and seen the surveillance camera.

That was good and bad luck for her. It was bad because it meant she had to immediately report the murder which would put her right where she was now—in a freezing meat locker of an interrogation room with possibly the rudest man alive.

But it was good because it meant Sasha's killer had been videotaped going into her room.

"Why did you break into Mademoiselle Morrison's room?"

"Well, I'm not sure you could call it *breaking in*," Maggie said. She'd been tempted to say that the door was ajar and she'd just pushed it open but she was sure Dumas's forensic magicians would be able to determine that a plastic credit card had been used on the locking mechanism. As she was always telling Mila and Jemmy, lying was a bad idea.

Especially to police officers in a murder investigation.

"The door was locked and you had no key," Dumas said in a shrug.

"Yes, but the only reason I was forced to access the room without a key," Maggie said for the tenth time, "was because Sasha wasn't answering her door. And the reason she wasn't was because she was already dead. So when the hotel surveillance tapes show the person who came to Sasha's door *right before me*— and who had the door opened for them by an alive Sasha—well, then you'll know who the killer is."

"And in the meantime, we have you."

"May I say what a colossal waste of time it is for you to grill *me* when you know the video tapes will exonerate me? And you could be doing something constructive in the meantime?"

"Constructive in what way?"

"Should I do your work for you? But since you ask, why not talk to the guy Sasha brought home with her the night Bette was killed? Or talk around to see who saw her alive last? She'd been holed up in her hotel room since Bette was murdered. Did household see her? Did she make any calls out?"

Dumas smiled thinly. "You have an active mind."

I have an exhausted mind, Maggie thought. *I promised Jemmy and Mila I would be at Roger's by dinnertime and there's no way that's going to happen now.*

She felt the tears gather in her eyes and she fought to hide them. Dumas would take it as a sign of guilt. He probably didn't have a mother of his own. There was no doubt he was hatched.

"You should be asking if Sasha's death means there's a second killer on the loose." Maggie said. "I understand Etienne is not copping to killing Bette. Is that true?"

"Where did you hear that?" Dumas said with a frown. "And I will ask the questions here."

"Surely you have the lab work back from Bette's crime scene by now?"

"I am not sharing results from our laboratories with you."

"Okay, fine. I'm just saying that since it was a unisex bathroom probably half the restaurant had been down there at one time or another, including the wait staff. Do you have any reliable eyewitnesses of someone down there when Bette was there?"

"Beside yourself, you mean?"

Maggie felt a schism of ice pierce her at his words. *He can't be serious.* But Maggie had experience dealing with little men with big shoes to fill. She knew first hand how desperate they could be when they needed to point the finger at someone.

The door opened and a policeman came in and said a few quiet words into Dumas's ear before leaving.

Dumas gathered up his folder.

"We are done for now," he said. "Your one phone call is

waiting in the hall. He has agreed to take responsibility for you so that you may leave with him."

Maggie could not believe how paternalistic the French legal system was but right at the moment she was so tired and vulnerable that she didn't care. She stood up and felt her knees turn to rubber and she gripped the table to steady herself. Then she turned and walked out of the room.

He stood in the hall, his head cocked to one side and frowning as though trying to determine if she'd been treated well. Then he opened his arms and Maggie walked gratefully into them. She felt him wrap them protectively around her.

"Thank you for coming," she whispered into his shoulder, allowing the tears to finally come.

"*De rien*," Roger said.

23

T he hard fact was that there was just no way Maggie could have called Laurent.

Not after everything they had said to each other. The last thing she could do was call and tell him she was being interrogated by the police for having found a second dead body in twenty-four hours.

Besides, she reasoned, Roger knew the players. He was familiar with the case notes, and could at least help her figure things out. Because of his own status as a Police Inspector, he could get information that the police would certainly never have shared with Laurent.

Plus Laurent had a criminal record.

On the off chance that someone in the Cannes police department had a good memory and remembered Laurent, the last thing Maggie needed would be the help of an ex con artist famous for working the Côte d'Azur.

Roger found a small restaurant not far from the police station. He led them to an inside table. Most diners anywhere in Cannes would logically prefer the patio in summer. After all, the weather was exquisite. But dining inside gave Roger and Maggie the privacy their conversation needed, and the incessant attention from the waiter that Roger—like most food-obsessed Frenchmen—desired.

The tables were small, only two or four plates to a table, each draped with starched white tablecloths against eggplant-colored walls. The resulting effect was spare yet elegant. It had the look of a restaurant that intended its food to do all the shining.

Like Laurent, Roger ordered for the both of them. It occurred to Maggie—just as she was in the first flush of being grateful she didn't have to think about what to order—that she had not been consulted.

She knew Laurent believed that *he* knew more about what was good and would therefore ensure that she had only the best. But as she was always reminding him with the children—people need to be allowed to make their own mistakes.

"For the entrées we will have *ravioli à la ricotta et huile de truffe*," Roger said, "Also a *tartare de salmon avec l'avocat et pomme Granny Smith*." He then ordered steaks for them both and gave clear orders of exactly how they should be cooked.

"*Oui, Monsieur*. And to drink?"

"A bottle of your house *rosé*."

By the time the waiter left with their order, Maggie's hands had finally stopped trembling.

"I still can't believe it," she said.

"Did you know the victim well?"

"Not before this week. I had dinner with her the night before last."

"Maggie, what is going on? Why are you involved in all this?"

Maggie looked at Roger. He was good-looking in an intense, European way. Thick brown hair like Laurent, but nowhere near as tall. Then again, at six foot five, few men were.

Perhaps the biggest distinction though was that whereas Laurent's eyes were dark brown and unreadable, Roger's were clear blue and always probing.

Would he ever move on? Didn't a big part of Maggie hope he never did?

"I came here with an old friend of mine," Maggie said. "I hadn't seen him since I left Atlanta nine years ago."

"He?"

"Yes. He's an old boyfriend. No, he was more than that. We were childhood friends. Our *families* were friends. And along the way…I let him down."

"Ah."

"What does that mean?"

"He allowed you to think you owed him."

"Are you trying to tell me I didn't owe him?" Maggie said impatiently. "That I didn't wrong him?"

"No, I am sure you did. I have first hand experience in such things, do I not?"

Maggie winced and focused on her ravioli as the waiter placed it before her. She was surprised to realize how hungry she was.

"But perhaps," Bedard continued, "he allowed you to believe your debt was greater than was the truth. Did he tell you he needed your help?"

"Yes. But it was for his wife who was being held for Bette's murder. He *did* need my help."

"I am sure."

"Okay, Roger, you're saying that like you *don't* believe it. If you think Brownie manipulated me, I have to tell you he's not like that. He's extremely forthright."

"Nine years is a long time. Perhaps he has changed."

"Not that much"

"*Bon.* So you stayed to help. Dare I ask in what form this help took?"

Maggie quickly outlined her last two days—from following Etienne, to swimming for the Île de Sainte-Marguerite with her hands tied while heavy objects were lobbed at her head, to finally discovering Sasha's body.

She wasn't sure at what point in her tale Roger had begun shaking his head but she was surprised he wasn't dizzy by the time she stopped talking.

"Maggie, Maggie..." he said solemnly. "You have told your husband none of this?"

Maggie sighed. "Every time Laurent and I've talked in the last two days we've had a fight. So no, I haven't shared my adventures with him."

"He will become unhinged, *certainement*," Roger said matter-of-factly.

"It couldn't be helped."

Roger gave her an admonishing look and then touched her bruised cheek. She blushed. Of course, if she'd thought about it, she hadn't really *needed* to go after Etienne through the dark streets of the seedier section of Cannes. *Or* used her credit card to break into Sasha's room. Those were two things at least in hindsight that stuck out as possibly less than sensible decisions.

Their steaks arrived and for a moment—like any true Frenchman—Roger was distracted enough to be able only to focus on his plate. The *pommes frites* were crispy and drizzled with *sauce béarnaise*. As usual, when Maggie was presented with exceptional cuisine, she thought of Laurent.

"How is it that Laurent ended up dropping the kids off with you?" she asked.

"He had exhausted all other avenues," Roger said with a shrug. "I understand this meeting in Arles is quite important."

"It must be if he couldn't wait one more day for me to get home."

"Perhaps he was not confident that you would *be* home in one more day." Roger arched an eyebrow at Maggie.

"I see you've joined Team Laurent," Maggie said tartly. "But in any case, I couldn't leave and now I'm not sure I'll be allowed to."

"You may leave. I have cleared it with Dumas."

"Will they want to talk to me again?"

"They know where to find you. You're not leaving the country I assume?"

"Very funny."

Maggie felt a gush of affection toward Roger. Regardless of how he felt about being with her—or how painful that might be for him—he was always there when she reached out for him.

"Thanks, Roger. Thank you for coming and for running interference. I really appreciate it."

"*Pas du tout*," he said gruffly, clearly not comfortable with the softer undertones between them. "Now. What do we know about these murders?"

"Well, you probably know more than I do. But here's what I know." Maggie put her fork down to concentrate. "The gossip is that my friend Brownie was sleeping with Sasha."

Roger nodded as if this was not news to him.

"Whether he was or wasn't, I don't know. When I ask myself who could have killed Sasha I have to think of Brownie's wife JoJo. She had motive, opportunity and she's cold-blooded."

"In your opinion," Roger said.

"I'm not *jealous* of JoJo, Roger," Maggie said in astonishment. "These are completely objective observations."

"Of course."

"Stop saying it like that. Brownie is a *friend*. I don't still have feelings for him."

"Continue."

Maggie tapped her finger on the table as she tried to assemble her thoughts.

"Okay, well, when Bette was killed and JoJo was the prime suspect, Brownie flipped out and begged me to look into it because I could speak the language."

Roger tore off the end of a large baguette and looked around the table for the saucer of olive oil.

"I talked to our waiter at the restaurant where Bette was killed and he confirmed that he saw JoJo go to the toilet at the same time as Bette."

"*Vraiment?*"

"Yeah, but when I talked to him the next day, he denied saying it."

"Interesting."

"Isn't it? So then Sasha slipped a note under my door saying I should talk to these two jurors, Jamison and Yang because they had a very different story to tell."

"Why did she not just hand you the note?"

"Presumably she didn't want me to know it was from her. I mean, first thing I'd have done is ask her how she knew what they saw? Say, that reminds me! Dumas should check the note for fingerprints! It's in my overnight bag under the—"

"The police have the note, Maggie."

Maggie's mouth fell open. "They went into my overnight bag?"

"Of course. And your room. Anything forensically that can be found on the note at this point will be found."

Maggie blinked and tried to imagine what the young woman behind the desk must have thought when the police confiscated her bag.

"Continue," Roger said.

She tried to block out the image of her bag being rifled through by a team of policemen wearing disposable gloves.

"So I tracked down Jamison and Yang and they said they were sitting in the restaurant bar in the sightline of the stairway to the toilet most of the night and nobody went down. Not JoJo or anyone—except for Etienne Babin. They described his jacket which was very memorable."

"So you called this information in to the police," Roger said, "and then went to apprehend Monsieur Babin yourself?"

"In my defense," Maggie said heatedly, "you should have

heard how the cops reacted when I called it in. I was sure they were just blowing me off!"

"And so you followed Monsieur Babin at which point he assaulted you, kidnapped you, attempted to murder you and then escaped back to Cannes in order that he might blow up the main convention hall. Is that the size of it?"

Maggie made a face at him.

"At which point," Roger continued, "he was quickly apprehended by the police—"

"Thanks to me."

"Thanks to the fact that they had in fact registered your earlier phone call," Roger said pointedly.

"I suppose," Maggie conceded. "Except now it turns out that Etienne *didn't* kill Bette?"

"There is no forensic evidence to support that he was downstairs when Madame Austin was killed."

"What about JoJo?"

"The same. Even her fingerprints are circumstantial. It was the knife she used to eat with so of course her prints would be on it. Plus as I understand it, the police didn't want to get sued by big bloodthirsty American lawyers for wrongful arrest. And her husband was threatening exactly that."

"What about Sasha's murder?"

"At this time the police have no leads."

"But the surveillance cameras in the hallway? Surely they'll know who else besides me went into Sasha's bedroom?"

"They are going through those right now. But until they can narrow down time of death, that might not be all that helpful. I understand Mademoiselle Morrison was...popular."

Maggie frowned. "Sasha was stabbed. Same as Bette, right?"

"No, *Madame Austin* was stabbed. Mademoiselle Morrison had her throat cut. There's a difference."

"If you say so. My point, Roger, is that not everyone can do something like that. I can understand a moment of passion with a knife, say a wife flips out and stabs her husband. But *two* knife murders? That's cold."

"You are assuming it's the same person."

"What are the odds that there would be *two* murderers walking around the festival?"

Roger shrugged as he poured more olive oil into the ceramic dish on the table and then caught the waiter's eye to signal that they needed more wine.

"Let me ask you," he said, "The jurors, Jamison and Yang. Why would they wish to give you false information about Etienne Babin?"

"It turns out Rick Wilson, who owns an ad agency in Atlanta, paid them to lie."

"And why would Monsieur Wilson do that?"

"I was thinking maybe you and I could ask him that together," Maggie said.

"I do not have jurisdiction here."

"That never stopped me."

"Nothing stops you, Maggie."

Maggie and Roger exchanged a fond look. There was no doubt in Maggie's mind that if it wasn't for Laurent, Roger would have made a good life partner for her. He loved her, he understood her. In some ways, maybe even better than Laurent did who was often hampered by the fact of his background. Roger's childhood—the product of an upper middle class family in Lyons—was much closer to Maggie's own.

"Where does your friend Brownie fit into all this, do you think?"

"I think he's been a fool," Maggie said slowly. "I think he married a hard woman and he stupidly turned to an affair when the going got tough."

"He has spoken to you about this?"

"No," Maggie admitted. "I'm just guessing."

Roger's phone rang and he glanced at the screen and then took the call.

"*Oui, chérie*? Oh yes? Give us five minutes. Madame Dernier will call Jemmy right back. Okay?"

Maggie felt a rush of warmth toward Roger as he orchestrated her callback to Jemmy. It made her feel like he was part of the family, like a beloved uncle. She felt so grateful to have him in her life.

Roger disconnected the phone and reached for his wineglass.

"Is that all?" he asked.

"Pretty much. Everything except the answer to the question of who killed Bette? And who killed Sasha? If what you've heard from the Cannes Police Department is correct, there's no evidence right now pointing to anyone."

Roger nodded sagely.

"That is true," he said. "Except you."

24

It was early evening when Laurent finally left Domaine St-Buvard. He was fairly sure he'd distracted Jean-Luc sufficiently that the old fellow wouldn't drop by tonight. But it wasn't the end of the world if he did.

He felt mildly uneasy about keeping Jean-Luc in the dark. But Laurent had gone to a lot of trouble for this little scenario to play out a certain way. And if he'd needed any further evidence of Jean-Luc's inability to keep his mouth shut, he only needed to look back as far as yesterday when Jean-Luc had burbled out all of Danielle's trusted secrets mere minutes after she'd begged him not to.

No, Jean-Luc was a good man and a dear and beloved friend.

But he was not to be trusted with anything more valuable than an old family *bouillabaisse* recipe.

Laurent had spent most of the day putting all the pieces in place for his crew's work tonight. He still had plenty of time to think about Maggie—and he attempted to call her once or twice. But just as he'd tried before, his calls only went to voice mail. When he called her at the hotel the front desk said she was out.

None of it made any sense. Maggie was the last person on

earth that Laurent would call mysterious. She wore her intentions, her emotions, and her desires on her face such that the basest, most idiotic of people might read her every wish and mood.

Which made her behavior the last few hours so...unsettling.

Was there a good reason why she was not answering her phone? Or why she had not spoken to her children? Or why she was unable to be reached in an emergency? Was this the same woman who could not drive to the village market without her cellphone?

Had Maggie left her phone uncharged? Had she lost her charger?

Was she trying to deliver a message?

But Laurent knew that was not like Maggie. It was difficult for her to dissemble. She would blurt out the truth if it killed her.

And there was a time or two when it nearly did.

That last thought gave Laurent a chill remembering times when Maggie's natural curiosity or inclination to help had led her into situations that she'd been lucky to escape from alive.

He turned on the radio and found a music station that didn't annoy him too much.

He was an hour from Arles. His meeting wasn't for another two hours. He'd planned on shopping for one last item for his special project tonight with the extra time. Marseilles would have been better but Arles would work too. It wasn't the nicest part of town but he'd heard he might be able to find what he wanted there.

On the other hand, he was only forty minutes from Cannes. If he were to skip the Arles meeting entirely...

His phone vibrated and he picked up, hoping it might be her.

It was Jean-Luc.

"Yes, Jean-Luc," Laurent said.

"Laurent, you are not at home?"

"*Non*, my meeting is tonight. Remember? Is everything all right?"

There was a pause on the line.

"Jean-Luc?"

"I thought I saw someone on the tractor road."

He meant the road that dissected Laurent's vineyard and led to the back of the Dernier *mas*. Laurent cursed silently. He'd instructed his men to use the road but not until after dark. It was seven o'clock. It wouldn't be dark for at least another three hours.

"I am sure it is nothing," Laurent said. "Kids on their bikes. How is Danielle?"

"She is beside herself," Jean-Luc said. "She has bitten my head off, Laurent! Have you talked to Maggie?"

"She will be home tomorrow," Laurent said. "Tell Danielle that she will be home tomorrow."

"I don't think it will help," Jean-Luc said morosely.

"I am getting another call, Jean-Luc. Ignore the teenagers on their bikes, eh? The house is fine. I have a security system."

"Oh, that's right. I had forgotten."

"*Adieu*, Jean-Luc," Laurent said and switched to the incoming call. "*Allo*?"

"We can't get the equipment up the back way. It is too steep."

"You were to have waited until dark. You were not to be seen."

"No one saw us. But we can't get the truck—"

"Don't use the truck. Carry the equipment on foot but *not until after dark*. Do you understand?"

"What if we're caught?"

"Don't be caught," Laurent said hanging up in mounting frustration before reminding himself *why* he was doing all this.

It is the end result that matters, he told himself. He knew Maggie didn't believe that but for him, it was simply one more habit that could not be broken.

He saw the sign for the turn-off for Cannes ahead but as he

put on his turn signal his phone lit up again. The screen showed an unidentified number.

"*Oui?*" he answered.

"I just talked to the vineyard magazine people," Bernard said. "They said they are holding the feature story for us! They will write it tonight so that it might be in the next issue. This is very big for us, Laurent. Are you on the way?"

Laurent snapped off his turn indicator and sighed heavily before moving out of the turn lane and back on the road to Arles.

AFTER MAGGIE SPOKE with both Jemmy and then Mila, giving them multiple kisses over the phone and prompting more than one snort of annoyance from diners surrounding them, she handed the phone back to Roger. She waited until he'd ordered the cheese course before tapping him on the wrist to get his full attention.

"You're not seriously suggesting the police will look at *me* for these murders?" she said.

"You did discover both bodies. And stepped in the forensic evidence. Both times."

"I had no motive to kill either of them!"

"Lower your voice," Roger said evenly. "People are trying to enjoy their dinners. As for motive..." He shrugged. "Some could say jealousy."

"You have got to be kidding. Jealously over what? Bette was a dried up old hag who had no one to love her and an empty apartment to come home to each night. Why would I be jealous of her?"

"Your husband will be delighted to see your priorities seem to be back in order."

"You've been talking to Laurent?"

"What about the younger woman? Did *she* not have an enviable life?"

"Roger, I lived that life. Trust me, there wasn't a thing Sasha had that I wanted."

"Not even her relationship with Monsieur Brownie?"

"You can sit there and ask me that? Really?"

"A cheap shot, as you Americans say. *Je suis desole*," Roger said. "Forgive me. But if you will allow me to make a suggestion?"

"Well, as you know, I love all your suggestions," Maggie said sarcastically as the waiter brought a wooden tray of cheeses and another basket of bread. He refilled their wineglasses and retreated.

"Why not call your husband and have him come for you?" Roger asked.

"I'm capable of driving myself home."

"Of course you are. Perhaps your husband needs to drive you home."

"That's ridiculous. Do you even know Laurent? Besides, I don't play games, Roger."

"Maybe you should."

"Spoken like a true Frenchman."

"Thank you. I am happy to loan you my phone so that you might sort things out with him."

"I have a phone. By 'sort things out,' you mean apologize."

"Is that really so hard? Or is it more important to you to be right?"

"It's not a matter of being right, Roger. The fact is, Laurent bosses me. All the time. And I'm sick of it."

"Who is it you are suggesting does this with you? Because I have seen you with your husband."

Maggie frowned. "You don't think he bosses me?"

As soon as she said it, she knew how she sounded. Like she'd been listening to someone else. Someone who had no real understanding of her marriage or her relationship with Laurent.

"I'm an idiot, Roger."

"I wouldn't go that far," Roger said as he cut into a large wedge of *Brie de Meaux.* "But I can confirm that your head, she is very hard, yes?"

Maggie burst out laughing and then realized it was the first laugh she'd had since arriving in Cannes.

RICK COULDN'T DECIDE if he felt like a kid again or if he felt like the lowest kind of felon.

It probably amounted to the same thing.

He'd spotted Maggie on *rue d'Antibes* getting out of a large sedan with a handsome man who he could only assume was not her husband. They didn't act married. Not at all.

They acted secretive.

He watched them as they parked and then entered the restaurant. At one point, Maggie put her hand on the man's arm and he laughed.

Rick prided himself on being able to read people. He wouldn't have gotten to the top of his game in the ad world if he didn't have *some* skills in that department.

And while he could tell these two weren't married he could also see that they were clearly sleeping with each other.

You'd be a fool to look at them and think otherwise.

When they disappeared into the restaurant, he toyed with the idea of going in too. It was a popular restaurant and he was confident he could hide himself among the diners. On the other hand, most of the action was on the patio and the couple had chosen the restaurant's dark interior for their illicit canoodling.

Should he take photographs? Except, she was married to a Frenchman. Her husband might not care that she was having an affair. Rick had heard that that sort of thing was widely accepted over here.

He pulled out his phone.

But Brownie would care.

Still he hesitated. Making Brownie thrash on the line wasn't the same as watching Maggie Newberry squirm.

He put his phone away.

Rick watched the restaurant a few moments longer from his position on the street while trying to make up his mind whether to go in or stay and watch.

Finally, he decided he'd stay. He'd be able to see her when she left. If she went in the car with the guy, Rick would lose her.

But he knew where he could find her again.

But if she didn't go in the car with him, he would follow her.

One way or the other eventually she would be alone.

Just the thought of it made Rick's pulse race and his mouth go dry.

Because when *that* happened, he thought, wiping his damp palms on his khaki slacks, *well, that was when the magic happened.*

25

A fter driving Maggie to the police station to pick up her overnight bag, Roger drove her back to the Carlton. A quick phone call confirmed that her room was still available and registered to her.

It had been a long hard day and Maggie wanted to get an early start back to St-Buvard in the morning. Roger had not caved on his refusal to confront Rick Wilson and Maggie had to be satisfied with his assurances that the police would be informed of Wilson's meddling.

Unfortunately, in her experience, a soft lead—a lead that may or may not have anything to do with the murders—would never be followed up on. Cannes was notoriously short of resources, especially manpower. The police would undoubtedly wait for whatever the forensics told them about both murders and go from there. Gone were the days when they might extensively canvass a murder site and interview everyone within a five-mile radius.

In Cannes? In the middle of a prestigious international festival? *Incroyable!*

Maggie heard a roar of laughter from the bar as she passed

through the lobby to the front desk. She was grateful that the beautiful young girl wasn't working the desk tonight.

She got her key and went upstairs to her room. She was grateful a second time that she ran into no one she knew along the way.

It wasn't even eight o'clock in the evening but she didn't have the energy for talking to anyone. Not after the day she'd had. And not if she had a prayer's chance of having the energy she needed for the phone call she intended to make.

The minute she turned the lights on in her room, her stomach lurched at the thought of the police going through the room this evening. The pillows? Her towels and sheets?

She was so tired she decided she wasn't even sure it mattered. She found a small demi bottle of rosé in the room refrigerator and opened it, then stripped her clothes off and stepped into a hot shower. Moments later, the bathroom pleasantly fogged with a lilac cloud of scent and soap, she pulled on her nightgown—pushing away the image of a stranger's hands touching it and examining it—and settled on the bed with a glass of the wine, and her phone.

Just do it. Don't think.

She punched in the number.

From where she was sitting she could see the night lights of Cannes as they stretched in a pulsating curve up the *Promenade de la Croisette* that hugged the coast of the Mediterranean.

"*Allo?*" Laurent's voice came on the line, suspicious and guarded.

He doesn't recognize the number.

"It's me. I lost my phone."

"How?"

Oh, we don't want to go there, Maggie thought, taking a quick swig of her wine.

"I'll tell you all about it when I see you tomorrow. Where are you?"

"I have just pulled into the parking lot of the restaurant for my meeting. I am a few minutes early."

"Laurent, I heard about what happened to Jemmy. I'm so sorry I wasn't there when he needed me. It just broke my heart."

Laurent gave the barest of pauses and then said, "It does not matter. He was very brave. It was good for him. You have talked to him?"

"I did. Twice."

"So you know…"

"…that he's at Roger Bedard's, yes."

"I had no choice," Laurent said gruffly.

"I know. Both kids adore Chloe. And I understand there's a cat too."

"That will of course assuage all wounds."

Maggie laughed. "Laurent, I'm so sorry. Sorry for all our ugly words."

"*Non*, I am sorry for this, *chérie*. Have you talked with Danielle today?"

"No, but I will as soon as I get home. I don't know what got into me. Can we start over?"

"*Bien sûr.*"

Deciding that tonight was not the time to reveal she'd tripped over yet another dead body, Maggie focused on telling Laurent about the *Best of Blogs* panel she'd discovered and how energized it had been to see it.

"Was it like what you are doing here in St-Buvard?" he asked.

"Some of it was. It was reassuring to know I was on the right track as far as that goes but some of the things I'm doing are more inventive, if you can believe it. I got the idea that the *best blogs* are doing things I did last summer and moved on from."

"I am not surprised."

"Well, I was, I can tell you."

"I do not tell you enough, *chérie*…" Laurent began.

Maggie was sure he was going to tell her how much he loved

her and she was getting ready to tell him it wasn't necessary to say when he surprised her.

"...what you are doing for the village with this blog makes me very proud."

A burst of joy blossomed in Maggie's chest. She knew Laurent respected what she was doing and he never trivialized her work on the blog. With its accumulated sponsorships and advertising, it usually brought in four figures a month. But because Laurent was always so taciturn, Maggie just assumed he believed that what he did with the vineyard was the important job and what she did was tantamount to the little woman baking cookies to keep from being bored all day.

"Our friends and neighbors count on the benefits they receive from your work," he said. "You have affected them in a way that I could not have imagined possible. And only you could have done it."

"Laurent, I..." Tears stung Maggie's eyes.

"I am remiss for not telling you," he said sternly. "For assuming you know that I see every day how *formidable ma femme* is. I am not ever taking you for granted, *chérie*. And I am sorry if I sometimes tell instead of ask. *Vraiment desole.*"

"Laurent, I'm blubbering here on this end," Maggie said, warmth radiating throughout her body.

"I know I don't always put it into words..."

"You don't have to. I don't want to make you be...someone you're not."

"I am the someone who loves you."

Maggie felt a rush of love toward Laurent so powerful that she got to her feet.

Why had Brownie suggested that Laurent dominated Maggie? Was it because he was jealous and Laurent's strength was the only thing he could think of to use against him? Was it because Brownie saw how in love Maggie was—always wanting to do things for her husband? And did he mistake that for servitude?

"When will you be back home?" she asked. "Because if I leave right now—"

"*Non, chérie*," Laurent said firmly. "It is late. Go to bed and dream of me, eh? Leave in the morning. We have the rest of our lives together. A few hours more won't kill us."

LAURENT HUNG up the phone as he pulled off the D36 and crossed Le Sambuc.

His heart was lifted by his conversation with Maggie. It had been too long since they had talked. Misunderstandings find their way into the cracks of any relationship when you are not continually smoothing and checking for them, he thought.

The last two days would not have happened if he had been more vigilant about what Maggie was feeling.

He saw the restaurant situated off the main road. *La Chassagnette* was shabby from the outside and had only two cars parked nearby. This did not signify the quality of the food inside in any way.

Not that that mattered.

Laurent was not staying for dinner.

He pulled in next to a nondescript SUV—the size of which was unusual for France—and immediately someone rapped sharply on his window.

The hulking shape of Bernard Faucheux materialized by Laurent's driver side window.

"*Allo*, Laurent? We will walk in together."

Laurent scanned the backseat of his car to confirm that he was leaving nothing. There were few streets in this part of Arles that were safe from a break in. He got out of the car, locked it and set the alarm.

As he joined Bernard on the sidewalk, his phone dinged to herald a new text message.

Expecting it to be a good night text from Maggie, he smiled as he glanced at the screen.

<We got in. But there is a barking dog>

Cursing, Laurent quickly typed back.

<Throw it the meat I told you to bring.>

"Laurent?" Bernard asked questioningly, waiting for him on the sidewalk. "*Ça va?*"

"*Oui, ça va,*" Laurent said, shoving the phone in his pocket and joining him.

26

I n spite of what Laurent said, Maggie got dressed.

She was sure she couldn't sleep now. She was too excited to see him again and to start eradicating the unhappiness that the two of them had manufactured in the last couple of days.

Just a quick two and a half hour night drive and she would arrive home at about the same time he did. The kids were safely at Roger's house for the night.

It was a perfect set-up for sealing the deal on their making up.

She would play *Linda Ronstadt* at top volume on the ride home and imagine all the different scenarios of what Laurent would say when he saw her walk through the door. A loving scolding when he knew she'd gotten in the car and driven back home would quickly turn amorous. This she had reason to know from experience.

As she was pulling on her jeans, a tentative knock at the door made her pause. She glanced at the clock. It was a little before nine.

She quickly finished dressing and went to the door. JoJo stood there looking luminous in a pale lemon silk gown that clung to every curve. Her three-inch high heels made her tower over Maggie.

"Goodness!" Maggie said as she took in the sight. JoJo really was a magnificent creature and done up to the nines as she was now, Maggie could already feel herself shrinking in comparison.

JoJo stepped into the room.

"I'm so sorry to barge in on you like this, Maggie. I just had to see if you were okay. I asked at the front desk and they said you were back. Surely the cops don't think you had anything to do with poor Sasha?"

"No. They were just fishing."

JoJo looked behind Maggie and saw her bag on the bed.

"You can't be thinking of leaving?"

"I can be in St-Buvard by midnight if I leave now."

"But Brownie's getting his *Top Ten Start-Ups* award at the festival banquet tonight."

"Well, you'll just have to cheer him on for the both of us."

"I can't talk you into staying? Are you sure?"

"Yes. But I was glad to have met you and I—"

"Then have one last drink. Please. Just for me to say thank you and I'm sorry and goodbye."

"None of that's necessary."

"Please, Maggie. I know what Brownie means to you and I've been a pig. I don't think things will be right between me and Brownie unless he knows that you've forgiven me."

"Fine. Okay. One drink. Downstairs?"

"Do you mind if we go someplace away from the hotel? I have to run down to the *Palais des Festivals*. Give me thirty minutes to be in my seat smiling and clapping as Brownie gets his award and then I can slip away while he's being carried off on the shoulders of all his admirers. Where's your car parked?"

Maggie hesitated. "It's off *rue Chabaud*."

"That's perfect! That's only a few blocks away from *rue Macé* where I've heard there are about a million bars. One quick drink and then you can hop in your car and head to the highway."

"Sure, okay," Maggie said, annoyed that she couldn't just tell JoJo *no* and head out right now. But if she did have to cool her heels for thirty minutes, it occurred to her that she did have one little bit of unfinished business she might attend to before she left.

"You're an angel, Maggie," JoJo said, flushing with excitement and relief. "I'm so glad Brownie has you for a friend."

Then JoJo turned and hurried down the hall toward the elevator.

Maggie glanced at her watch and did a quick look around the room to make sure she wasn't leaving anything behind.

Downstairs, she checked out and on her way to the front door glanced into the bar. Most people would be at the awards presentation to see the non-judged awards being handed out—or at private parties happening in apartments up and down the *Jetée Albert Edouard* or on multi-million dollar yachts in the harbor.

When Maggie spotted Courtney in the bar she wasn't surprised to see she wasn't alone. Courtney had always been popular, even nine years ago. And that was *before* she became a mover and shaker in the Atlanta advertising world. If anything, Courtney's star had only burnished brighter since then.

Courtney sat at a corner table with the same man who'd interrupted Maggie and Courtney's drinks the night before. Courtney saw Maggie approaching and her face lit up.

"Maggie! There you are!"

The man turned around but Courtney instantly took his hand.

"Darling, let me have a minute, will you? Fifteen minutes?"

"Of course. Glad to see you again," he said to Maggie.

Maggie took his empty seat.

"I wanted to see you before I left," Maggie said.

"Do you have to go?"

"Boy, do I ever," Maggie said with a laugh.

"Oh, darling, really? Why?" Courtney took a sip of her champagne and knit her brow.

"Well, honestly, it's not as much fun as you might think being the fattest person in the room. I mean, it's great for all you toothpicks, but for me, not so much."

Courtney burst out laughing. "You always said the funniest things,"

"They're funnier when they're about someone else," Maggie said.

"Well, I think you look great."

"Thanks."

"I bet you never even count calories any more, do you?"

"You can look at me and ask me that?" Maggie said wryly.

"But I know you, Maggie," Courtney said, her eyes twinkling. "You'll have replaced that obsessive little trait with something else."

"What do you mean?"

"I mean, obviously something else is a priority for you now. I don't know what it is but whatever it is, I'll bet you nail it. I bet you nail it every day. Maybe your kids? Or the blog you write?" Courtney shrugged. "Something else is more important to you than size two pants."

Like a thunderbolt, Maggie realized her friend was right.

"And while we're getting real here," Courtney said, "did you know I've been in Cannes for three days and haven't eaten over five hundred calories in any one day?"

Maggie frowned. "Really?"

There was a plate of golden *gougères* on the table. Without thinking when she sat down, and even though she'd had a full dinner not two hours before, Maggie had reached over and popped one in her mouth. It melted on her tongue in an explosion of feather-delicate cheese and butter. She would have expected the Carlton to have a good pastry chef. And they clearly did.

"Tom ordered those," Courtney said nodding at the plate. "They smell amazing and I'm hoping he hasn't noticed that I haven't had one. I'm drinking a little bit more than usual to give me strength to resist but I really, really want one."

"You're serious?" Maggie said. "You're in the south of France and you're not eating anything?"

"Crazy, huh? See that's something else that's changed since you and I used to hang out. I'm older now and my metabolism has slowed. I have to work out longer for the same results and the occasional treats I used to allow myself? Those are now in the category of *never* or *when the apocalypse comes*."

Maggie had to stop herself from reaching for a second *gougère*. They were *so* good. But she didn't want to torture poor Courtney.

Had she just thought the words *poor Courtney*?

"You are so lucky, darling. You can eat anything you want and I'll bet your gorgeous hunk of a husband doesn't even care about a few extra pounds, does he?"

"Not really," Maggie admitted.

"You've got it all, girl," Courtney sighed. "Don't ever think for a minute that you don't."

Maggie flushed with pleasure—both in anticipation of seeing her "gorgeous hunk of a husband" and at Courtney's words.

"Are *you* seeing someone these days?" Maggie asked. "Back in Atlanta?"

"I am. But we're not exclusive. I happen to know the other woman he's dating is ten years younger than I am."

"You're not old."

"Thirty-nine still can't beat twenty-nine."

"Jeez, Courtney. He doesn't deserve you."

"Oh, he's a great guy. Really. It's just the world I live in. But trust me, I'm tired all the time. It's hard enough keeping the business going without trying to compete with a twenty-something too. I'll bet you sometimes curl up with your hubby in flannel PJs on the couch and watch TV, don't you?"

Maggie nodded. "It gets cold in Provence in the winter."

"Yeah, well, I don't own flannel PJs. I'd *kill* for one evening with flannel PJs. And someone who thought I looked sexy in them."

"Oh, Courtney."

"Oh, don't listen to me!" Courtney laughed. "I'm only whining because I really want those *gougères!*" They both laughed and on impulse Maggie leaned over and gave her friend a hug. She would love to be able to urge Courtney to eat the damn *gougères* but she knew that for the life that Courtney led back home, a perfect figure was important—or at least Courtney thought it was.

It wasn't Maggie's place to try to reroute Courtney's values. Her friend's goals—like her life—were different from Maggie's now.

Thank God.

She saw Courtney's friend Tom hovering in the shadow of a nearby palm.

"Well, I just wanted to say goodbye," Maggie said. "It was such a treat seeing you."

"I know. Me, too. Will you be back in Atlanta any time soon?"

"Maybe Christmas," Maggie said as she stood up. "We sometimes go home then."

"I'd love to see you."

"I'll call you."

Tom edged closer and Maggie leaned over and hugged Courtney again.

"I better go now," she said. "I've got a hot date with a Frenchman who doesn't know it yet."

"You're a lucky girl, Maggie," Courtney said as Maggie walked away.

Don't I know it? Maggie thought, her heart soaring as she made her way to her meeting with JoJo.

THE MOMENT LAURENT entered the restaurant he knew something was wrong.

First he felt Bernard hang back and then turn and disappear. Laurent forced himself not to go after him. Regardless of what Bernard was up to, Laurent came here for a meeting.

Although it was now clear it was not a meeting with a pair of magazine writers.

He entered the main dining room and was not surprised to see it empty except for one guest.

She sat with her back to him. It was a cool move and one that impressed Laurent in spite of the budding irritation welling in his gut.

Adele Bontemps. He should have known.

Laurent strode to her table. A *charcuterie* plate sat before her, untouched. There was a bottle of local *rosé* and two glasses. One of the glasses, Adele held in her hand, the other was waiting for Laurent at his table setting.

This whole charade was clearly Adele's plan and so far Laurent had unwittingly accommodated her perfectly by following every twisted decree and edict, stupidly, trustingly.

Merde. Where was his head lately?

"You are not going to sit, *chérie*?" Adele purred as she sipped her wine.

Laurent pulled the chair back roughly and sat. He examined the wine label, grunted, and poured a glass.

"What is this all about, Adele?"

She reached over to the *charcuterie* plate and delicately extricated a piece of *giardiniera* in the form of a pickled carrot. She brought it to her lips and nibbled it, her eyes finding his.

"You are in a hurry, *chérie*?" she asked sweetly.

"You have gone to a lot of trouble to speak with me alone and away from St-Buvard," Laurent said. "What is it you want?"

"I am sure you must be very curious."

"I will consider a glass of decent *rosé* worth my drive. And then I will leave. Nothing you have to say is of interest to me."

"No?" Adele took a piece of the duck prosciutto and wrapped it around a thin stick of provolone cheese. She examined her concoction carefully.

Laurent would always readily agree that Adele was beautiful and incredibly alluring. It was in fact her life's work to promote the illusion. She was in her early forties but she looked more beautiful than when she was in her twenties. He'd known her then.

She'd been dangerous even then.

"No interest? Even if I were to tell you that I have set in motion something that will damage your perfect life?"

"I wouldn't believe it."

Adele slid the duck between her full lips. Fat glistened in a single drop on her bottom lip as she chewed.

Laurent drank the rest of his wine and stood up.

"I require you to sell the crushing operation back to Bernard," she said. "Or, if you'd like, to me. But it amounts to the same thing."

"It is not for sale."

She took a sip of her wine.

"I thought you might say that. Which is why tonight a friend of mine visited your home." She eyed the *rillettes* on the platter before her.

Laurent stiffened. "He will find no one at home."

Adele shrugged. "His purpose isn't to talk with you. Or *her*."

Laurent felt a rush of relief that Maggie and the children were out of the way.

What if they'd been home tonight?

He looked at Adele as if he hadn't really seen her before. In some ways, it was possible he hadn't.

He had not thought Adele to be a threat in a serious way. Not to him. Not to his family.

Was he losing it? Had he been wrong about how dangerous she was?

But when Adele shrugged again and began to delicately wipe her fingers on her napkin, he realized her game was not about threatening his family. She had arranged this gambit specifically for a time when there would be nobody at home.

"Why is your man there?" Laurent asked patiently.

Adele looked at him and smiled angelically.

"His mission is to plant a single photograph in your home. Much like a scavenger hunt, it will be placed somewhere not easy to find. But eventually, yes."

"A photograph?"

"Yes, *chérie*. A very special photograph."

Laurent massaged the bridge of his nose. This was becoming extremely tiring and very annoying all in one and yet he knew Adele wouldn't be rushed. Her game had taken days, perhaps weeks to construct, and she would see it through until every *i* was dotted and every last hoop jumped through.

"A photograph of you, *chérie*, looking very handsome, I must say. Naked. And in my arms."

"Doctored, of course."

"*Mais, oui, chérie.* Unless something happened I don't remember!" Adele laughed.

The blackmail was a bald, crude attempt and something he would have thought unworthy of Adele. But she was a woman scorned—at least in her view—and so perhaps he shouldn't be surprised.

In any case, it was time to end it.

"Interesting," he said simply.

"That is all you have to say, Laurent? May I imagine the

horror and hurt your wife will experience when she sees this photograph? When she is happily dusting a shelf and suddenly finds something, *Oh, qu'est-ce que c'est?* she might say as she pulls the photograph out only to see her husband in the arms of another woman."

"Are you finished?" Laurent asked.

"I have just told you that your house has been entered tonight without your permission," Adele said. "I wonder why you do not immediately call this crime into the police? Is it possible you have a reason for not calling them?"

Laurent felt his pulse speed up but he kept his face placid and his hands still at his side.

She knows. One of the idiots I hired for tonight's job must have talked.

He pulled out his phone. *This is the last time I hire a job locally.*

"What are you doing?" Adele said as the smile faltered on her face.

"As you so sensibly suggested. I am calling the police to report the break-in."

"But...but you...I mean, is that wise?" Adele's face hardened but she quickly recovered her smile, obviously convinced he was bluffing.

"*Allo?*" Laurent said into his phone. "This is Laurent Dernier of Domaine St-Buvard. My wife and I are out of town this evening but a neighbor has reported a break-in at our home. Yes, that's right."

Adele was blinking rapidly, her mouth opening and closing in disbelief.

"Oh, one more thing. I have workmen onsite who should be able to give an eyewitness description. Yes, it *is* very unusual to have a crew working at this hour of the night." Laurent looked at Adele and smiled. "It is a little surprise I am planning for my wife."

After he hung up, Laurent picked up his keys from the table.

"It doesn't matter," Adele said. "Even if they catch him, the photo is still where he hid it, ready to be discovered unless you sign over the crushing operation."

"I'm afraid this time the ugliness between us will amount to more than just a fine from the police, *chérie*," Laurent said. "Unless you agree to leave St-Buvard for good, I will find it necessary to reveal to the *flic* your personal involvement in this instance as well as a few other escapades of which I am aware."

He walked to the door where he stopped and looked back at her. She was turned in her chair, staring at him with all the venom and hatred clearly visible across her face.

"As for Maggie," Laurent said, "I'm afraid you don't know *ma femme*. She could find a hundred such photos and her eyes would never believe what her heart knew to be false. I am sorry for you, Adele, that you do not know what that kind of love feels like."

Then he turned on his heel and walked out the door.

27

T he sounds of the *La Croisette* lifted up like a giant wave and rolled across the sky. Maggie heard the laughter as if it was much nearer than she knew it was. The winding back streets of Cannes alternately blocked and liberated the noise so it was difficult to determine how close the source was.

The party must still be going strong, Maggie thought, as she moved up a narrow street lined on both sides with restaurants whose facing awnings nearly touched. All were shuttered and closed.

Maggie hurried up the street, past the closed Lacoste store, the upscale lingerie shops, the locked and darkened grocery stores toward the parking garage where she'd left her car. As she walked, she thought what an idiot she'd been to have envied anyone here even for a minute.

The whole point of coming to Cannes had been to see an old friend—perhaps heal a wound that she'd caused—and see if there was anything new in the way of marketing that could be of help to her and her blog.

In truth, she'd also looked forward to a relaxing break from the nonstop demands of motherhood.

Instead, she'd become bogged down in making comparisons and second-guessing herself.

Well, that and tripping over two dead bodies, she reminded herself.

She shifted her overnight bag on her shoulder. She should have left it at the hotel. No, that was the whole point of meeting JoJo here—so Maggie could just hop in her car afterward and head out of town.

She looked at her watch. It was getting late. She would stop by the garage first and throw her bag in the car so she didn't have to lug it to whatever brasserie JoJo had found that was still open.

She looked over her shoulder.

It occurred to her that it was strange that JoJo would want to meet her tonight. Wouldn't she want to celebrate with Brownie after his big win? On the other hand, Maggie had definitely picked up tensions between JoJo and Brownie so perhaps it wasn't that odd for JoJo to want to be on her own.

After all, hadn't JoJo been doing just that ever since they arrived?

Maggie shivered in spite of the fact that the night was warm. She flashed back to the last time she'd walked the darkened streets of Cannes—and remembered all too well how that had ended. She still had a lump on her temple and a fading bruise on her cheek to remind her.

She heard a faint roar of applause and cheering and wondered briefly what amazing thing must have happened on the beach. Perhaps another performer? Or a bigger award being given out? Or maybe everyone was just drunk and ready to cheer at anything.

Maggie still didn't know if Brownie knew that JoJo was sleeping around—or if that was even true. Now that she thought of it, she realized she was only taking that idiot Jamison's gossip for gospel.

Is it because I want to believe it? Is it because I don't like JoJo so I secretly hope her marriage to Brownie is a failure?

Annoyed with herself for the downward turn in her thoughts, Maggie approached the parking garage and another thought suddenly occurred to her.

How did JoJo know where my parking garage was located?

ROGER NAVIGATED onto the A8 heading west toward Aix. He'd be home in an hour if he kept the pedal down. He leaned back into the driver's seat and flooded the car with the sounds of Patrick Bruel coming through his radio speakers from his iPhone, singing along with the throaty tenor until he became aware that he was taking no real pleasure in it. He snapped the speakers off.

It had been a long time since he'd spent so much time with Maggie. They'd not been alone for any length of time since before her children were born.

He thought back to the afternoon at the restaurant and how she'd looked. In spite of the swelling on her cheek and the discoloration there to herald the run-in she'd had with Babin, she looked beautiful as usual. Her hair was long and unruly around her shoulders—just as Roger loved it. And her eyes sparkled with intensity as she spoke.

So American, he thought. The way she interacted with him was as familiar and affectionate as ever. Even, perhaps as intimately as if she did not have a husband.

No, much as Roger might like to imagine it, he couldn't take it that far. Maggie had been grateful to see him, of course. After all, she had allowed him to be the one to mount the white stallion and rescue her from the castle keep.

He grimaced at his own imagery. Pathetic, this hold the

woman had on him. Apparently even her obvious devotion to a husband and two children could not weaken it in him.

And what of his own girlfriend, Ezzie, who was ten years his junior and looked like she had stepped from the pages of *Vogue*? It was not like Roger was going to bed alone every night curled up with a detective novel.

Was it only because he could not possess Maggie that made her so desirable to him?

He had to admit that was part of it. But he also had to admit he simply enjoyed her company, and her very American conversational style. He especially enjoyed watching the way her mind worked.

He frowned as he thought back to their conversation. Maggie was right about the need to question Rick Wilson. As soon as they'd parted Roger had risked stepping on sensitive toes by texting that very suggestion to Dumas. It had thus far been met with silence. Roger had expected no less. But still. *Someone should talk to Wilson. He might well have relevant information to the murders, one or both.*

Roger watched the upcoming exit off the A8. It wouldn't take much time to circle back to Cannes and find Wilson himself. Maggie said he was often in the Carlton Hotel bar. Roger glanced at his watch. It was early, he thought as he shifted lanes toward the exit. Plenty of time to get a few answers before heading home.

His phone vibrated and he saw the screen light up into a photo of Ezzie.

"Where are you, *chéri*?" Ezzie asked. "Can you come by tonight?"

Roger felt a flutter of excitement in his chest at the sound of her voice.

"But of course," he said nonchalantly.

"I have a special surprise for you if you can get here soon," she teased.

"I think that can be arranged," Roger said as he pressed down

on the accelerator and flew past the exit that would have taken
him back to Cannes.

MAGGIE STOOD at the corner of Chabaud and Marceau.

She could see the chain across the front of the garage but at
first she couldn't process it. She walked to it and tugged at it
where it was draped across the gaping opening. Inside the garage
was totally dark. There wasn't an office or cashier in sight. Maggie
cursed her stupidity.

*How did I not know when it closed? What kind of public parking
garage closes at all?*

She looked at her watch and cursed again. It was after ten
o'clock. The garage sign clearly announced it closed nightly at
ten except for *le weekend*.

She'd parked here because it was closer to the beach and
because it was cheap.

And now she was paying the price for that.

One way or the other, she was not going home tonight.

She shook her head and crossed her arms on her chest as
disappointment and fury battled for dominance in her.

Maggie felt an irrational surge of resentment towards JoJo.
She knew of course that her missing the garage closing time was
not JoJo's fault. But it felt good to trade disappointment for anger.
She gave the chain another frustrated shake, enjoying the sounds
of its discordant rattle as it echoed down the dark, empty streets.

Screw JoJo, she thought. *I'm going back to the hotel for a hot bath
and start over in the morning. Laurent was right. This was impetuous
and crazy thinking of driving home at this hour.*

Maggie heard the noise from the beach celebration climb
again until it crested into a climax of cheers and applause and the
sound made her even angrier.

Idiots! Mindless drunken idiots! she thought as she shifted her bag—biting into her shoulder now—to her other arm and began the trek back down the alley toward the hotel.

Her phone vibrated briefly. She pulled it out and saw it was showing the time of her appointment with JoJo. She was still a block away from their rendezvous point and now—if she was going to reconsider and meet her—she was late.

At the cross street, Maggie paused. She was positive she'd come this way but it didn't look familiar. Listening to the sounds from the beach, she headed down the street in the opposite direction.

After three more blocks she stopped in frustration and looked around. The street was claustrophobically narrow, with a line of dark apartment windows shuttered tight. A vein of unease throbbed between her shoulders and she began walking again. How had she gotten turned around? She wasn't even sure she could retrace her steps back to the garage.

Maggie turned to look back the way she'd come. Her heart was thudding in her throat. A sensation crawled across her skin like a thousand angry ants. She rubbed her arms and a thin sheen of sweat popped up on her face.

Then it came to her in a flash. She knew exactly what she was feeling. It was a feeling of foreboding that went beyond the dark shadows, the vacant alleyways, and the sound of her heart pounding in her ears.

A sixth sense that told her *she was not alone.*

The thought erupted with a fierce burst of fear that spiked her anxiety. She tried to force it away—to stay calm, to think.

She closed her eyes and willed herself to take slow, long breaths against her burgeoning panic.

The blow came from behind. Her phone flew out of her hand. Maggie heard it break against the stones as she clawed at the hands wrapping around her throat.

28

M aggie gasped. Her vision began to waver as her panic combined with her lack of oxygen. A scent of something familiar filled her senses. Lemons and something sweet. A man's aftershave.

A smell she recognized.

The fury of the knowledge of who held her shot a burst of adrenaline through her, fueling a reserve of energy she didn't know she had.

She drew her elbow back and jabbed her assailant hard in the gut. With a loud groan, he released her and stumbled against the crumbling stonewall of the alley. Maggie whirled around and grabbed his shoulders. She brought her knee up hard between his legs.

With a scream that ricocheted down the alley, Rick Wilson collapsed to the cobblestones.

Maggie was shaking as she worked to suck in gulps of air. For one mad moment, she looked around the alley to see if there was something heavy—something lethal—to finish him off with.

She flattened herself against the wall, her hands gripping her own shoulders as she hugged herself to stop the violent trembling that overcame her.

Wilson squirmed and moaned on the ground, his hands clutching his crotch and rocking in agony.

Maggie saw her phone on the ground—broken beyond use—and wiped the perspiration from her face. It was impossible to believe she'd been shivering in the summer air just a few moments before. Her face was now burning hot. She forced herself not to throw up the dinner she'd had hours earlier with Roger.

"Why are you following me?" she gasped.

"Just thought...we could...talk," Wilson choked. "Didn't mean to...startle you."

"You tried to strangle me!"

"No! I just wanted to...I'm sorry. I went too far," he said, leaning up against the wall but no longer holding himself. "I don't know what came over me. I wouldn't have really...hurt you."

Maggie realized that this was her chance to get the answers about why Wilson paid Jamison and Yang. But more importantly, if Brownie was involved in something he shouldn't be.

"Tell me what you're doing with Brownie," she said. "And maybe I won't call the cops on you for felony assault. You're trying to rig the votes at one of the juried panels, aren't you?"

Wilson narrowed his eyes and pushed himself into an upright seated position.

"Stay where you are," Maggie said. "If you don't think I can't put you right back down only this time with a broken bone, please, by all means try and get up."

"You think you're tough, don't you?" But he stayed on the sidewalk.

"What is your game with Brownie and the votes?"

He shrugged. "You're not wired, are you?"

She had to hand it to him. He had nerve. Or he mistakenly believed he didn't have anything to fear from her.

He should have been in my head fifteen seconds ago when I was looking for something to brain him with.

"Whatever it is, you won't get away with it," she said.

"Really? Are you going to turn in your dearest chum, Brownie?" he sneered. "Because if you turn *me* in, you turn him in."

Maggie let out a snort of exasperation. She had been hoping her guess was wrong. But Brownie had dropped too many telltale hints.

He'd missed all the preview panels that as a jury leader he should have attended. He spent more time in the bar talking with people who looked like they were either ashamed to be seen with him or way too eager to be talking to him.

What was the matter with Brownie? Does he not know how much he has to lose?

Somehow Maggie knew JoJo was behind this. She had to be. There was no way Brownie would get into this mess on his own.

"Why did he do it?" she asked.

"Money. Why else? He's drowning in gambling debts."

"What about Jamison and Yang?"

"What about them?"

"You paid them to lie in a murder investigation."

"That's not against the law, sweetie."

"Why did you do it? Five hundred bucks times two is a lot of money."

"Maybe to you."

"*Why* did you do it?" she repeated. "And Martin. You paid him too."

"If you say so."

"You paid Martin to implicate JoJo in Bette's murder and then to recant. You paid Jamison and Yang to implicate Etienne Babin. W*hy*? How are you connected to Bette's death?"

"Not at all as it happens."

"But you told me yesterday her death was connected to the Cannes festival."

"Did I?"

Maggie clenched her jaw. This was getting nowhere. Wilson wouldn't tell her why he'd done the things he had and for the life of her Maggie couldn't figure out how to make him.

Wilson laughed softly and then moaned as if the laugh hurt. "I knew you when you were in Atlanta. Do you remember me?"

"Not even for a minute. You can go now. But give me your phone."

"I'm not giving you my phone!"

Maggie held her hand out for the phone.

His nostrils flared as he handed it over.

"You're a Class-A bitch. You know that? You were back then. And you are now."

"You're wrong," Maggie said glancing at the phone. It was fully charged. "I'm a lot nicer now. Which is why I'm not calling the police to have your sorry ass dragged off to jail for assault. But I'd hurry and go before I change my mind."

Cursing her, Wilson stood up and with one last forlorn look at his phone, turned and limped off in the direction of the *Boulevard de la Croisette*.

THE AWARD WAS heavy and golden. Brownie knew it wasn't real gold, of course. More like the trophies he used to rack up in Little League a few centuries ago. Well, him and every other kid on the team. But this one had heft and it had writing on it.

He wished he could have added Sasha and Bette's name to it beforehand but he'd do it when he got back to Atlanta before he put it on display in the agency.

He scanned the audience for his wife. He'd seen her just before he went up to the podium. Because she'd arrived so late he hadn't been able to save her a seat but he'd definitely spotted her as he mounted the steps to receive the award.

As soon as they'd handed him the trophy he'd become so overwhelmed with needing to turn it into a tribute to Sasha and Bette that he pretty much forgot everything else. All he could think of was their faces—beaming—and looking down on him. He wanted to make sure he said just the right thing. If he had his way, they'd both live on in advertising history, never to be forgotten.

It occurred to him that because their tragic deaths happened at the biggest advertising awards festival in the world, now they very likely *would* live on forever.

That helped ease the pain of their loss at least a little.

He could still hear the roar of approval from the audience when he lifted his trophy up to the skies and said *I dedicate this award to the two best damn ad women I know! Sasha Morrison and Bette Austin!*

The wave of approval had rolled over him and more than one eye was wet with love and affirmation at his words.

Now he moved through the crowd, clutching the golden orb against his chest. A few people came up to him to offer their congratulations and Brownie shook hands and said he'd catch up with them later at whoever's party on whatever yacht before turning toward the open air bar that had been constructed on the beach.

Could the bitch not even wait for the applause to die down?

MAGGIE WANTED to be sure she gave Wilson enough time to be well ahead of her. She didn't trust he wouldn't jump out at her from one of the street corners.

One question she never got an answer to was why had he followed her and attacked her in the first place? Was it because she knew about the vote-rigging? But until she'd mentioned it to him, how could he have known she was on to him?

She put a hand to her throat to massage where he'd held her. She was willing to believe he hadn't meant to seriously hurt her. She wouldn't have let him go if she truly thought that. He'd been rough but awkward. He didn't know what he was doing and his claim that he'd gotten carried away felt true.

After all, Maggie had gotten a little carried away herself.

"Did you think I wouldn't come?"

Maggie whirled around to see JoJo standing behind her in the shadows.

"How long have you been there?" Maggie asked.

Could JoJo have seen her altercation with Wilson? If so, why hadn't she come to her aid?

JoJo emerged from the shelter of a dark building overhang. She had changed from her evening dress into jeans and a camisole top. Her eyes had a dazed look as if she'd had too much to drink.

Maggie decided that JoJo couldn't have had any idea of what had just happened. But she was sick and tired of everyone in Cannes and unwilling to indulge a single other person's shenanigans.

"Well, I'm not in the mood for a drink," Maggie said with annoyance. "I'm heading back to the hotel." As the words left her mouth, Maggie couldn't help but think there was something odd about JoJo. Even in the dark, her eyes looked wild as if she were on something. The ingratiating friendliness that JoJo had displayed an hour ago at the hotel was gone. And in its place was a preening mien of victory.

A foreboding overcame Maggie seconds before she saw JoJo make her move. And in those seconds, Maggie was only able to turn and take a single step in the direction of the hotel and the sounds of merrymaking on the beach.

And that was all.

The next thing she felt was a shattering vibration smash into her hip and travel up her spine until it exploded in her brain and sent her falling face first to the cold cobblestones beneath her feet.

29

Maggie remembered hitting the street, the curb coming up to crack her in the chin, her hips and legs vibrating in agony.

She smelled JoJo's perfume as the woman knelt near Maggie's face, her lips close to her ear. Maggie fought not to vomit.

"Just wanted to let you know I'm serious, sugar," JoJo said. "You'll move where I tell you to. Got it?"

Maggie nodded numbly, feeling a burning sensation in her hands and arms as she slowly became fully aware again. She felt JoJo pluck the barbs from her hip and then grab her by the upper arm.

With JoJo's help, Maggie staggered to her feet.

"Why are you doing this?" Maggie asked as she leaned against the stone abutment behind her. She glanced around but JoJo had chosen her moment well. They were completely alone.

"Time enough for questions later," JoJo said as she waved the Taser in Maggie's face. "Two blocks down. There are no street lights so watch your step." Then she giggled as if she just heard how ridiculous that sounded.

Maggie couldn't help the surge of fear she felt when she

looked at the Taser in JoJo's hand. The memory of the nerve-grinding pain of being tazed was so vivid, she swallowed hard to push the thought of it away. She turned in the direction that JoJo indicated and trudged along the rough cobblestones. Meanwhile, her mind raced. She'd dropped her bag when JoJo tazed her but she still had Wilson's phone in her front jeans pocket.

Roger said JoJo hadn't killed Bette so why was she doing this?

Maggie felt a wave of ice-cold dread descend upon her.

Sasha.

If JoJo killed Sasha and she thought Maggie suspected…

They walked without speaking until Maggie felt a sharp jerk on the back of her shirt. She stopped walking.

"What's that in your pocket?"

Maggie's heart sank as JoJo gestured to Maggie's front pocket.

"Dig it out. Right now, please. Slowly."

Maggie pulled Wilson's phone out of her pocket.

"Thinking of calling someone, Maggie?" JoJo said. "Drop it on the street and stamp on it. Hurry up!"

This phone was her only chance to let someone know where she was! Maggie hesitated but JoJo jerked her arm out straight until the Taser was eye level with Maggie.

"Do you think I'm joking?" JoJo hissed. "Do it!"

Maggie dropped the phone and heard it crack as it hit. She braced herself against the wall and drove her foot into it over and over again as the sounds of breaking plastic filled the quiet alleyway.

"That'll do," JoJo said, kicking the pieces into the gutter. Then, holding the Taser on Maggie, she dug out the key that opened the dark wooden door.

The street was deserted. Maggie could still hear the music and even laughter from the beach. *It's because sound rises,* she told herself. *I can hear them.*

But they'd never hear my screams over the music.

"Inside," JoJo said, waving the weapon at Maggie.

The last thing Maggie wanted to do was go into a place where she had nowhere to run, no hope of being heard if she shouted for help. But JoJo's finger on the trigger made it clear she'd be happy to shoot Maggie again and drag her lifeless body inside. Maggie stepped into the dark room. JoJo came up behind and shoved her hard. Maggie stumbled through the door and her shins hit a chair just as JoJo shut the door. All sounds from the beach cut off like the slam of a coffin's lid.

LAURENT HUNG up the phone with Phillipe, the leader of his crew. All in all, it was a satisfactory report. Phillipe admitted that there was what he referred to as a *bit of a mess* as he called it but the job was done. Laurent wasn't entirely sure what *a bit of a mess* looked like. But he had the rest of the night to deal with it, whatever it was.

He'd treated himself to a stop along the route from Arles to St-Buvard at one of his favorite brasseries, *Le Jardin*. Undiscovered by tourists, *Le Jardin*—with nary a hint of a garden in sight—was renowned in the area for its duck dishes.

After a pleasant hour alone with his thoughts and a superb *duck confit croustade* accompanied by an *herbes de Provence* salad and a glass of a very good *Côtes du Rhône*, Laurent was back on the road and headed toward home. He was grateful for Roger's offer to bring the children to Domaine St-Buvard tomorrow so he could skip going to Aix tonight.

Depending on when Maggie arrived in the morning, they should have sufficient time to repair the gaps between them that had been created in the last couple of days. He smiled in anticipation. He had been sorely tempted to allow Maggie to come home tonight even in the dark but he couldn't take the chance of her returning too soon.

Laurent now had the entire night if he needed it—without

worry about children or a too-curious spouse— in order to tie up any and all loose ends of this night's escapade.

He'd already promised himself that this would be the last job like this. He must be getting old. The secrecy and near misses had taken a toll on him. He thought of how easy it had been for Adele to find out *at least partially* about tonight's caper.

In the old days, none of the typical setbacks he'd experienced with this job would have bothered him. Perhaps it was just as well that he was retired from that old life.

He stopped at the traffic light before the turn off to the A8 and impulsively entertained the thought of driving to Cannes instead to surprise his *femme* in her big bed at the Hotel Carlton. He could still get back to St-Buvard in the morning in time to tie up any loose ends that needed to be dealt with.

His heart began to beat a little faster. He could be in Cannes in less than two hours.

His phone rang as the light changed and Laurent frowned to see that the number on the screen was not one he recognized.

"*Allo?*" he answered cautiously, well aware that Adele might yet have a trick or two up her sleeve.

"Laurent? This is Babette Zimmerman, Roger Bedard's mother-in-law."

A sudden clutch of fear shot an image of Jemmy, his wound possibly more serious than the idiot doctor at the ER had believed...

"*Oui*, Madame Zimmerman," Laurent said. "Are the children—?"

"Oh, yes, they are well but the little one, Mila, has awakened and is crying for her *maman*. I know Roger arranged that he would bring the children to you tomorrow but is there any way you could come for them tonight after all?"

Laurent let out a sigh of relief.

Aix was much closer than either Cannes or St-Buvard. He could be there in thirty minutes, collect both children and bring them home to tuck them away in their own beds. Then, as they slept, he would do whatever he needed to do to clean up his crew's mess. And of course, seeing her children as soon as she arrived home would be a very good surprise for Maggie.

In fact, this might work out even better, he thought.

Except, of course, for the part where he and Maggie would be able to privately demonstrate to each other how much they had missed each other. That would have to wait.

"Of course, Madame. Tell Mila her papa is coming."

As he turned the radio on for the short drive ahead of him, Laurent marveled at how the pull of his child could make him reroute his most happily anticipated plans without complaint or rancor. He'd learned long ago that his own needs would forever come unquestionably second to those of his children.

It was a realization that never ceased to amaze him. And one he presently mulled over with good humor as he passed the exit to Cannes and headed toward Aix-en-Provence.

30

The room JoJo pushed Maggie into off the alley was crudely furnished. A wooden table was by the door and two hard-backed chairs sat under a small window on the far wall that probably looked out over the train station.

Maggie could hear the faint sound of trains. In the distance but there. She looked around in the gloom.

Had JoJo been planning this all along? Who was she in it with? Rick Wilson?

"How did you know where I parked my car?" Maggie asked.

JoJo snorted. "I didn't. But Dennis Beaker said he had a room near Chabaud avenue and you said your garage was on Chabaud. So *voila* as the Frogs say."

"You're talking about the creative director at Wilson, Burt & Lewis? Is he in on this?"

JoJo narrowed her eyes at Maggie before walking to the door.

"Dennis rented this place for the festival week," JoJo said. "I think he had an idea he might use it for an illicit rendezvous or two."

"What kind of rendezvous would be so illicit he couldn't just use his room at the Carlton?"

JoJo raised an eyebrow. "I have no idea what Dennis gets up to in his personal life," she said. "I said I needed a place for a few hours. He gave me the key."

"So he knows I'm here?"

"Don't get your hopes up. I didn't tell him why or when I needed it."

"So why did you bring me here?" Maggie asked tersely.

JoJo opened the door and looked out and then closed it again. Maggie noticed she didn't lock it.

She is expecting someone, Maggie thought, her fear beginning to ratchet up higher. *Who?*

"Tell me what the police asked you today," JoJo said, walking back to Maggie.

"They wanted to know what state I found the...found Sasha," Maggie said.

"They didn't ask you about me or Brownie?"

"No."

"And they let you go because they ruled *you* out?"

"That's right," Maggie lied. "They have video evidence of the person who murdered her."

JoJo frowned. "What do you mean?"

"The surveillance cameras in the hotel hallway," Maggie said. "It showed the killer going into Sasha's room. The medical examiner was able to match up the time stamp with the time of death."

Of course, the camera footage hadn't been processed yet. And the medical examiner had only just started his examination on Sasha.

But JoJo didn't know that.

JoJo chewed her lip and glanced toward the small window. Her face looked as if it had aged ten years since they'd left the alley. Or perhaps it had always looked withered and ravaged. Until JoJo dropped the exaggerated smiles, it had been impossible to see.

Maggie waited for JoJo to ask her the obvious question. She

studied JoJo's face as the urge to do just that cramped the woman's features before JoJo finally turned away.

The only reason JoJo won't ask is because she already knows what the surveillance camera footage shows.

"You never should have interfered, Maggie," JoJo said, going again to the door. This time she put her ear against it, listened for a moment and then came back to Maggie. She held the Taser tightly in her hand.

"Brownie asked me to," Maggie said. "For your sake."

JoJo snorted. "My lovable idiot. What is that old saying? The truth will set you free? If Brownie had just stopped trying to *help* so much the truth would have set us all free."

"I have no idea what you're talking about."

"I was never in any danger of being held for Bette's murder! Never!"

"Is that because you had an alibi in the form of the Saatchi's art director?"

JoJo's face hardened. "You think you're so smart, Maggie Newberry. So much smarter than everyone else."

It was absolutely stunning to Maggie to realize that all along these people had actually felt insecure around *her.*

"But to answer your question," JoJo said, "I was never in any danger because Etienne Babin was the real killer and the evidence would have revealed that just as soon as these idiot French police got around to dusting off their microscopes and fingerprint kits."

"I think you should go back to being relieved you ran into the Saatchi guy that night," Maggie said.

"What are you talking about?"

"Etienne didn't kill Bette."

"Yes, he did. He confessed."

"No, he didn't. One of the detectives on the case had concerns about what kind of murderer wears a lime green jacket to kill someone. Murderers usually want to blend in to their surroundings. Plus Babin denied killing Bette."

JoJo frowned as if something bothered her about what Maggie was saying but she didn't respond.

"Why did you drag Brownie into the voteing scam you were running?" Maggie asked, hoping the switch in subjects would disarm JoJo.

"My, my. Don't tell me you still care about him?"

"I'll always care about him. Doesn't mean I want to be with him."

JoJo let out a short bark of a laugh. "Please. As if I could be jealous of *you*. Do you *own* a mirror?" She shook her head as if bewildered by the suggestion.

"But I don't suppose there's any harm in telling you," JoJo said. "The vote went down this afternoon without a hitch. The fifty grand was deposited into our account. It's all over and there's nothing anyone can do about it now."

"Wow. That's a lot of money. Mind telling me the specifics?"

"Sure," JoJo said with a shrug. "Although it sounds as if you've already worked most of it out. Brownie agreed to sell his vote in addition to swaying two other jurors in the *Palme d'Or* category for Advertiser of the Year."

The *Palme d'Or* was one of the top five biggest awards in the festival. It showed just how naive Brownie was to think he could get away with it.

"I assume that would be for the Wilson, Brut and Lewis Agency?" Maggie said.

"Aren't you clever?" JoJo said with a sneer.

"I can't imagine what kind of hook you have into Brownie to get him to do something like that."

"Hey, I wasn't the one who approached him. I just told him what a great opportunity it was."

It must have been Rick Wilson who approached him. Figures.

"It's hard for me to believe that the Brownie I know could do something like that," Maggie said.

"Maybe you don't really know him any more. For example, he is utterly devoted to me. Totally and completely."

"I wonder. Will he still stand by you once he learns you killed Sasha?"

JoJo's jaw clenched and her eyes probed Maggie's.

"Who says I did?" she asked.

"If it wasn't you, any reason why she was killed?" Maggie asked.

"Someone must have thought the world would be better off with one less skank," JoJo said bitterly.

"I guess that means you found out about her and Brownie."

"She thought she was God's gift. And the way Brownie treated her—like she was some sort of creative super genius. It was disgusting to watch."

Maggie felt a shiver of sorrow for poor Sasha.

"Plus," JoJo said, "it turned out Sasha heard some of the other delegates talking about Brownie selling his vote and she threatened to go to the *ethics* panel! Give me a break. I didn't even know they had such a thing in advertising."

That didn't make sense. Wasn't Sasha in on the voting scam, too?

"But Sasha sent me the note," Maggie said. "The one leading me toward Etienne."

"Did she?" JoJo said smugly. "Are you sure?"

"I recognized her handwriting on it." But now that Maggie thought about it, this wasn't true. She'd really only recognized the unique ink color and the fact that it was a fountain pen—not the penmanship.

"But I don't understand," Maggie said running her hand through her hair in frustration. "If it wasn't Sasha, then who gave me the note?"

"Here's a clue. The fifty thou goes into a *joint* checking account, "JoJo said, smirking.

When the realization hit her Maggie felt sick.

"Brownie?" she said dully.

"Rick told him what he had to do to get me off the hook for Bette's death. And he did it. After all, I could hardly tell him I already had an iron-clad, could I?"

"Why would he...I just can't believe..." That Brownie would sell his vote was bad enough, but to frame an innocent man for murder?

Maybe JoJo was right. Did Maggie really know him any more?

"And you're okay with Brownie giving the police false information leading to a wrongful arrest?" Maggie asked.

"I think that was *you* who did that. Besides, the police will never know they got the wrong man."

"I told you. They know it wasn't Etienne who killed Bette. And now I can testify that Rick Wilson paid people to implicate Etienne."

"Can you, darling? I'm not sure you'll be able to do much of anything after tonight."

"A threat, JoJo?"

"You tell me," JoJo said as she walked to the door and put the Taser down on the table. "After all, you're the wordsmith." When she turned around, Maggie saw that JoJo had pulled something bright and shiny from her bag.

"The fact is," JoJo said as she walked slowly toward Maggie, "and as our dearly departed Sasha used to say: When it comes to clipping loose ends, I really do believe *you're done*."

JoJo held up a short folding utility knife.

"*Well and good*."

aggie had a split second to react before JoJo lunged at her with the knife. She twisted her body sideways and lashed out a hard kick to JoJo's stomach. Maggie felt a cold stinging sensation as JoJo's knife blade skinned her ankle.

Maggie didn't waste time checking the damage. She turned and ran for the unlocked door, her heart pounding in her ears. She had to get out! If she could just get to the street...

"Stop her!" JoJo shrieked.

Just as Maggie reached the door, it swung open and a man's body blocked the doorway. He grabbed her in a vice-like hug, lifting her feet off the ground.

Instantly Maggie recognized the feel of him.

Brownie! Thank God!

"Are you out of your mind, JoJo?" Brownie said as he held Maggie and kicked the door shut behind him.

"What the hell took you so long?" JoJo said. "Did you get lost on the way back from the awards show?"

"I'm so sorry, Maggie," Brownie said as he set her down on her feet. "Are you hurt?"

"Why are you fawning over her?" JoJo asked indignantly, her eyes flashing. "She just kicked the hell out of me! Did you miss *that* part?"

"Dear God, JoJo," Brownie murmured, "have you lost your damn mind?"

"Is that what you think?" JoJo shrieked at him, waving the knife in the air. "That I'm crazy?"

"Put the knife down, JoJo," Brownie said.

"What is going on, Brownie?" Maggie said. His grip on her tightened.

"Go ahead. Tell her, Brownie," JoJo said. "Tell your ex-girl-friend—I assume she's still your ex? Because after you screwed Sasha for half of last year I'm really not too sure what's true and what's false any more. Unless maybe it's you, Brownie."

"Can you just put the knife down, JoJo?" Brownie said. "I can't believe how you're behaving right now!"

"Really?" JoJo said. "So you're protecting her? Is that really how this is going to go down?"

"We said nobody would get hurt. Come on. Put the knife down."

"Is that what you want? For me to put it down?" JoJo's eyes darted from Brownie to Maggie. "Sure. Okay. I'll put it down. I'll put it down where it counts!"

JoJo lunged at Maggie, slicing wildly with the knife. Maggie felt Brownie push her to the floor. She braced herself to feel the piercing impact of the knife as it struck her. But it didn't come.

She turned on her knees and tried to make out what she was seeing.

JoJo was on the floor writhing wordlessly, her arms flailing about her head.

Brownie stood over her, the Taser in his hand.

He must have picked it up as he came in.

"Brownie," Maggie said, her voice full of pain and bewilderment.

He turned to her and held out a hand to help her up.

"I'm so sorry, Maggie," he said. "So sorry about all of this. I can't imagine what you must think."

"Is JoJo...?" Maggie gestured to JoJo on the floor still convulsing. Her eyes had rolled back into her head.

"The crazy thing is I really thought for a moment that JoJo and I could work things out," Brownie said, tucking the Taser in his belt. "What a mess."

He shook his head apologetically at Maggie.

"JoJo and I have been having some problems," he said.

Is that what you call it? Maggie thought in astonishment, still watching JoJo who definitely did not look like she was anywhere near regaining consciousness.

"She needs help, Brownie."

Brownie chewed his lip but didn't answer. Still gazing at his wife on the floor, he murmured softly to himself, "I've been such a fool. First Bette and now...this."

At first, Maggie didn't register what Brownie said. But as the silence between them filled in the spaces of the room the horror of his words—of what he was implying—sank in. Maggie's mouth fell open.

All of a sudden she remembered how surprised JoJo had been when Maggie told her Etienne had *not* confessed to killing Bette. *Someone* had told JoJo that Etienne had confessed. And it wasn't any of the French detectives.

In fact the only one who *could* have told her was Brownie.

And there was only one reason why he would.

"Oh, God," Maggie said. A sinking feeling spread throughout Maggie's body. "You killed Bette."

Brownie turned to her, his eyes sad as he regarded her.

"Maggie, please don't look at me that way."

"Why? Why did you do it?" she said in anguish.

Brownie held out his hands to Maggie as if he was pleading with her. As if he wanted to take her by the shoulders. Something in the gesture reminded her of when they were children. It was a familiar gesture when he would appeal to her when she was beating him at a game or teasing her in a private way as only two best friends could do. He dropped his hands without touching her.

"Bette's husband came to me..."

Maggie shook her head in stunned denial. "You said Bette was divorced."

"No. She was separated. She was hoping for a reconciliation but she had a will..."

"Cut to the chase, please. Her husband inherits on her death."

"Yes."

"So he wanted you to kill Bette. Got it. And he was going to pay you five mill?"

"One million."

"You know what? It doesn't matter. You're a murderer, Brownie. Five million or five bucks. It comes to the same."

"Maggie, please don't turn away from me. You don't know what it's been like for me! I have crippling debts! They broke my brother's legs last month! You remember my brother Bobby! I had to do this!"

She honestly didn't think she could look at him, hear his familiar voice, and listen to the foul words coming out of his mouth.

Not without vomiting.

"Tell me *how*. You were never out of my sight that night. Not for a second."

"Well, I must have been," Brownie said with a sigh. "Because I managed it. With time to spare."

Maggie reran the tape in her mind. She saw Brownie go into the bar after Bette. She watched him nearly the whole time.

Nearly.

She remembered turning to speak to JoJo for maybe a total of five minutes. She'd *assumed* Brownie never left the bar. But five minutes was enough time for him to go downstairs, stab Bette and run back up.

She shook her head in disbelief.

"You killed Bette and then framed your own wife?"

"No! Of course not. When Rick heard that I was backing off the votes buying thing—I mean, I was going to make a million dollars. I didn't need to risk losing my business on a lousy fifty thou—and then when Bette…died, he took advantage of the situation."

"By framing JoJo for it."

He nodded and regarded JoJo on the floor. She had calmed down but her limbs were still twitching. And she hadn't regained consciousness.

"Rick paid off a waiter and a few other people to say they'd seen JoJo go down to the toilet. That was his message to me to *get back in line.*"

"And then to get JoJo released Wilson had to find some other fall guy," Maggie said, the light finally dawning. "Somebody expendable like Etienne."

"Etienne Babin is well known around the festival circuit. A real lunatic."

"Perfect for what you needed."

"Don't feel sorry for Babin, Maggie. He was thinking of blowing up the *Palais des Festivals!*"

"And Sasha?" Maggie asked, not wanting to hear the answer but needing to.

"I loved Sasha!"

"Is that why you killed her? Because you loved her so damn much?"

"You're going to think I'm terrible," he said.

"*That* ship has already left and crashed on the rocks with no survivors. I already think you're the worst scum on the planet. So *why?*"

"It wasn't my fault. She…she wouldn't listen to reason. I mean, even though she cheated on me the night Bette was killed," Brownie said, "I was willing to forgive and forget. But she didn't want my forgiveness! She wanted out!"

"Is that because she found out about the votes-buying or because she learned that you killed Bette?"

"I had to tell someone. JoJo doesn't even know about Bette."

"So you confessed to Sasha and then you became afraid she'd go to the cops."

"You should have seen the way she looked at me, Maggie! I knew I couldn't trust her any more."

Maggie glanced at JoJo on the floor. She was finally quiet and Maggie had a bad feeling about that. Brownie had tazed her from close-range. Could he have killed her?

He'd already killed Sasha and Bette. And now possibly JoJo.

A thin line of sweat formed on Maggie's top lip. Brownie was running his hands through his hair and staring out the small dark window, absorbed in his own thoughts. She looked at the door but even if she made a dash for it, Brownie could cut her off in three steps. She'd never make it.

The only thing she knew to do was stall.

"So you used me as your alibi for Bette's murder and to funnel lies from your paid informers to the police."

"That was all Rick and Dennis. They did all that."

"Did they know it was you who killed Bette?"

He shook his head. "I don't think they cared who killed her. Her death was just an opportunity for them."

"How did you make the fire alarm to go off when it did? That was you, wasn't it?"

He grinned.

"Actually Bette gave me the idea. As she was falling, she reached out for the alarm button on the wall. She never even got close but it got me thinking. I saw the make and model of the system. It was archaic. I knew it would be a piece of cake to hack in with a GUI port scanner app, which I downloaded once I got back to the table."

Maggie had a flashback of Brownie sitting at the table focused on his smartphone.

"So you triggered the alarm to go off remotely," Maggie said tonelessly. "Making it look as if Bette was being attacked while you were upstairs sipping Pinot."

"Surrounded by witnesses. Pretty smart, huh?"

"Except it won't last. If Bette never touched the button, trust me they already know that. At this moment they're going through the restaurant online system to see if the fire alarm malfunctioned or if someone interfered with it. When they do, they'll revise time of death and you'll become a suspect."

"I'm leaving France tonight on the red-eye. I'd hoped it would end here in Cannes but if it doesn't, I'll simply make it difficult for them to extradite me. They don't have circumstantial evidence tying me to Bette..."

"They *will* once they give you a thorough DNA swabbing. They'll find *something* of you left in that toilet, Brownie. And when they do..."

"Look, I know you're upset, Maggie, but in my defense I wasn't planning on killing Bette that night. It just... happened. I saw the opportunity and I went for it. It was sort of brilliant in a way. Very organic."

Maggie stared at him in horror.

"I mean I couldn't have planned it any better! Bette stomped away from the table. My natural instinct really was to go check on her. I picked up the steak knife as I got up—"

"Your *wife's* steak knife."

"It was just an impulse. Anyway, I ran after Bette and stopped in the bar to get my bearings. Well, to be honest, I stopped to put on the disposable glove I'd put in my pocket back at the hotel."

So much for impulse, Maggie thought, a shiver of ice skittering down her spine. *And it explains why only JoJo's prints were found on the knife.*

"I went downstairs and caught Bette as she entered the bathroom. There was nobody else there so I just stuck the knife in her. No talking. I just did it. Then I raced upstairs and came back to the table."

"Where you talked to me the rest of the evening as if nothing was wrong."

"Well, I know what you're thinking Maggie. How could I have done that? But you've never felt the amazing relief of knowing your money problems were finally over. It was the best moment of my life. You're here in the south of France with your perfect husband and your perfect life and you don't know what hell my life has been. The feeling I had when I ran up those stairs from the restroom after killing Bette was bliss compounded by extreme joy."

Maggie's mouth was dry with the horror of what she was hearing.

"And Bette?" she asked. "The fact that you'd just killed your friend?"

He gestured helplessly. "I mourned her later, sure. I'm not heartless."

He walked over to JoJo and gently kicked her shoe.

"Do you think she's dead?" he asked.

"I've known you since you were eight years old, Brownie. You're a monster."

"You don't know how I've dreaded you finding out about all this," he said sadly.

"I never realized how much of your life was manipulated in order to make your life as easy as it could be. Your parents, your school—your career—everything you ever did was to make it easy on you, Brownie. Maybe I shouldn't be surprised by any of this. And to think I felt guilty about dumping you for Laurent."

"I hated you for that, Maggie. I don't mind saying. It took me a long time to get over it."

Brownie looked at his watch and then went to the door and glanced out. He was waiting for someone. That explained why he'd been willing to natter on without concern for all the confessions he was giving.

"What's happening, Brownie?" she asked softly. "What are you going to do now?"

"I have a flight back to the US in about two hours."

"Not bringing JoJo home with you?"

Brownie looked at Maggie and his shoulders sagged.

"I'm doing the best I can, Maggie. I don't know what else to do. I can't let you just leave here and tell the cops what you know."

"By now the cops already know it was you, Brownie. Don't you get it? You confessing to me is irrelevant!"

"Well, maybe not if I can get out of the country in time."

"Are you nuts? France and the US do prisoner transfer agreements all the time. You'll be arrested as soon as your plane lands in Atlanta. If you kill me, you'll just compound your problems."

"I am not going to hurt you, Maggie! How could I? Do you know me at all?"

"So you're going to let me go?"

"No, I can't do that. But you won't be harmed. I've been promised."

"By whom?"

"I know someone who knows someone. You'll be taken away. Some place safe."

"What are you talking about?"

"Some men are coming for both you and JoJo in a few minutes. But it's going to be okay. You'll both live. That's what's important."

Maggie felt her knees begin to shake. She could barely stutter out her words.

"Who? How do you know them? Where...where did you meet them?"

"I didn't actually meet them. They're just some guys that someone knows who Dennis knows."

"So nobody has actually met these people."

"It doesn't matter! Everything is going to be fine."

"If you give me to these men I'll be taken offshore and then I promise you I'm dead as surely as if you used that knife on me right now. The only difference is that Laurent has no closure, and no idea of where I am or if I'm ever coming back. You consign him and my whole family to a living hell of wondering and never knowing what happened to me."

Brownie shook his head as if to shake away Maggie's words.

"I've been promised you won't be hurt. You'll live a life of luxury...peeling grapes and splashing in infinity pools."

"Do you hear yourself? This is *human trafficking*. There is no life of luxury. Only drug addiction and early death after being raped over and over again!"

"Maggie, calm down! I swear to you—"

"And I swear to *you* that you won't get away with this. I not only have Laurent but a very good police inspector who will hunt to the ends of the earth until they find out what happened to me —*and who did it to me*. They'll find you, Brownie."

"What are my options, Maggie? I can't kill you. I love you."

"You have no concept of the word."

Suddenly, JoJo came to life from beneath their feet, screaming in rage.

"You bastard!"

She lunged at Brownie, the knife still in her hand. She stabbed him twice in the back. Brownie grunted and tried to turn to face her. But JoJo spun away from him and slashed at his face and neck. Futilely, his blood soaking the front of his shirt, Brownie tried to bat JoJo's hands away.

Maggie watched in chilled horror as Brownie sagged to his

knees, his hands clutching his chin as the blood oozed out of him.

Breathing heavily and sobbing, JoJo turned to Maggie. The madness was evident in her eyes as she pointed the knife at Maggie.

"You need to listen to me, JoJo," Maggie said as she scanned the room for something she could use to protect herself or throw at JoJo.

"You turned him against me," JoJo said, the tears streaking down her face.

Maggie knew Brownie had the Taser but she also knew that by the time she got to him, JoJo would be on her.

"JoJo, listen! You have not done anything yet to send you to prison. Brownie confessed to both murders. If you put that knife down—"

"What? If I put it down you'll give me a character reference at my trial?" JoJo said, wiping the tears and streaked mascara from her face with the back of her hand.

"I'm just saying..." Maggie said spying one of the wooden chairs nearest her. "France still uses the guillotine in their capital cases. Think about *that* before you do anything crazy."

"What if the cops think I already *have* done something crazy?" JoJo said, as she glanced at Brownie on the floor.

"That was self-defense," Maggie said, moving closer to the nearby chair. She had to get out of here. If what Brownie said was true, some very ruthless men were on their way at this very moment.

"Two stabs in the back?" JoJo screamed, her voice was laced with incredulity as she pointed to Brownie lying in a growing pool of his own blood. "Does *that* look like self-defense to you?"

Maggie didn't have an answer to that and they were running out of time. She grabbed the chair nearest to her and lifted it protectively in front of her.

Instantly, JoJo charged.

Maggie tried to back away as JoJo slashed wildly at Maggie's hands. Her knuckles erupted in fire as she felt the blade slice across them. Goaded by the pain and the fear that JoJo was too strong for her, Maggie sucked in one last reserve of strength and rammed the chair into JoJo's face.

JoJo screamed and dropped the knife, grappling instead at her face. Ignoring the throbbing agony in her hands, Maggie tossed the chair aside and kicked the knife out of reach.

JoJo was in much better shape than Maggie and could easily catch her if Maggie tried to run.

Maggie licked her lips as JoJo, her midriff exposed, held her battered face. Maggie had to disable her. It was her only chance.

No thinking! Just do it! Maggie took two steps toward her and drove her fist as hard as she could into JoJo's stomach.

JoJo made a long groaning sound and crumpled to her knees, her arms dropping to cradle her midsection.

Maggie looked desperately for the knife. *Where had she kicked it?*

JoJo moaned but Maggie knew she wouldn't be down long.

She tried to remember the sound when she'd kicked the knife away. There hadn't been a clatter as there should have been if it had hit a wall or skittered across the tile floor. She went to Brownie and found it wedged against his pant leg where it had lodged.

She grabbed it up, her hands trembling and now slick with Brownie's blood. She turned to see JoJo was on her feet again.

"You won't use it," JoJo said, gasping, one hand to her bleeding face. She pointed at Brownie, but her finger shook convulsively. "You think it's easy? Come at me! Let's see!"

Could she really stab JoJo? Maggie swallowed and held the knife in front of her.

"JoJo, please. Brownie needs help. And you and I need to get out of here before—"

"You broke my nose! I'm going to take that knife away from you and show you how it's done."

Maggie licked her lips. Could she really use this knife on JoJo? Even to protect herself?

Brownie was so quiet on the floor. Maggie didn't dare take her eyes off JoJo to look at him. He might already be dead. The thought made her feel exhausted and sad all at once. Then another thought came to her. *The Taser.*

"I don't have to stab you," Maggie said, her eyes on JoJo as she blindly reached for the Taser in Brownie's belt.

As soon as JoJo realized what she was doing, she charged.

Before Maggie had a chance to grab the Taser, JoJo tackled her hard on the floor. Both women slid in the blood. Maggie was on her back grappling with the knife between them. Her hands were too slippery. She was losing her hold on it.

JoJo was strong and she was fueled by fury. She grabbed Maggie by the hair with both hands and slammed her head against the floor. Agony shot up into Maggie's head in black star-bursts. She jerked the knife out between them and jammed the point of it under JoJo's chin.

They both froze. The only sound in the room was JoJo's labored breathing. The knifepoint was sticking into her but not pressed deep.

Not yet.

JoJo released Maggie.

It was in that moment, the moment that Maggie thought she might stab another human being to save her own life that she heard the sound that made her blood turn to ice.

Men's voices. Outside.

It was them.

The human traffickers had arrived.

33

L aurent strode across the lobby of the Hotel Carlton.

As soon as he'd reached Roger's townhouse an hour earlier, he'd been met at the door by Madame Zimmerman who apologized profusely for his trouble. It seemed both children were sleeping soundly and she was sure it would be better to just leave them until morning.

Realizing his sacrifice had somehow turned into the possibility of being able to make love to his wife after all, Laurent had quickly agreed and turned around and drove to Cannes.

He approached the registration desk.

"Could you please tell me the room number for Madame Dernier?" he asked the young woman behind the desk.

She smiled amiably, indeed suggestively, and turned to her computer screen.

"I am afraid Madame Dernier has checked out with us," she said demurely.

Laurent cursed silently. So Maggie left after all? At this time of night?

"Can you tell me when?" he asked.

She checked her records. "Nearly two hours ago. But she was in the bar for at least one of those hours."

The way Maggie drove, she wouldn't be home for at least another hour. Even so, she had a good head start. While disappointed to have to wait yet again before he held his wife in his arms so that they might adequately forgive each other, Laurent nonetheless knew it was a pleasure that would not be deferred for long.

He thanked the receptionist and turned away to hurry back to where he'd parked the car.

If he did twenty kilometers over the speed limit on the A8 he could reach home at roughly the same time as Maggie.

MAGGIE PUSHED JoJo off her and lurched toward the door. She twisted the deadbolt, giving thanks that there was one, then turned and faced a stunned JoJo who was staring at Maggie as if she'd gone mad.

Immediately the door erupted in a furious pounding that made Maggie jump away from it.

Fear crawled up her bare arms like a living thing. Her mind raced so fast she couldn't keep a coherent thought.

All she could hear was the monster at the door.

She backed away from it.

"Brownie arranged for both of us to be taken out of the country tonight," she said.

"What are you talking about?" JoJo's chin was bloody where Maggie had pricked her with the knifepoint.

Maggie snatched up JoJo's purse from the floor and upended it, spilling pens, a wallet, passport, a box of tampons and a Taser cartridge across the floor.

"Come on, JoJo," Maggie said, sorting through the contents in frustration. "You've seen the movie *Taken*. You know how this works. Where's your cellphone?"

"You're lying. Brownie would never do something like that to me."

Maggie pointed to Brownie on the floor, the pool of blood surrounding him.

"He *tazed* you! You're lucky you're still breathing. Does *that* sound like the behavior of someone who's going to ride off into the sunset with you?"

A man shouted through the door in strongly accented English, "Open the door! We're here!"

JoJo turned in the direction of the small window across from the door. For one mad moment Maggie thought she might try to climb out of it. But even at a size zero, there was no way she would fit through it.

The sound of a key in the lock made both women turn and stare at the door. Maggie spontaneously moved closer to JoJo. The voices outside were louder now.

"They'll break it down when the key won't open it," Maggie said. She snapped her head to JoJo. "Your cellphone!"

JoJo looked at Maggie with wide eyes as if she didn't understand and then appeared to wake up. She pried her phone out of her back jeans pocket. Maggie grabbed it and stared at it.

"Dammit!" Maggie said. "It's fried. Probably when he tazed you."

Maggie dropped the phone and ran to Brownie. He was still now but she didn't have time to see if he was breathing. She patted his pockets for his cellphone and found it in his back pocket.

The sound of the door being hit with something heavy echoed through the room and JoJo cried out. Maggie felt a wave of dizziness and forced herself to slow her breathing down to remain calm.

"Hurry!" JoJo said urgently. "They're getting in!"

Brownie's phone was turned off. Maggie had no idea how long it would take to power back on. Cursing, she pushed the *on* button and got an icon on the screen showing that the battery was depleted.

For one moment she thought she might actually throw up. The phone was dead. She stared at the icon on the screen. She couldn't think of what to do next.

"Open the door!" an angry man's voice roared from outside.

Maggie dropped the phone and pulled the Taser out of Brownie's belt. Quickly she checked the charge.

Empty.

With mounting fear, she ran back to JoJo's purse on the floor and scooped up the Taser cartridge.

"How does this thing go in?" Maggie asked, turning to JoJo who was gripping her hands to her chest and staring at the door. Maggie tried to slide the cartridge into the Taser. Her hands shook.

It wouldn't fit.

"JoJo!"

Another blow to the door reverberated throughout the room making both of them jump. Maggie forced the cartridge into the Taser. It loaded.

She checked the battery charge. Weak.

Would it be enough? Even if it did work she only had one shot and there were three of them.

She hurried to stand next to JoJo and face the door. There was another terrible thud on the door as the top hinge popped off and skittered across the tile floor.

It wouldn't take much more to bring the door down.

"What are we going to do?" JoJo asked in a hoarse whisper, her face white with shock.

Maggie handed JoJo the knife.

"I guess here's where you show me how it's done," she said grimly.

34

Charles Dumas inhaled a lungful of the Gauloises cigarette as he watched the video for the fifth time.

The surveillance video was black and white, grainy and stuttering. It clearly showed the American William "Brownie" Henderson going into Sasha Morrison's hotel room well within the medical examiner's range for time of death. Except for Maggie Dernier, Henderson was the only visitor to the victim's room.

That in itself might not have meant much.

Added to that was the fact that Henderson was having an affair with the victim and that Dumas's men had searched his room and found a pair of sandals in the trash with what Dumas felt sure would reveal Sasha Morrison's blood on them and Dumas was confident he had a prime suspect for her murder.

Combined with the surveillance video, Brownie Henderson was finished.

After Dumas's team discovered the restaurant bathroom fire alarm system had been triggered remotely, and that Madame Austin did *not* in fact expire at the moment it sounded, he'd been able to revise her time of death which put Henderson back in the picture for that murder too.

A double homicide solved in less than twenty-four hours?

And an *American*—soon to be in custody—for both murders? Well, that just made everything all the sweeter.

At the very least Dumas would be looking at a commendation. Likely a pay rise. Was there any higher to go than chief of police in Cannes? Perhaps Lyons? Paris? He felt a pleasant warmth spread throughout his body.

He pulled out his phone to see if his mistress had responded to his earlier suggestion. That would make this night fairly perfect in every way.

She hadn't yet answered, which was annoying. As Dumas scrolled down the list of texts to see if he'd missed it somehow, his eye fell on the two messages that had been sent earlier in the day from Roger Bedard.

Arrogant, presumptuous bastard, he thought sourly. He dared come to Cannes to tell *him* how to handle this investigation? Was Aix or wherever the hell it was that Bedard came from even in the same league as Cannes? Did Aix deal with world-famous celebrities on practically a daily basis?

Dumas himself had personally touched the shoulder of Jennifer Lawrence in order to direct her to a public restroom. And of course there was that time he'd handed George Clooney a back stage pass the star had dropped at the *Palais*. There was not a police officer in the south of France who had not heard that story!

No, Cannes was a completely different world. It was a way of life that could only be understood—and competently maneuvered—by someone who understood the life of very famous people—how they thought, their dreams and desires.

Dumas snapped off the video.

As for the matter at hand, there was no hurry.

He knew who his man was. He knew where he'd find him...

eventually. There was only one flight out of France tonight to the States and Dumas had posted men at both the Nice International Airport and Marseilles with orders to prevent "Brownie" Henderson or "JoJo" Henderson from boarding.

He tapped a pen against his bottom lip and frowned. He didn't really see Americans taking the train to Paris to fly out. He wouldn't waste precious resources to cover bases there.

He turned to his adjunct officer to order an espresso.

"Make it hot this time," he said, pursing his lips in reproach.

He felt a wave of satisfaction at the thought of his phone ringing—as it would any moment now—to report that Henderson was in cuffs and on his way to Cannes in the back of a squad car.

It was always sweeter when the perpetrator came to him.

And that sweetness would certainly be tasted tonight.

All Dumas had to do was wait.

MAGGIE KNEW they had only seconds before the door broke completely.

"Go stand behind the door," Maggie said in a low urgent voice. "Wait for my signal. Don't just charge them when they come in."

JoJo nodded, never taking her eyes off the door. Maggie pushed her toward it and watched as JoJo slid into place behind where the door would normally open. Maggie knew that once the men kicked the door down it was anyone's guess which way it would fall.

They had a fifty-fifty chance it would at least temporarily hide JoJo from view.

Maggie just had to hope they'd get lucky.

She stood ten yards away, forcing herself not to look at JoJo, the knife held limply in her hand, her knees visibly shaking even from where Maggie stood.

Maggie kept the Taser at her side. She didn't want to tip them off that she had a weapon—in case they had a real one—but not having it raised when they entered meant she'd lose precious seconds lifting it up to use it.

She had no other choice.

The final blow against the door was loud and followed by a half-hearted cheer from the men in the street. Maggie didn't look at JoJo. Terror fluttered in her chest like a trapped bird. She'd been wrong about the door bursting open. Once freed from its restraints, it just stood, teetering on edge until one of the men pushed it and it fell crashing to the floor. Maggie had to fight the urge to raise the Taser.

Not yet. Net yet.

She could see JoJo out of the corner of her eye. She was facing Maggie—waiting for her signal.

"Is there only one?" a male's foreign-accented voice thundered out, followed by a large bear of a man who entered the room, stepping over the door. As soon as he entered, he saw JoJo in his peripheral vision and turned to her.

Maggie could see two more men behind him. She had to act now. She ran toward the bear man as he turned to confront JoJo. The two men coming through the door saw her and shouted to him.

She was close now. The bear man turned from JoJo—who stood frozen against the wall.

Maggie pushed the Taser within inches of his face and pulled the trigger.

Nothing happened.

"*Now*, JoJo!" Maggie shouted as she futilely pulled the trigger again and again.

The blow came from out of nowhere.

Maggie felt herself slammed up against a wall where no wall existed. Her world exploded in black nuclear bursts of agony.

All sound screeched to a stop.

The pain came in relentless waves but she was floating. Being carried. Her body weightless and gradually...pain free.

35

M aggie couldn't see. She couldn't hear.
But she was becoming aware of her body. It was
cold and wet. She was lying on a hard floor. It was
vibrating.

No, moving.

She heard sobbing. And under the sobbing, men's voices in a
language Maggie didn't know. She tried to open her eyes but they
wouldn't work. She heard a groan. It was coming from her.

"Maggie, please don't be dead," JoJo sobbed. "Maggie, please
wake up."

The smell came to Maggie before her vision did. A rank,
rotting odor of fish and mildew.

She pried her eyes open and struggled to sit up but she
couldn't move. Her hands were zip-tied in front of her. Her feet
too. She was in the back of a van. JoJo sat beside her. In the
gloom, Maggie could see JoJo's lip was split and bleeding. She
was also tied.

"Maggie," JoJo said in a hoarse whisper. "What are we going
to do? Where are they taking us?"

An ice-cold fear needled its way through Maggie's spine. The helplessness she felt was like a raw, livid wound—it was all encompassing. It was final.

An image of her children came to her but she forced the thought of them away. She couldn't think of Jemmy and Mila. She mustn't think of them. *Not now.* The image in her head of Mila's gap-toothed smile made Maggie want to bash her head against the wall of the van. She couldn't think she would never see them again.

Laurent.

He will go mad.

She pushed herself up to a sitting position and looked around. They were still in Cannes. She could tell by the tight corners the van was making, throwing her and JoJo back and forth, and the fact that they weren't traveling fast.

Maggie took hope from the fact that they were still in town. When they got on the highway, all hope would be gone.

"What are we going to do, Maggie?" JoJo asked again.

"Be quiet," Maggie said. "Let me think."

Let me think. As if that will do anything. What were their options? The van had no windows. Did that mean anything? Maggie looked around the darkened interior. There was nothing that could possibly serve as a weapon of any kind. What good would that do anyway?

Even if there was a crowbar back here, was she going to wait the six hours as they drove her to Marseilles or whatever port they obviously intended to take them to so they could dump them on a tramp steamer heading to the Mideast? And what would Maggie do then? Hit one of them before she was subdued?

Maggie fought the feeling of claustrophobia and pain that seemed to radiate from her chest, lungs and throat. The fear was everywhere in the van, suffocating her.

She could hear the three men squeezed into the front driving cabin. A sliding door partition blocked the cabin from the cargo area where she and JoJo were.

That was a bit of luck that she and JoJo were not able to be seen by the men. But Maggie wasn't sure how to use it to her advantage.

Even if she and JoJo somehow managed to get out of the van, their feet were zip-tied. Only a knife would free them.

"Did they search you?" Maggie asked.

"Search me?"

"For weapons. For your cellphone. Car keys...anything."

"All of that is on the floor back where they grabbed us."

"What happened to the knife?"

"I...I tried to stick him when you yelled," JoJo said, her eyes watering as she remembered back to the moment. "But he... ripped it out of my hands. Who are these men? Did Brownie really arrange this?"

Maggie ignored her. One way or another JoJo would have plenty of time later to reflect on Brownie's treachery.

The van slowed.

"We're stopping," JoJo said in a raised voice.

"Shhhh! Be quiet!" Maggie hissed. She edged to the back of the door, her feet toward the doors. "Can you hear what they're saying?"

"No! I can't understand them!" JoJo said loudly.

"Be quiet!" Maggie said urgently. "Try to listen!"

Maggie strained to hear why they had stopped. She could hear music more loudly now where she couldn't before. They were clearly approaching a more populated neighborhood.

There was only one way out of Cannes unless you went by boat and that was by the outer loop. Maggie knew the shortest way there would be to cross the *Place de la Gare* by the train station. There was no other way.

The *Place de la Gare* would be crammed with partygoers. It might not be as congested as the *La Croisette* by the beach, but in sheer numbers would still double any other street in any other mid-sized town in France.

Maggie felt her hopes rise.

If the men who'd taken her and JoJo thought they were incapacitated by fear they might not have bothered to lock the back door.

On the other hand, if they've done this a lot, that's probably the first thing they did.

In any case, it was their only hope: wait until they were in a more highly trafficked area—and try to get the back door open. With her feet tied even if she fell to the street and was unable to run, there was at least a chance someone might help her before she was stuffed back in the van.

It wasn't much.

But it was worth a try.

36

R oger had been nearly home to Aix and Ezzie's flat when the overwhelming urge to return to Cannes in order to question Rick Wilson made him take the next exit and drive back.

He'd berated himself the whole way: *Fool! In love with a married woman! Would give up a gorgeous woman like Ezzie to run down a ridiculous lead that will almost certainly amount to maximum personal embarrassment! And for what?*

For nothing. Nothing except his inability to let anything go that had to do with Maggie Newberry Dernier.

In spite of that, as he drove back to Cannes Roger couldn't help feel that he was finally going in the right direction.

And a policeman's instinct could not be ignored. In the past twenty years, that instinct had done more than serve Roger well. It had saved his life more than once.

Maggie's too, now that he thought of it.

Yes, he was an idiot in love with another man's wife. That was simply a fact. He could no more deny it than argue that the sun would come up in the morning.

It was what it was.

So he had driven back to Cannes. He'd found Wilson in the Carlton bar and with less than gentle French interrogation methods had discovered Wilson's earlier run-in with Maggie tonight.

"*The bitch stole my phone! If you really are with the police, I want to file a complaint.*"

"*Where did you see her?*"

"*Hell if I know. All these winding streets look alike to me.*"

"*Then you will come with me, Monsieur, to jog your memory.*"

"*The hell I will!*"

"*As you wish, Monsieur,*" Roger said, grabbing his hair and slamming his face into the bar. "*Je suis desole,*" he said to the startled barman. "*This patron has reached his limit.*"

It had only taken a few more moments from there to get a fairly accurate description of the crossroads where Wilson had met with Maggie.

Not knowing why, but feeling certain that Maggie needed him and that time was of the essence—and perfectly willing to look the fool if that should *not* be the case—Roger called in an emergency triangulation on Wilson's phone to his own police department in Aix.

Now he stood in the matrix of the maze of narrow streets. In his hand he held Maggie's overnight bag.

Finding it was the single most alarming discovery since he'd begun looking for her. There was no way she would have left it behind—not with her passport and car keys inside.

A few feet away he found her broken cellphone where Wilson had said she'd dropped it.

Had she been attacked after she left Wilson?

"Maggie!" he called and then paused to listen. There was no reply.

The woman named Courtney had stopped him at the hotel as he was interrogating Wilson and said that Maggie was to meet

Brownie's wife JoJo tonight. Nobody had seen either JoJo or Maggie since the awards ceremony.

It was not lost on Roger that nobody had seen Brownie since then either.

Now as he walked away from the crossroads where Maggie had met Wilson, and with no other clues other than an abandoned bag to tell him which direction she might have gone, he received an incoming text. His heart pounded with excitement when he saw what it was.

It was the GPS location for the last known location of Wilson's phone—not two streets away from where Roger was standing.

It was also the last location before the phone had been turned off. At exactly eleven fifteen. More than an hour ago.

Everything was adding up to a very dangerous picture.

It is late. Maggie has left her bag in the street. And now she has turned off her only phone?

There was no time to call Laurent or even for police support. If he was right, every second counted now.

He began to run.

MAGGIE DECIDED she needed to wait until the noise from outside was the loudest. If she could get the door open and fall into the crowded street she stood the greatest chance of being rescued.

"What are you doing?" JoJo said.

"Be quiet! Before you remind them that they didn't gag us!"

Maggie scooted to the back of the van. The seats had been taken out and there was only a metal floor.

"Is the door locked?" JoJo said even more loudly, her eyes glittering with hope and desperation.

Suddenly the men in front seemed to remember the women were there. An outburst of voices came from the cabin and Maggie saw the panel in the partition begin to slide open.

She rolled to the rear of the van and pulled herself to her feet.

One of the men appeared through the partition as Maggie desperately groped for the door handle. She saw the man's face when he realized what she was doing.

"Block him!" Maggie screamed. She fumbled to get a grip on the door lever with her bound hands.

It opened! The door was unlocked! Maggie was hit with a blast of noise and loud music seconds before she felt the sensation of flying backwards, slamming into the side of the van.

Groaning in vibrating pain, and with the world whirling around her, Maggie opened her eyes to see the man standing over her, one foot on her chest.

He slammed the back door securely shut.

37

Roger saw the smashed cellphone first. His flashlight illuminated the shards of plastic off the cobblestone alley in the gutter—exactly where the map had told him it would be. He ran towards it and immediately saw the gaping opening and the broken door.

"Maggie?" he called, his voice in equal parts hope and despair.

It was silent.

With his flashlight in hand, Roger stepped into the room and saw a body in the middle of the floor. His stomach clenched and then released when he realized it was a man's body. He moved closer and knelt by him.

Unconscious but still alive.

The door battered off its hinges and a wounded man inside.

Maggie's phone smashed on the stones outside.

He saw a woman's purse on the floor, its contents dumped out. He picked up an American passport belonging to Joleyne Henderson of Atlanta, Georgia.

Brownie's wife.

The woman Maggie was to have met tonight.

Quickly, Roger pulled out his cellphone and called for police assistance and an ambulance. He didn't have the authority to request a blockade on all exits out of Cannes. But he put an urgent call in to the man who did. And finally he texted Laurent with what he knew. He didn't call because he didn't have time to answer Laurent's questions.

Worse, he didn't have answers.

He pulled the man's wallet from his pocket and confirmed that it was Brownie. Someone had obviously attacked him, left him for dead, and taken his wife—and probably Maggie—in such a rush that his wife had no need for her purse.

Roger heard the sirens of the approaching police and ambulance.

He put his hand on Henderson's neck and felt a pulse. Weak but there.

His phone rang.

"Chief Inspector Bedard," Roger answered.

"This is Chief Inspector Charles Dumas of the Cannes Police Department."

Roger quickly described what he had found.

"Will you confirm the blockade?" Roger asked. His mouth felt dry and nausea edged up into his throat. "As I told your *sous-lieutenant* earlier, I have reason to believe both Madame Dernier and Madame Henderson have been assaulted—"

"When was the last time you saw Madame Dernier?" Dumas interrupted.

Roger felt his pulse rate rocket. Any moment he would drive his fist into a wall.

"This afternoon after we left the police station," Roger answered between gritted teeth. He needed that blockade. *Even now it may be too late!*

"We are interested in speaking with Madame Dernier," Dumas said. "She is a close contact of William Henderson who is now a person of interest in both of our recent homicides."

Roger shook his head and stared down at Brownie on the floor.

"Your suspect is here. Better hurry though. He's badly injured and I cannot stay to greet you."

Somehow I have to find her. Somehow I have to stop whoever took her.

"Where are you?"

Roger gave him the address.

Dumas cursed. "I know it," he said.

When the Chief Inspector of Cannes revealed to Roger *why* the address was significant to him, Roger's blood ran cold.

MAGGIE FELT the crushing disappointment cascade through her. The man reached down and picked her up by the shoulders and flung her against the side of the van. Her head hit the wall and the pain ricocheted inside her skull.

A harsh voice from the front yelled out something.

Maggie's assailant responded to him in kind. She opened her eyes and watched him put something on the door handle. She couldn't see what it was but she could guess.

She'd blown their one chance to get out. The door had been unlocked. And now it wasn't.

The man returned to the front with the other two and slammed the partition shut.

"Maggie?" JoJo said. "What did he do? He put something on the door."

Maggie closed her eyes. Her head hurt so bad. The pain felt like a kettledrum banging relentlessly in her skull.

"Too late," she whispered.

"No!" JoJo shrieked. "It can't be! We need out! Let us out of here!"

JoJo lifted her legs and began kicking the door with both feet.

She screamed in frustration.

The sight of her hysteria ratcheted Maggie's terror up into her throat.

It was true. All they had left now was fear personified, gripping, unending fear in its purest form—the form of hysterical, useless screaming, flailing and kicking.

No more tricks. No more plans. No more hope.

This was all they had left.

Maggie twisted her body and lifted her feet to the side of the van and kicked with her whole might, knowing it would deplete her, knowing it was futile, knowing it would call the man back into the rear of the van to drug them or beat them.

She and JoJo kicked in unison. Maggie threw back her head and screamed along with JoJo, over and over again. The partition slid open again and one of the men climbed in back.

The van stopped with a severe jolt and the man fell against the wall of the van. Cursing, he righted himself and reached for JoJo. She threw her head from side to side and continued to scream until he grabbed her head under his arm and stuffed a filthy towel in her mouth and duct taped it around her head. Maggie saw him: his eyes were inhuman and base. He drew back his hand and slapped JoJo hard. She collapsed limp against the van wall.

Maggie screamed.

She screamed because they were taking her away from her babies, and because her family would never know what happened to her. She screamed even when she felt the man grab her with his harsh, punishing hands. She kicked at the van wall with her heels and flung her head from side to side until she felt a thick cloth pushing into her mouth. She spat it out.

The man cursed and grabbed up the pad from the van floor. As he tried to ram it into her mouth again, she bit him. Her legs never stopped pummeling the van wall. Kicking, flailing as if they had a mind of their own. She saw him draw his hand back. She squeezed her eyes shut not to see it coming. Her ears rang in her head like an echoing gong when the blow came.

Then she lay on her back and all sensation seemed to fall away. She didn't have the strength to sit up. A relentless vibration in her head combined with crushing sadness. She felt herself drift into unconsciousness.

She saw Mila's face again in her mind…and Jemmy's. They were laughing in the sunshine on the back patio. *It must be an autumn evening after the harvest is in.* She and Laurent were sharing a mug of mulled wine and watching the children play, their voices and laughter rising up and down among the naked, harvested stalks.

The memory of Laurent's hand on her shoulder would be something that would comfort her and give her strength for the rest of her life no matter what happened now.

She could hear the soft rumble of his voice. His French accent thick and soft in her ear like butter.

She could feel the cool air of the autumn breeze off the vineyard.

His voice.

The cool air on her skin.

The outside noise was louder now, hurting her dream. People were talking. Laughing. The music. It made her head hurt.

"Maggie, open your eyes, *chérie*. Look at me."

She wanted to open her eyes. To make the dream be real. She tried to see through the darkness in the van and then realized the vehicle was no longer moving.

Slowly the darkness in the van gave way to light. She felt his hands on her—large and sure—as he pulled her into the light and the noise.

She opened her eyes then and saw his face. She saw it where she knew it was not possible for him to be.

"I am here, *chérie*," Laurent said as he held her, his familiar breath on her face. "It is over now."

38

Hours later, Maggie and JoJo sat wrapped in blankets at an empty café near where the van was stopped. The road was blockaded by a swarm of police to prevent vehicle and pedestrian traffic while the crime techs processed the scene.

Laurent sat with his arm around Maggie. When the shaking got too much, she leaned into him and he held her tightly. She knew she was still in shock, still only half believing that they were safe and that it was really over.

JoJo sat beside her, ramrod straight in her chair. Her hair hung in her face, her broken nose, a split lip and the stunned look in her eyes that hadn't left since the moment Maggie told her that Brownie meant to betray her.

Maggie had to admit to feeling a sort of survivor's kinship with JoJo. Although it was true JoJo *had* tried to kill her at least twice tonight, she'd also been the one whose hysteria at just the right moment had reminded Maggie that giving up was not an option.

If JoJo hadn't flipped out and started kicking the side of the van, Maggie would have sunk into heartbroken reverie.

And they would be on their way to Mumbai or Shanghai by now.

Maggie figured she could forgive the woman a few murder attempts for that.

Although JoJo left out the part about attempting to kill Maggie with a knife she answered the police questions truthfully. She also admitted to attacking Brownie and gave no justification for it.

Maggie couldn't blame her. From the terror of their abduction and Brownie's betrayal to their ultimate rescue, there was just too much to process tonight without attempting to lie or dissemble on top of it.

Two of the kidnappers had been taken into custody. One had been badly beaten before the police arrived. One ran but was quickly apprehended. The other had escaped.

The van itself was still parked in the middle of the road. Every time Maggie looked at it, she shivered.

Roger Bedard came over to where the three of them sat and said a few quiet words to Laurent that Maggie couldn't catch. Although it had been Laurent who'd found the van they were in, Maggie knew Roger had been the key to their rescue.

If he had not come back to Cannes, if he had not tracked down Wilson, if he had decided to wait for the information on Wilson's phone back at the Carlton bar instead of calling Laurent and going to look for her, it would have been too late for anyone to help JoJo and Maggie.

They would have been long gone.

As Roger had already told Maggie, he was driving back to Aix when he changed his mind and decided to find and question Rick Wilson after all. When he did and discovered that Maggie had taken Wilson's phone, Roger was able to call that phone number into his office to triangulate its last known coordinates.

Roger had then called Laurent to tell him what was happening. That's when he found out that Laurent was in Cannes. They met up and went together to the crossroads where Wilson claimed to have last seen Maggie. There Laurent quickly found and identified Maggie's overnight bag. At that point, he and Roger split up to search for Maggie street by street.

"When Roger found where you had been held," Laurent said, lightly stroking Maggie's arm, "he sent me a text saying we were at a dead end. We did not know where to go from there."

"Well, *Laurent* did," Roger said. "Dumas informed me that the storage room you were held in was suspected of being used by a human smuggling ring. When I told Laurent that, we both knew that unless you were taken by boat the only way out of Cannes was the outer loop. We raced to the *Place de la Gare* which was the closest access point from where you'd been taken. We separated again to look for a van with no windows."

"What if we'd been put in a car trunk instead?" Maggie asked.

"Dumas said that this was not the first time for these men," Roger said. "They always used a van for transport."

"I did not see the van you were in," Laurent said, shaking his head as if realizing how close he'd come to losing her. "I was interested in another suspicious vehicle. I stopped it in the street. If you had not started screaming, I would not have found you."

He brushed a stray tendril from her forehead and then cupped her bruised chin, not unlike how Roger had done earlier that day.

"I know I look a mess," she said.

"You look beautiful, *chérie*."

Maggie turned to Roger. "What made you come back to talk to Rick Wilson?"

Roger shrugged, clearly uncomfortable. "Just a gut feeling," he said vaguely.

"In the course of your questioning," Maggie asked, "did you happen to find out why he attacked me in the first place?"

"It seems he noticed you many years ago back in Atlanta. He wanted to get your attention."

"Why didn't he just say so instead of tackling me to the ground?"

"He said he tried," Roger said with a shrug. "Just tonight he said he asked you: *Do you remember me?* And you replied: *Not even for a minute.*"

"Well, in my defense," Maggie said, "I was in the middle of a very stressful moment. Am I supposed to feel bad about how I treated him?"

She looked from Roger to Laurent.

"No *chérie*," Laurent said, surprising her with a kiss on the mouth. "Not even for a minute."

The four of them sat quietly for a moment. The coffees in front of them had been drunk, refilled, and had now grown cold. Maggie snuggled up against Laurent and hoped they were about to be allowed to finally leave. She watched as police and workmen maneuvered a tow truck in position to take the van away.

It looked like any other van, she thought. Like a thousand she'd seen driving through Aix or on the A8 delivering vegetables or other goods.

"Will catching these men help free the poor women they've kidnapped in the past?" Maggie asked in quiet voice.

Roger shrugged and glanced at Laurent. "Very possibly," he said.

Maggie could tell he was lying.

She turned in Laurent's arms, feeling the strength of him envelop her.

"Take me home, Laurent," she said.

CHAPTER 39

The morning after Maggie returned home, Laurent drove her to Danielle's house. He hadn't needed to tell her that something was wrong. Maggie had worked that out for herself.

When they drove up to Danielle and Jean-Luc's two hundred year old farmhouse, Maggie found Danielle sitting by the front window—as if waiting for her. Without a word, Maggie went to the older woman and they embraced.

The news of Danielle's illness was devastating to Maggie. Later that same morning while Maggie was still there, Danielle's doctor called and reported that the latest lab work looked very encouraging. Whatever happened next, Danielle knew she had the love and support of her family and dear friends. With their strength behind her she could face anything.

Now three days later Maggie stood beside Danielle in the center of the St-Buvard village square and watched as the many different vendors worked to put the finishing touches on their booths and tables at the St-Buvard Lavender Fête.

Jemmy and Mila joined the other village children who were squealing and running between the many gaily-colored booths until they were corralled by the two teenage girls who'd been hired to watch them.

It promised to be a warm day but the huge plane trees surrounding the square would provide ample shade for the festival.

Unlike last year's fair when the number of sellers had outnumbered the shoppers, Maggie had insisted that this year the booths be limited to only those that could fit around the village square. Even so, there were nearly fifty stalls, tables and kiosks.

"Everything looks great," Maggie said to Danielle.

"It will be our best yet, I think."

Maggie squeezed her hand. "You did all the work."

"Nonsense. You returned in time." Danielle winked at her. "Just in the nick of time."

"You sure you don't regret not getting Madame Lampé to help you?" Maggie asked teasingly.

Danielle laughed. "I do not believe it was ever a credible threat, was it?"

Maggie smiled but turned to look again at the activity of the fair coming together. She saw Laurent drive up and park on the street. In an hour it would be impossible to find a spot. She waved to him but he didn't see her. Both children ran to him, jumping around his knees as he turned to unload a large wooden crate from the trunk. He had brought a selection of wine for tasting at the *fête*. While not strictly having to do with lavender, what could be more French at a Provençal fair than wine?

Maggie watched Laurent move to one of the booths opposite the square. He wore jeans and a cotton shirt with the sleeves rolled up. His muscles rippled as he positioned the crate of wine.

Maggie was fairly sure it had *not* been Laurent who'd beaten one of the kidnappers. She heard that the crowd had gotten involved when they realized there was a kidnapping in progress.

It was possible however that Laurent had not done all he could to rescue the poor man until a hospital stay had been guaranteed.

Laurent turned now to catch her eye. He must have known she would be watching for him.

Will I ever stop watching for him?

He smiled and gave a barely perceptible nod before turning to talk with Jean-Luc at the booth.

"Hey," Maggie said to Danielle, "did you tell Madame Benet that she could sell her home-made t-shirts at the fair?"

"I did *not*," Danielle said emphatically, frowning as she headed off in the direction of the offending booth.

Maggie looked around the square, at her friends and neighbors—and their excitement about the fête. She loved seeing the booths and tables full of lavender sachets with hand-sewn embroidery, row after row of dried lavender stalks tied with twine, and of course the soaps, honey, lavender butter, marinades, perfumes, and lavender–infused liquors, not to mention the racks and racks of watercolors, vintage and new, depicting the beautiful lavender fields of Provence.

Cannes seemed like a long way away.

At one point on the drive home from Cannes, Laurent had asked her if she wanted to enter her blog in the international advertising conference next year. When Maggie had looked at the various blogs on display at the Carlton, she remembered entertaining that very thought herself. But as she stood here at the fête and watched her friends, neighbors, and family on this beautiful June day, she realized it didn't matter to her if the whole world thought her blog was the best.

It only mattered that her family was proud of her, that her village benefited from it and that she loved doing it.

Her time in Cannes had underscored that belief more than a trophy or award ever could. It truly was all about how she lived her life.

Maggie knew the genesis of that revelation might have gotten

its start in Cannes but its culmination came the minute she
stepped across the slate foyer of Domaine St-Buvard that first
night home from Cannes.

Right away, Maggie knew something was off.

It wasn't just the muddy footprints in the foyer or the fact that
the antique vase that normally sat on the hall table was now carefully arranged in three large broken pieces on the floor.

It had more to do with the fact that Laurent didn't seem
surprised by any of it.

The reason for that soon became evident when Maggie
followed the trail of dirt and debris to the back of the house.

There, where before had been only a single door at the rear of
the living room leading to a mudroom, was now a massive barn
door hanging from a rustic wrought iron rod with *fleur de lis*
brackets.

When she turned to look at Laurent, he was examining the
door with interest and obvious approval.

"What is this?"

He slid the door open.

All Maggie could do was stand and stare at what was behind
the door. The room they had used to store paint buckets, rubber
boots, dog bowls and flower pots had been transformed into a
home office with gleaming hardwood floors and a dramatic set of
French doors that led to the garden. Maggie's computer sat on her
desk which was positioned against the wall beside a new wooden
bookcase.

She turned to look at Laurent with her mouth open.

"For me?" she said.

"Do you like it?"

She moved into the room as if in a daze. She could tell by how
the French doors were positioned that this room would be
flooded with light from the garden in daytime. The view would
encompass the whole of the vineyard beyond.

It was easily the most beautiful vantage point in the house.

"But, *you* should have this office," Maggie said.

"Why, *chérie*? Because you don't work as hard as I do? Because your work is not as important as mine?"

She slid into his arms.

"Oh, Laurent. It's beautiful. Thank you."

"Nobody knows as well as I do the value of what you do, *chérie*. I am sorry it took me so long to show you."

THAT NIGHT after the lavender fête was over and once the children were finally in bed, Maggie went to her new office. She ran her fingers along the hand-carved floral designs in the hanging door. They matched the designs carved in the French doors.

Laurent said he'd used an artisan in Aix who was renown for creating hand-carved furniture for some of the most famous homes on the Riviera. Her eyes filled with tears at the thought of how Laurent had done all this—in secret—and during his busiest time of the year.

And in spite of all the ugly words between them this week.

As Maggie went to look out the French doors and watch the glow of the dropping sun bathe the vineyard in red-golden hues, she still couldn't believe how she could have been swayed *even for a moment* by Brownie's belief that Laurent didn't respect her.

She felt an ache in her chest as she thought of Brownie. After a few touch and go nights in critical care in Nice he had survived JoJo's knife attack although his health would always be compromised. Whether or not he would be allowed to go back to Atlanta before his trial he would almost certainly spend many years, if not his lifetime, inside a French prison.

Roger Bedard had called this morning to say that a disposable glove found on Brownie the night he was taken to the hospital had tested positive for Bette Austin's blood. For Brownie, it was the proverbial nail in his coffin.

Somehow, Maggie couldn't bring herself to feel sorry for him.

Courtney had texted her that Rick Wilson was fined for attempting to influence a juror's vote and barred for life from the Cannes advertising festival. His attempts to interfere with an ongoing police investigation by purchasing false testimony was being dealt with by his lawyer and would likely result in a hand slapping in honor of Franco-American relations.

Dennis Beaker was still being held in Cannes and questioned for his contact—however remote—to a known human trafficking ring.

Martin the waiter had slipped out of the country before anyone could question why he'd flip-flopped on seeing JoJo that fateful night. Maggie imagined the cops wouldn't bother tracking him down. They had their prime suspect.

As for JoJo, since Brownie had declined to press charges against her, she had gone back to Atlanta to file for divorce. She'd have a great story going forward about her first husband and there would be a decent enough settlement so that she'd never have to worry about having time to practice her forehand on the Atlanta Lawn Tennis Association circuit.

As Maggie stood gazing out onto the vineyard Laurent appeared at the door to her office, a glass of wine in one hand and Mila half-asleep in the crook of his arm.

"You are working, *chérie*?"

"No. Just marveling at how lucky I am," she said, walking to him to give him a kiss and take the child from him.

"What is that you are wearing?" he asked.

Maggie glanced down at her flannel PJs.

"Just my comfy clothes. I guess it's weird for June."

Laurent leaned over and kissed her again, his hand dropping to her waist to pull her close.

"I like you in your comfy clothes," he said in a low voice.

"Let me put this one to bed and I'll meet you on the patio for a night cap," she said.

As she turned toward the stairs with her sleepy child in her arms, Maggie felt a surge of satisfaction and peace at the same time that she realized that Brownie did at least get one thing right.

There *were* moments in the south of France that were pretty damn perfect.

To find out what happens next, be sure to order *Murder in Grenoble*, the next book in the *Maggie Newberry Mysteries!*

WHAT'S NEXT

If you want to see what happens next to Maggie and Laurent, check out *Murder in Grenoble, Book 11 of the Maggie Newberry Mysteries*!

Here are the beginning chapters of *Murder in Grenoble*.

1. The Nights Grow Colder

Maggie snuggled down under the duvet, resisting the moment when she would have to face the world—starting with the assault of a nasty spate of February weather. Opening one eye, she saw what she knew by scent and habit would be there: a steaming bowl of *café au lait* on her bedside table placed there by Laurent who of course had been up for hours.

The aroma of the coffee did its work and she pushed herself up to a sitting position and reached for the bowl. Knowing how she enjoyed the view first thing in the morning—and how the creeping sunlight would help wake her—Laurent had pulled back the drapes in the bedroom.

Through the steam rising from the bowl she could see the outline of the antique Juliette balcony outside the window and the dramatic sweep of the vineyard beyond. She took a sip of her coffee, relishing its rich flavor as well as the warmth of her bed. From this distance the pruned vines were just black stumps sticking out of the ground. After seven years and seven harvests, Maggie knew there was life in what looked like a field of devastation. There was in fact the beginning of next August's harvest although its merit would depend on sunshine and the spring and summer rains.

Maggie could also see the distant truffle oaks and cypresses that framed the borders of the vineyard, and the rows of olive and fig trees leading from the back garden along a pebbled path to the vineyard.

"*Maman!*" a child's voice cried out. It was immediately followed by the low, rumble of Laurent's voice.

Maggie sighed. Her peace was coming to an end. Not that she didn't adore the moment when her children flung open her bedroom door and climbed onto the bed to greet her as they often did. But there was something about this morning that made Maggie want to linger.

Want to put off getting out of bed to face the day.

And she knew very well why.

She looked up as her bedroom door swung open. Laurent stood in the opening, their daughter Mila in his arms. His light brown hair hung to his shoulders. His eyes were dark, nearly pupilless. Maggie always found them sexy but a little disconcerting too because she could never read them. His eyes were a lot like Laurent, himself. Mysterious.

A big man, Laurent stood over six foot five, with broad shoulders and even edging toward his mid-forties carried not an ounce of fat. It always amazed Maggie how Laurent seemed to effortlessly manage that—especially since he was such an amazing cook.

"See?" Laurent said to the child as he stepped into the room. "*Maman* is alive and well. Now it is time for everyone to get dressed." He raised an eyebrow at Maggie to underscore his statement.

"I'm up. I'm up," Maggie said, pushing back the warm covers. "Race you downstairs for pancakes?"

The child kicked her feet to be let down. Laurent put her down and Mila quickly disappeared out the door. Maggie's little dog Petit-Four jumped out of her dog bed and followed the child downstairs.

"Is everybody up?" Maggie asked as she put on her slippers. Her parents had come to France for Christmas and never left—unusual for them. Maggie's niece Nicole had spent three weeks with them at Domaine St-Buvard, Maggie and Laurent's *mas*, but had recently flown back to Atlanta to go skiing with school friends.

Nicole was seventeen now with no apparent memory of the traumatic first few years of her life. She excelled in school and was a loving cousin to Maggie's children Jemmy and Mila.

"Of course," Laurent said wryly as if to imply that only Maggie could still be asleep with so much noise going on in the house.

Maggie's friend Grace Van Sant and her ten-year old daughter Zouzou had gotten in late last night.

Maggie and Grace had been the best of friends when Maggie first came to France over nine years ago. But their friendship had taken a serious hit two years ago—one that Maggie was sure they would never come back from.

"Zouzou is a problem," Laurent said flatly. His comment surprised Maggie first because there were very few things that Laurent ever admitted were a problem for him, and secondly because all children everywhere routinely adored him. As gruff and bearish as he was—or perhaps *because* he was so gruff—children tended to gyrate toward him. And problem children? There was no such thing as far as Laurent was concerned.

"Seriously?" Maggie said. "You can tell that already? She's been here, what, eight hours and asleep for most of them?"

Laurent shrugged. As usual, his response was enigmatic. But if Laurent said Zouzou was a problem, that meant something.

Maggie sighed. "Are you going to be okay with her?" Maggie and Grace were scheduled to leave that afternoon for a five day retreat at a ski resort in Grenoble where they would try to work out their problems and find their way back to a friendship again. The plan was for Zouzou to stay at Domaine St-Buvard with Laurent.

Laurent only snorted.

"What is it with Grace and children?" Maggie said with annoyance as she slipped into her robe. "First Taylor and now Zouzou."

Grace's oldest child Taylor had always been a trial but Zouzou had been the cheerier and more docile of the two. Any way you looked at it, Maggie thought, it looked like Grace had taken a perfectly sweet kid and somehow turned Zouzou into a horror show just like her big sister.

Or maybe Maggie was just feeling down on Grace these days.

Eighteen months ago Grace had been living with Maggie and Laurent while the rest of Grace's life was falling apart around her. *Correction*, Maggie thought—*while Grace was singlehandedly dismantling her life around her*. Grace had gone on a spending spree with money she didn't have for a business that gave every sign of failing from the beginning, while ignoring both her daughters and leaving the care of them to Laurent and Maggie or anybody else who'd take them.

In the end Grace's bad judgment had led to Mila's being abducted at a public fête providing Maggie with the worst nine hours of her life.

So, yes. Grace had a long way to go to prove she was a friend to Maggie.

"People don't change," Maggie said.

"I think what we have been saying is the exact opposite of that," Laurent said.

"Yes, well, I'm talking about Grace now," Maggie said. "Not Zouzou."

"Get dressed, *chérie*," Laurent said ominously as he turned to leave. "And dress warmly. It is cold inside and out today."

2. *Wash, Rinse, Repeat*

Laurent was right about Zouzou.

Maggie was standing next to her mother Elspeth Newberry in the kitchen and watched as the truculent preteen sat apart from the group, her iPad in her hands, a permanent scowl on her face. Zouzou was short for her age with long blonde hair down her back. She had a heart-shaped face and bow lips with lively blue eyes. She had been chubby the last time Maggie had seen her. She was bordering on fat now.

Was she stress eating? Was it genetic? Grace was willow slim and Taylor was as skinny as a wire. It was true Zouzou's biological father had not been skinny but nothing like this.

"Are you going to be all right, darling?" Elspeth asked her.

Maggie looked at her mother in surprise.

"Why wouldn't I be?"

Ever since she'd arrived at Domaine St-Buvard five weeks ago Maggie's mother had hinted at how tired she was and how busy and overwhelmed her schedule was given all of Nicole's school activities and Elspeth's own daily round of bridge parties and country club luncheons with friends.

And then of course there was Maggie's father. John Newberry, on the surface, often appeared to be his old jolly self during the holidays—only half listening to what anyone said and responding to even serious inquiries with a laugh and a good natured shrug. But there had been a few instances of temper that Maggie had never seen from him before.

And then there was his memory. Not just short term. There were moments when he would look at the children and Maggie would swear he wasn't sure who they were.

Was that what was bothering her mother?

Has there been a diagnosis that she's trying to bring herself to tell me about?

Maggie knew her parents had had a rough last couple of years, mostly because of Maggie's older brother Ben. Their granddaughter Nicole who they were raising had been nothing but a joy to them but Nicole would be going away to college soon.

"You just seem a little tense, is all," Elspeth said and looked away.

I could say the same of you, Maggie thought. But she'd long since given up trying to get her mother to tell her what was on her mind before she was ready. Elspeth was a lot like Laurent in that way.

"Laurent's concerned about Zouzou," Maggie said.

"Zouzou is fine and Laurent knows it," Elspeth said. "It's you he's worried about."

Maggie nearly laughed. "That's ridiculous. *He's* the one on the front lines this week. I'm going on *vacation.*"

"*Are* you, darling?" Elspeth said, raising an eyebrow before glancing across the room where Grace sat with a cup of coffee.

Except for a brief greeting last night when Grace and Zouzou got in, Maggie hadn't said much to Grace. She figured they'd have plenty of time to hash all that out during their five days at the ski resort—although Maggie was really hoping to get some skiing in. She hadn't skied in years and she'd so loved it when she was in college and used to make the weekend jaunts up to Sugar Mountain in North Carolina from Atlanta.

"I'm fine," Maggie said firmly. "Danielle will come over if you need anything and otherwise Laurent has everything under control."

"As he always does."

"That's right. As he always does. You are acting so strange," Maggie said with exasperation. She looked around the room. Laurent had finished making the last plate of pancakes and was handing them out to Jemmy and Maggie's father. Her father smiled dotingly at his grandson.

"We'll be fine here," her mother said, following Maggie's eye to where John Newberry sat next to Jemmy. "Your father comes alive when he's with Jemmy."

Maggie was startled to hear her mother say that although she knew it was true. *Is it because of the whole mess with Ben?* Was her father so discouraged by all that had happened with his only son that he'd jumped a generation to pin all his hopes and dreams on the next one?

All through the holidays, her father had spent much more time with Jemmy than with Mila. It was true her father was a man's man—down to the hunting dogs, the cigars, the glass of bourbon in the library at night and the expectation that the women in his life would honor him and his decisions no matter how misguided they might be.

The quintessential Southern gent, Maggie thought as she watched her father. She'd always loved that about him.

But she didn't want it for her son.

"Your father thinks Jemmy will make an amazing lawyer some day," Elspeth said. "When you move back to the US."

And there it was.

Maggie bit her lip to ensure she didn't over react. This wasn't the first time this visit that her mother had mentioned how she hoped Maggie and Laurent would move back to the States. Maggie didn't know which she was more upset about—the fact that her parents were already pushing their own preferences for Jemmy's future—or that they believed Maggie would come back to the US.

But now was not the time to respond.

"Laurent hopes Jemmy will become a *vigneron* like him," Maggie said and then cursed the fact that she'd responded in spite of her best intentions.

"Oh, not seriously, surely?" Elspeth said. "Jemmy is so smart."

Are you saying Laurent isn't? But this time Maggie managed not to say it outloud.

Laurent looked over at Maggie and frowned. She knew he couldn't hear their conversation from where he stood—no matter how acute his hearing was—but he seemed to be able to tell things from the vibrations in the air.

She forced herself to smile at him as if to say *No problem. All is well.*

He probably can read the lie in that too, she thought

"After all, our children are who they will be," Elspeth said, blithely continuing the conversation. "Remember that, darling. You and Laurent are just along for the ride."

"Yep," Maggie said, biting her lip hard. "Good to know."

An hour later, Maggie stood by the taxi parked in the front drive of Domaine St-Buvard. Laurent stood beside her, a leather Louis Vuitton train case on the ground in front of them.

Grace was having a last minute tête-a-tête with Zouzou on the front steps of the house. Their words were muted but the intense expressions on both their faces left little doubt that a warning was being issued and *not* received well at all.

"Promise me you won't wallop her while we're gone," Maggie said to him, only half joking.

"I make no promises."

Maggie shivered and Laurent automatically put an arm around her. It was cold with a light dusting of snow already on the ground. The strong scent of roasting grapevines filled the air. Laurent had been pruning and burning the vinestocks already this morning. She could smell the woodsmoke in his jacket as she leaned into him.

For a moment, she was sorry he wasn't going with her. It had been ages since the two of them had gotten away—before Mila was born four years ago.

She looked up at the façade of their home. Sometimes she

indulged herself by trying to remember how it felt to see Domaine St-Buvard for the first time. How seeing it nine years ago had filled her with hope and longing and delight. And a little fear.

A large stone terrace splayed out from the front door in three stepped tiers to the curving gravel drive. Oleander and ivy clustered against the fieldstone walls of the house in thick tangles of dark green. A black wrought-iron railing framed the second-story balcony that jutted out over the front door. The three sets of bedroom windows on the second floor were tall and mullioned and framed with bright blue shutters.

As a country *mas*, the house was bigger and older than most in the area. After years of renovations and gradual design additions it was now a stylish and comfortable family home for the family of four.

"You think this is a bad idea, don't you?" she said. "Me and Grace going off like this."

"*Pas du tout*," he said with a shrug.

Which meant, in Laurent-speak, *very probably yes*.

Maggie blew lightly on her hands and stamped her feet. A thick band of clouds overhead had sunk the front terrace steps into deep shadow and she felt the chill.

As Grace turned away from Zouzou, who turned and stomped into the house, pushing past Jemmy and Mila as they came outside, Maggie squeezed Laurent's hand. He leaned over and kissed her.

"Keep your cellphone on," he said.

"You're one to talk."

Laurent was notorious for forgetting to carry his phone or letting the battery die.

Jemmy and Mila ran over to hug Maggie goodbye. She kissed them both.

"Be good for Papa, okay?" Maggie said, smoothing down Jemmy's wild hair, so very like what Maggie imagined Laurent's must have looked like as a boy. The two were so similar in so many ways. Just maybe not in the important ones?

"Of course," Jemmy said. He'd taken to speaking only English since his grandparents had arrived—another point of contention, Maggie knew, with Laurent. Her ears still rang with Laurent's comment last night after dinner when her father had announced how proud he would be when Jemmy joined his Uncle Ben's old law firm.

"I would rather he join the flic than become un avocat," Laurent had said as he and Maggie got ready for bed last night. *I'd rather he be a cop than a lawyer.* And in light of Laurent's past life as a criminal on the *Côte d'Azur, that* spoke volumes as to how much he did *not* want his son to take the law as his vocation.

Maggie hugged both children again and gave Laurent one last kiss before getting into the taxi beside Grace.

Grace was wearing a Burberry quilted parka that hugged her every curve that Maggie knew couldn't have cost less than a thousand US dollars. Maggie wasn't sure how Grace was doing for money these days but clearly she wasn't shopping the sales bin at Macy's.

"Are you ready for this?" Grace asked lightly as she smoothed the nonexistent creases from her coal black wool slacks.

"Of course," Maggie said, waving to her family as the car drove away. "Why wouldn't I be?

3. Blowing Smoke

Laurent watched the taxi creep down the long curving drive of Domaine St-Buvard. The snow had turned into brown sludge that now clumped down the center of the gravel drive.

When Laurent had inherited the *mas* and surrounding hectares of vineyard from his Uncle Nicolas nine years ago he'd merely hoped that some day he might be able to bring the ancient vineyard back. At the time he'd wanted only to be able to produce a simple *vin de pays.* Something he could put the Dernier name on. Maybe pass on to his children.

At the thought of Jemmy, Laurent turned toward the house.

Towering Italian cypress trees and Tatarian dogwoods flanked the massive front door. In summer hollyhocks would push out in a riot of bushes by the front steps. But now there was just the stone lion—its head bowed, one ear chipped as it had been for a century—standing guard on the stone threshold that led into Domaine St-Buvard.

"She'll be fine, Laurent," his mother-in-law Elspeth said to him as he stepped into the ancient *mas*. She was a beautiful woman, Elspeth. Laurent had no doubt that her lifelong wealth had helped preserve the affect. But he had to admit she was essentially good-humored. Born that way if he had to guess.

"I am not worried about Maggie," he said, his full lips curving into a smile. "Only what there is for dinner tonight."

"Well, I can hardly believe that," Elspeth said. "I'm sure you have everything in the kitchen under control."

Laurent was known for many things in the family but his ability *dans la cuisine* was the most prominent.

"Where are the children?" he asked as he scanned the foyer and hall leading to the living room.

"I am here, Papa!" Little Mila piped up from the kitchen. "Waiting for you!"

Laurent smiled at the sound of his daughter's voice. If someone had told him a decade ago that he would receive an immediate jolt of warmth and joy in response to a little girl's voice, he would simply not have believed it.

"I believe they are all waiting for you," Elspeth said as she moved ahead of him into the kitchen.

The kitchen was painted a pale ochre yellow with sporadic persimmon touches. The window over the sink was wide and faced the front driveway. Most days it brought in the Mediterranean sun that infused the kitchen with a yellow glow. The floors were terracotta and featured a matching backsplash. Maggie would have preferred something a little more feminine—

perhaps something with hand-painted flowers—but this was Laurent's space and it was designed for utilitarian use. The resulting look was clean, airy, and masculine.

As Laurent entered the kitchen he saw their neighbor Danielle Alexandre sitting at the counter with a cup of coffee before her. She was flanked by both Mila and Jemmy. In the absence of their American grandparents who normally resided in Atlanta, Danielle and her husband Jean-Luc had taken up the challenge of being acting grandparents to the children.

"*Bonjour*, Laurent," Danielle said. Her eyes looked hollow and her face gaunt. The chemotherapy had taken its toll on her but all agreed it was for the best. She was in remission now. As Laurent came into the room and kissed her on both cheeks, he immediately sensed that there was something wrong.

"I did not want to distract from your goodbyes," Danielle said, smiling wanly. Her brown hair heavily streaked with grey was twisted into an attractive but unfashionable bun at the nape of her neck "So I came in the back."

"I saw her first, Papa!" Mila said excitedly. Mila was a beautiful child, blonde with dark blue eyes and a rosebud mouth. Except for Maggie's dark hair, Laurent always thought Mila looked like her mother.

"Did you, *ma petite*?" Laurent said, cupping the child's cheek lightly before moving into the center of his kitchen. He had been in the process of making a *tagine* for lunch and went to his mortar and pestle to begin creating the spice mixture he'd use in the African dish.

Elspeth sat down next to Danielle. A large potted lavender plant perched on the breakfast counter.

"Danielle was telling me that Jean-Luc isn't feeling well," Elspeth said, her eyes too bright as she spoke.

"*Ah oui*?" Laurent said noncommittally as he shook out equal amounts of ginger and cardamom into the heavy marble bowl.

"It is nothing," Danielle said. "The flu I'm sure."

"Jemmy," Laurent said, "go find Zouzou and tell her to come down."

"She wants to be alone," Jemmy said.

Laurent turned and glanced at him, one eyebrow shooting high into his brown fringe. Jemmy got down from his stool with a sigh and went to walk upstairs to the bedrooms.

From where Laurent stood he could see through the main salon past the back terrace and to the sweeping fields of his vineyard.

The vineyard was cut by two narrow dirt and gravel roads into quadrants. Last year's harvest had been a good one, easily the best of all seven so far. But the spring rains had bleached the sweetness from the grapes and the Mistral had destroyed nearly a quarter of the vines—whisking them away back to Morocco or wherever the hell the demon winds came from.

Next year will be better, Laurent thought and then grimaced at the thought.

"Papa? Can I cut some rosemary sprigs from the *potager*?" Mila said, jumping down from her stool and snatching up the shears from a hook by the stove. Laurent's *potager* was through the dining room and off the back terrace.

"You must not run with those," he remarked to the child before glancing at the two older women at the counter. "You will stay for lunch, Danielle?" he asked.

"*Mais non*, Laurent. *Merci*," Danielle said. "I just came by to say hello."

And to tell me about Jean-Luc.

"Tell Jean-Luc I will come by later," he said as he turned back to his stove. Through the window over the sink he caught a glimpse of movement in the front drive and saw that it was Zouzou. The child moved sluggishly, trudging up the drive and then turning and walking back down. Was she doing it for exercise?

Jemmy returned to the kitchen. "I couldn't find her. What do you want me to do now?"

"Supervise your sister," Laurent said without taking his eyes off Zouzou. What was the girl doing?

As Danielle got up to leave, his cellphone rang

"I will tell Jean-Luc you will come," she said to Laurent as she and Elspeth moved through the salon and out the back terrace door.

"*D'accord*," Laurent said and then accepted the call.

"I have not yet decided," he said curtly into the phone and then hung up.

His emotions juddered through him as he held the phone in his hand and waited for his feelings to settle. He could see Zouzou again and he watched her as she went to the end of the drive where it connected with the road that led to the village.

Laurent's eyes were good. Very good. But he didn't need to see that well to recognize the motions of what Zouzou was doing as she pulled something out of her coat pocket and stuffed it into her mouth.

4. So Far Apart

The temperature had fallen rapidly with the late afternoon by the time Maggie and Grace's taxi arrived at the front door of the *Chalet Savoir Faire*. The fog that had accompanied their drive from the *Gare de Grenoble* was thinner now having evolved into faint wisps that hovered close to the cobblestone pavement in front of the ski chalet.

As Grace got out of the taxicab the brief arctic bite of breeze gave her a rush of memory of happier times. She pushed the memories of Kitzbuhl and St-Moritz from her mind. Those places were from a time long ago.

A time when I had money and a family.

She immediately performed a mental exercise that her therapist Ruth back in Atlanta had taught her called thought-stopping.

Whenever Grace found herself thinking of how she'd sabotaged her life—her friendships, her relationships with her children, not to mention her marriage to Windsor—she would mentally pinch herself and say "ouch" as softly as possible to bring it to her attention.

You manage what you monitor, Ruth would say and, as tiresome and ultimately annoying as Grace always found the woman, she knew she was right.

Maggie hadn't said three words on the train ride to the village. That was so unlike Maggie that Grace figured it had to be deliberate.

Or who knows? Maybe Maggie really doesn't have anything to say to me.

A prick of melancholy pierced Grace at the thought and she pinched herself. It didn't help to go there. She'd learned that if nothing else.

"Ouch," she murmured.

"Did you say something?" Maggie asked politely, looking around as if to find the reason for Grace's utterance.

"Not really, darling," Grace said with a smile. "Just excited about our retreat."

She could see a wince of emotion flit across Maggie's face. Grace had had to seriously talk her into this trip and she knew it was only the prospect of being able to ski that ultimately had gotten Maggie on board.

Maggie doesn't want to be friends again.

Grace swallowed hard and pushed the thought away, mentally pinching herself for all she was worth.

Don't think that. It doesn't help.

This time she voiced the *ouch* only in her mind.

As she stepped out of the taxi, Maggie observed the front of the ski lodge. It was made of brick and stone—unusual for the area—and featured a small bay window showcasing a pair of posed mannequins wearing colorful ski resort clothing. Each mannequin was leaning on a pair of skis, their pom-pom knit hats perched jauntily on their heads to give an almost macabre sense of premonition to the place.

While the chalet was clearly very old, it did appear as if it had been recently renovated, which Maggie could tell from the tacked-on modern additions on either side. But the main section of the building—ancient soot-stained yellow brick—looked as if dated back to the time of the French Revolution. One look at its ancient beams and the elaborately carved front lintel that hung over the front door made Maggie believe that guess was entirely possible.

As long as they had Wi-Fi and decent coffee—and what resort mountain chalet didn't?—it was perfectly fine as far as Maggie was concerned. A fissure of pleasurable spite stung her when she thought how differently Grace must be viewing all of this.

Instantly, Maggie scolded herself. Envisioning—and then reveling—in the thought of Grace's reaction to staying at a one-star hotel was beneath her.

Satisfying, but beneath her.

Once through the front door Maggie didn't wait for the handsome-if-aging bellhop or Grace for that matter—but strode purposefully to the front desk.

It had freshly snowed in Grenoble that morning but her phone's weather app had accurately predicted the sun would be out all afternoon—making for amazing weather for downhill. Clear, cold, very little wind. She only hoped the next five days would be as nice.

Grace trailed behind Maggie as she stood at the registration desk and hit the front desk bell. The lobby was full of people dressed for the slopes or for travel. It had been Maggie's idea to book the trip for after the weekend so that they might take advantage of lower rates and fewer people. If even only half the people in the lobby were leaving, it bode well for having a pleasant uncrowded experience on the slopes.

"*Oui*, Madame?" A woman wearing the nametag *Alys Chaix* hurried around the counter. In her early thirties, she had curly chestnut-colored hair that framed large brown eyes and the bowed lips of a Botticelli angel. She brought with her a wafting of floral fragrance. Maggie was instantly reminded of her grandmother.

"Welcome to *Chalet Savoir Faire*," the concierge said.

"*Merci*," Maggie said. "We have two rooms reserved through February 27."

"Great minds," a male voice in an English accent bellowed over Maggie's shoulder. She turned to see a man with ruddy cheeks and a bulbous nose standing behind Grace. He grinned at Maggie. "I'm staying through the twenty-seventh as well."

Before Maggie could respond, Grace turned to address the man.

"How nice for you," she said sweetly.

That was classic Grace. Polite on the surface but a slow burn when you thought about it. It was clear that the guy hadn't really looked at Grace—which he definitely did now—because he reacted the way most mortal men did when they laid eyes on a goddess incarnate.

Grace was a beauty and there was no mistake about that. She was Grace Kelly with all the poise and style you'd expect from a mythical creature.

In Grace's case however, Maggie knew exactly how much myth was involved.

"I...I...well, I..." the man stuttered as he gazed dumbfounded at Grace.

Grace turned from him and gave Maggie a small conspiratorial smile and for just a moment Maggie was tempted to return the smile. But she didn't. She turned back to the concierge who was pushing two room keys across the counter at her.

"The Wi-Fi code is on the back of the resort brochure," Madame Chaix said with a smile and then looked past Maggie and Grace at the Englishman. "Monsieur?"

Maggie stepped away from the desk and spotted the bellhop standing with their luggage. He looked too old to be a proper bellhop but he was still quite handsome. His nametag read *Max Fountainbleu*. Behind him was a table with a series of stacked glossy brochures and a sign that read in English "Ski Lesson Signup." A picture of Max from years earlier was on the sign.

"I guess he does double duty," Grace commented as she and Maggie approached the man and handed him their room keys.

Before they reached the stairs, Maggie saw a set of French doors that opened onto what looked to be the dining room. She tapped Max on the shoulder to indicate he should wait.

"I just want to see the view from here," Maggie said to Grace. "TripAdvisor said it was magnificent."

"Of course, darling," Grace said as the two stepped into the dining room.

The entrance to the dining room featured an open entryway with a vaulted ceiling supported on rows of squat ornate pillar and a large crystal chandelier. A massive display window immediately afforded a dramatic view of Peak Etendard—the major summit of the French Alps' Grandes Rousses—soaring three thousand meters above sea level.

As Maggie gazed at the stunning view, she felt a ping of excitement race through her at the thought of skiing the mountain tomorrow.

Branching off from the dining room was a hallway that opened up on the other side of the kitchen. From where they stood Maggie could see a massive aquarium built into the wall that made up nearly one whole side of the hall wall.

It occurred to Maggie that a narrow passageway en route to the restrooms was an odd place to put such an enormous fish tank. While it was true that guests would be able to see the pretty fish on their way to and from the restrooms, the hall was too narrow to afford more than an extremely truncated view.

Scanning the rest of the dining room, Maggie was surprised to see that there were still people eating. It was late afternoon and she would have expected lunch to be long over. A tall man wearing a toque and chef's jacket stood next to a table positioned closest to the window and the view of the mountain. A young Indian couple sat at the table. The Indian man was not happy.

The chef leaned over the young Indian man to say a few words that Maggie couldn't hear which prompted the young man to fling down his napkin and jump to his feet.

"I say! That is total rubbish! I'll have the management know immediately, you racist cretin!" the young Indian man said hotly, his face shoved close to the chef's.

"*Pardonez-moi*," Max said politely and pushed past Grace and Maggie. He strode to the table and spoke to the chef in a low voice. Maggie saw the chef turn on Max as if he would transfer his ire to *him* but when he saw that he was being observed by her and Grace his face flushed and he stormed out of the room.

Max quickly delivered his apologies to the young couple and then rejoined Grace and Maggie. He collected their bags and carried them upstairs to the first two rooms on the second floor. He set the bags down on the carpet to manage the keys. As he did, the door to the room across the hall opened and a man in his mid-forties stepped out followed by a woman of about the same age with a thin, sharp-boned face and a severe pixie cut.

"*Attends*, Max!" the man called out. "Glad we caught you! Can you fit us in for a lesson tomorrow morning, say about ten?"

Max nodded. "*Oui*, Monsieur Toureille," he said. "No problem." He nodded at the woman. "Madame Toureille."

At his words the couple giggled and, holding hands, retreated down the hall toward the stairs.

"If they're married to each other," Grace said, "I'm Katy Perry."

Max opened the door to Maggie's room but she noticed a sly smile from him at Grace's words.

So he understands English, Maggie thought. *Good to know.*

"I take it you are the ski instructor?" Maggie asked, knowing perfectly well he was.

"If you are interested in lessons," he said, "I should warn you that weather conditions are thought to be worsening."

Maggie pressed her lips together.

"Do you mean there won't be enough snow?" she asked. "Or that high temps are coming to melt the snow on the ground?"

He shook his head. "A front is coming through."

"So that would mean *more* snow, wouldn't it?" Grace asked helpfully.

"*Oui*, Madame. *Too* much snow. Very dangerous conditions."

Maggie sighed, tipped him and went into her room tossing a cavalier, "see you in the dining room" over her shoulder to Grace who stood expectantly in the hallway.

Maggie closed her door.

To continue reading, order *Murder in Grenoble, Book 11 of the Maggie Newberry Mysteries.*

RECIPE FOR SOUPE DE POISSONS

Few dishes are as evocative of the Côte d'Azur as this one. As Laurent well knows. In his version, he uses:

2 lbs firm white fish
½-lb raw shrimp, boiled and shelled (save the water)
½-cup olive oil
1 tomato
Orange rind
1 onion, finely chopped
3 garlic cloves, crushed
White bread
Parsley, bay leaf, saffron, fennel
Parmesan cheese

Cut the fish into two-inch pieces. Put some heat under a big saucepan and add the oil, a few sprigs of the parsley, the chopped onion, 1 bay leaf, a pinch of saffron, the fennel, tomato, rind and the garlic. When it gets aromatic (sorry to be so nonspecific but this is where your nose and your eyes work better than words) add the fish and cover with 1-1/2 quarts of the shrimp water. Salt and pepper it liberally and bring to a boil for 15-20 minutes. Turn off the heat and replace the wilted cooked parsley with another sprig of fresh parsley.

Ladle the soup into bowls.

Toast the bread and cut into squares or rounds. Put big healthy dollops of aioli on them and add them to the bowls so that they are bobbing on top. Grate fat curls of Parmesan cheese onto them.

ABOUT THE AUTHOR

USA TODAY Bestselling Author Susan Kiernan-Lewis is the author of *The Maggie Newberry Mysteries*, the post-apocalyptic thriller series *The Irish End Games, The Mia Kazmaroff Mysteries, The Stranded in Provence Mysteries, The Claire Baskerville Mysteries,* and *The Savannah Time Travel Mysteries.*

Visit www.susankiernanlewis.com or follow Author Susan Kiernan-Lewis on Facebook.

Books by Susan Kiernan-Lewis
The Maggie Newberry Mysteries
Murder in the South of France
Murder à la Carte
Murder in Provence
Murder in Paris
Murder in Aix
Murder in Nice
Murder in the Latin Quarter
Murder in the Abbey
Murder in the Bistro
Murder in Cannes

Murder in Grenoble
Murder in the Vineyard
Murder in Arles
Murder in Marseille
Murder in St-Rémy
Murder à la Mode
Murder in Avignon
Murder in the Lavender
Murder in Mont St-Michel
Murder in the Village
Murder in St-Tropez
Murder in Grasse
Murder in Monaco
Murder in Montmartre
Murder in the Villa
A Provençal Christmas: A Short Story
A Thanksgiving in Provence
Laurent's Kitchen

The Claire Baskerville Mysteries
Déjà Dead
Death by Cliché
Dying to be French
Ménage à Murder
Killing it in Paris
Murder Flambé
Deadly Faux Pas
Toujours Dead
Murder in the Christmas Market
Deadly Adieu
Murdering Madeleine
Murder Carte Blanche
Death à la Drumstick
Murder Mon Amour

The Savannah Time Travel Mysteries
Killing Time in Georgia
Scarlett Must Die

The Stranded in Provence Mysteries
Parlez-Vous Murder?
Crime and Croissants
Accent on Murder
A Bad Éclair Day
Croak, Monsieur!
Death du Jour
Murder Très Gauche
Wined and Died
Murder, Voila!
A French Country Christmas
Fromage to Eternity

The Irish End Games

About the Author

Free Falling
Going Gone
Heading Home
Blind Sided
Rising Tides
Cold Comfort
Never Never
Wit's End
Dead On
White Out
Black Out
End Game

The Mia Kazmaroff Mysteries
Reckless
Shameless
Breathless
Heartless
Clueless
Ruthless

Ella Out of Time
Swept Away
Carried Away
Stolen Away